"I thought I was just a hot one-night stand."

She averted her gaze. "You were."

There was a long moment of silence.

"Now who's the liar?" he whispered and lowered his head.

His lips were scorching, rivaling the fire that blazed behind him. He didn't punish her with a hard, devouring kiss. Instead, his warm, moist mouth gently slid over hers. Cassie tried to collect herself enough to give him the hell he so richly deserved, but her body wouldn't cooperate. Her eyes slid shut right before he slipped his hands to her waist. The edge of her sweater was lifted and cold, callused hands tingled over her bare skin, then encircled her and easily lifted her to the top of the desk.

She trembled and placed her hands on his chest. The fact that she was kissing James Sutton—a lying, conniving jerk—didn't seem to matter to her treacherous body. The hormones that had been so easily controlled with a simple shower nozzle were now raging out of control. And all it had taken was one little kiss.

Or one big, tongue-twisting—heart-stopping—soul-wrenching kiss.

Whatever it was, it was too good to let her mind take control. So she released her brain and let her body do what it would....

Praise for **The Deep in The Heart of Texas Series**

CATCH ME A COWBOY

"4½ stars! A heartwarming return to Bramble, Texas, with many familiar faces. This is an emotional story that will bring the reader to laughter as well as tears and spark a desire to see more of the characters, both new and old, who live here."
—*RT Book Reviews*

"Lane gives readers a rip-roaring good time while making what could feel like a farce insightful and real, just like the characters themselves."
—*Booklist*

"Nosy townsfolk, Texas twangs, and an electric romantic attraction will leave readers smiling."
—*BookPage*

"Katie Lane is quickly becoming a must-buy author if one is looking for humorous, country romance! This story is an absolute hoot to read! The characters are real and endearing...the situations are believable (especially if one has ever lived in a small town) and sometimes hilarious, and the romance is hot as a June bug in July!
—*Affaire de Coeur*

MAKE MINE A BAD BOY

"A delightful continuation of *Going Cowboy Crazy*. There's plenty of humor to entertain the reader, and the people of the town will seem like old friends by the end of this entertaining story."
—*RT Book Reviews*

"Funny, entertaining, and a sit-back-and-enjoy-yourself kind of tale." —RomRevToday.com

"If you're looking for a romance true to its Texas setting, this is the one for you. I simply couldn't put it down."
—TheSeasonforRomance.com

"I absolutely loved Colt! I mean, who doesn't like a bad boy? Katie Lane is truly a breath of fresh air. Her stories are unique and wonderfully written...Lane, you have me hooked." —LushBookReviewss.blogspot.com

"Another fun read and just as good as [*Going Cowboy Crazy*]...a perfect example of small town living and the strange charm it has. I really enjoyed reading this one and hope that Katie Lane is writing a third."
—SaveySpender.com

"It will make you laugh, and then make you sigh contentedly. *Make Mine a Bad Boy* is a highly entertaining ride."
—RomanceNovelNews.com

GOING COWBOY CRAZY

"Romance, heated exchanges, and misunderstandings, combined with the secondary characters (the whole town of Bramble), who are hilarious...This is the perfect summer read. Katie Lane has a winner on her hands; she is now my new favorite author!"
—TheRomanceReadersConnection.com

"Entertaining...[with] a likable and strong heroine."
—*RT Book Reviews*

Hunk *for the* Holidays

Hunk *for the* Holidays

Katie Lane

FOREVER

NEW YORK   BOSTON

Forever
Hachette Book Group
237 Park Avenue
New York, NY 10017

www.HachetteBookGroup.com

Printed in the United States of America

First Edition: September 2012
10 9 8 7 6 5 4 3 2 1

Forever is an imprint of Grand Central Publishing.
The Forever name and logo are trademarks of Hachette Book Group, Inc.

The Hachette Speakers Bureau provides a wide range of authors for speaking events. To find out more, go to www.hachettespeakersbureau .com or call (866) 376-6591.

The publisher is not responsible for websites (or their content) that are not owned by the publisher.

To my mother, Helen Marie, who loved Christmas and her family and who never once doubted that her daughter would become a published author

Hunk *for the* Holidays

Chapter One

I want James Sutton taken out, Cass."

Cassie McPherson smiled at her father's gangster phrasing. It wasn't that hard to picture Al McPherson toting a Tommy machine gun and issuing orders like the Godfather. As reigning chieftain of the McPherson clan and founder and president of M & M Construction, Big Al wasn't a man you messed with.

"I don't think we have anything to worry about, Dad." She cradled the phone with her shoulder and shifted through the stacks of paper on her desk, looking for her day planner. "We both know that Sutton is low-balling. Either his employees are working for dirt cheap or he's losing money."

"Either way, I don't like it. The Calloway Complex is the fifth project we've lost to him this year." Big Al's voice became louder, as it always did when he was losing his temper. "And I heard from Michaels that he's wining and dining Steve Mitchell, hoping to get Slumber Suites away from us."

Cassie found the planner, but not a pen. "Now, Dad, stop getting upset. It's been only a few weeks since your heart surgery, and the doctor said you're supposed to take it easy. I shouldn't even be talking to you about work."

There was a loud snort on the other end. "Bullshit! It's my company, and I'm going to run it. And I'm sure as hell not going to let some young whelp straight out of grade school put me out of business."

She located a pen beneath a Snickers wrapper. She stared at the small smudge of chocolate on the side and had to stifle the urge to lick it clean. "Calm down. He doesn't have enough capital or clout to put us out of business. We could buy his company with pocket change."

Her father snorted again, but this time with less anger and more humor. "That's my girl. You think just like your dad."

"Which means?"

"I've been working on a plan to take care of Sutton."

"A plan? Dad, it better not be anything that's going to put you back in the hospital—or worse, in jail. Have you talked to the boys about it?" She used the edge of an envelope to wipe the chocolate off, then flipped open the planner to jot down the meetings she wanted to have after the first of the year. Unfortunately, the planner was only good through December. So instead she jotted down a list of things she needed to get done before the holidays— including her dreaded Christmas shopping.

"Why would I talk to your brothers about business?"

her father said. "They aren't the least bit interested. I have four sons, and it's my little girl who got the business sense in the family."

Cassie rolled her eyes and rocked back in the chair, resting her Frye boots on the desk and crossing her ankles. "Dad, they all have good business sense and work their butts off for the company. They just don't spend all their time thinking about business. Besides, who can blame them when you forced them to spend every summer vacation in high school doing the grunt work?"

"You did it and loved it." He chuckled. "The guys on the crews used to call you Cast-iron Cassie because you pulled your own weight. Hell, you can even drink them under the table, just like your old dad."

She sighed. "Okay, old Dad, enough already. Stop worrying about James Sutton. There's no way that Steve Mitchell is going with Sutton, not when his father was so happy with the hotels we built for him. But after the holidays, I'll set up a meeting with him just to be sure. No, you cannot be there. Mom would have both our hides."

"Speaking of your mother," her father whispered. "The vulture has landed."

Cassie laughed. "Give Mom my love, and I'll see both of you tonight at the Christmas party." She dropped her feet to the floor and leaned forward to place the receiver in its cradle, knocking over a stack of invoices.

She glared at the mess. This was the part of her job she hated the most. Paperwork. She would much rather be on site, whether in Denver or another city, planning and watching as simple steel and hard work turned into an architectural piece of art. She loved the smell of welded metal and the sounds of heavy equipment. Respected every carpenter, electrician, and steelworker. Her father was right: Her brothers might work for the company, but construction was in her blood.

Too bad her mother didn't think it was ladylike for Big Al's only daughter to be working on site. So Cassie was given the position of vice president in charge of accounts—pretty much a glorified accountant.

She heaved a deep sigh and bent down to pick up the invoices. It could be worse. Her mother had almost talked her father into sending her to interior decorating school. Which would have been a real disaster. She'd much rather do paperwork for M & M than stand around with some stuffy socialite while she decided between floral or stripes. One day she would get up the nerve to talk to her father about being an architect full-time. But not now, not after he had just gone through triple-bypass surgery. He didn't need something else to worry about. James Sutton was quite enough.

James Sutton.

What was the man up to?

Cassie flopped back in the chair. Everything her father had said was true. They *had* lost a lot of business in the last year to Sutton Construction. Until recently, she hadn't been overly concerned; they had lost jobs before and would lose them again. But now she wondered if maybe her father was right. Could James Sutton actually be stupid enough to think he could run them out of business? If so, she didn't believe in hiding out and waiting for the bomb to drop.

She sat up and reached for her phone just as her executive assistant walked in the door, looking like a cute blond

Christmas elf in her green business suit and bright red high heels.

"Hi, Amy." Cassie placed the phone back in its cradle. "Just the person I wanted to see."

"Aren't I the lucky one," Amy said sarcastically.

"Lucky for you, you're my best bud or I'd fire you for insubordination."

"Then who would be your whipping boy?"

"Good point."

A frown wrinkled Amy's smooth brow. "Did you skip lunch again today?"

Cassie stood up, smoothing out the wrinkles of her jeans while discreetly brushing away any chocolate crumbs from her lap. "No."

Amy walked over to the desk and lifted the Snickers wrapper. "I wouldn't call peanuts and chocolate lunch." She shook her head. "You should learn to eat a little neater, Cass. Then I wouldn't catch you every time."

"Okay, so I had a candy bar. Shoot me. I was planning on getting lunch. I just haven't had time."

Amy crumpled up the wrapper and threw it in the trash can. "Even when you have time, you get one of those foot-long, artery-clogging dogs from the vendor. Smothered in sauerkraut and hot mustard."

The mere thought of a hot dog smothered in sauerkraut and spicy mustard had Cassie's mouth watering. God, what she wouldn't give for a couple dogs and an ice-cold beer. Unfortunately, there were other things to worry about at the moment.

She walked around her desk and leaned on the edge. "Okay, I'll bring a tuna fish sandwich on Monday."

"Monday is Christmas."

"Okay, so I'll bring a turkey sandwich on Tuesday. Now, what have you found out about James Sutton?"

"You want it from the beginning?" When Cassie nodded, Amy started sorting through the piles of paper, organizing them as she talked. If there was a personality type that came before A, Amy was it. "Sutton was born in Pittsburgh and comes from a lower-middle-class family. His father worked in the steel mills, and his mother was a housewife until she died of cancer when he was fourteen. Which would probably explain why he goes through women so fast."

Cassie shot her a befuddled look. "Huh?"

"I read this article about how young boys—especially pubescent boys—can be traumatized by the loss of a mother. I guess sometimes it can affect their adult relationships—either they can't get enough women or they don't like women at all."

Cassie rolled her eyes. "Well, I don't care if Sutton is a womanizer or gay. I just want to figure out how he's underbidding us. What else did you learn?"

It took Amy a second to remember where she'd left off. "After high school, he went to Penn State, graduating with degrees in business and architectural engineering. Then, after college, he started building houses in Las Vegas. He got in right before the market exploded and made a fortune. After the bubble burst, he moved here and got into the commercial side of things."

Cassie turned and stared out the floor-to-ceiling windows at the steel-gray skies. "So the guy has more money than we thought."

"If he does, he doesn't show it. He lives in a nice but

modest neighborhood. Although maybe he spends all his money on women. From what his assistant said, he has quite a few."

Cassie whipped around. "You talked with his assistant?"

"Yeah, the Internet can give you only so much info."

"Who did you say you were?"

"Amy Walker, of course. The woman didn't have a clue. I told her I was thinking about doing an article on her boss for the business section of the *Denver Post*. She was more than willing to sit and gab. I think she has a major crush." She batted her eyelashes. "According to her, the man is a real hottie."

"Not in my book. In my book, he's the jerk responsible for my father's heart attack."

Amy looked up from the planner she'd been reading. "Right. Along with fourteen-hour work days, bad eating habits, and lack of exercise. Any of that sound familiar?"

Cassie ignored the comparisons. "Okay, so maybe Sutton isn't entirely responsible, but he played a big role in it." She grabbed the planner out from under Amy's nose and flipped to the next week. "Set up a meeting with him on Monday."

"Monday's Christmas."

"Right. Then Tuesday."

"Most people take the holidays off between Christmas and New Year's."

"I bet he doesn't," Cassie said. "Just try it."

"Speaking of the holidays"—Amy came around the desk and gave Cassie the once-over—"please don't tell me that you're planning on wearing jeans to the Christmas party."

"Of course not. I brought something to change into just in case I didn't have time to go home."

"You never have time to go home. So what did you bring?"

"My burgundy dress."

"No." Amy stared her down. "I refuse to let you wear that thing one more time. Not when it belongs in the wardrobe vault for *Saturday Night Fever.*"

"But it's a Liz Claiborne."

Amy looked at her in disbelief. "My God, woman, you need to read some fashion magazines once in awhile instead of *Architectural Digest.* Liz might be fine for tea with your in-laws. But if you want to make a statement—attract attention..."

She swept out of the office and in less than a minute returned holding a hanger covered in long white plastic. "You need Versace. I took the liberty of shopping for you today at lunch." She closed the door behind her. "I charged it to your credit card account, of course." With a smile a mile wide, she whipped off the plastic to reveal a slinky red—

Shirt?

Cassie lifted an eyebrow. "Where's the rest of it?"

"The shoes and accessories are in my office."

"No, I mean, where's the skirt that goes with it?"

"This is it." Amy held it up to Cassie and nodded her approval. "Perfect." She reached for the rubber band that held Cassie's hair back and tugged it out, along with more than a few jet-black hairs. "You desperately need a cut and some highlights." She plucked at the thick strands. "Lucky for you, men love long hair."

"Cut it out, Amy." Cassie grabbed back the rubber band. "I'm not you. The men who work for me would laugh their asses off if I tried to strut around like some froufrou girly girl." She jerked her hair back into a ponytail.

Amy crossed her arms and glared. "You're being stubborn again, Cass. Just because you dress femininely doesn't mean men won't take you seriously. Besides, you're the boss's daughter; no one would dare laugh at you. Not with Big Al as your daddy and four brothers. So live a little. Lighten up. Stop acting like one of the guys and start acting like a woman. A very attractive woman who needs to get laid before her female parts become an exhibit at the Smithsonian."

Cassie's eyes widened. "It hasn't been that long."

"Try eighteen months."

Eighteen months? Had it been eighteen months? She turned back to the window and quickly did some mental calculations. Yep, it had been eighteen months since she'd been dumped by Mike. And not really dumped. Their split had been a mutual agreement after she'd come home to find him wearing a pair of her thigh highs. She might've forgiven him the hosiery if he hadn't stretched out her most comfortable pair of black pumps.

She turned back around. "Okay, so it's been eighteen months. So what?"

"So what?" Amy stared at her. "Are you telling me you've been so busy you haven't had time to miss sex?"

No, she missed it. So much so that she just recently had to clean off all the hard water deposits from the pulse setting on her shower massager.

"So what do you want me to do," she asked, "grab the

first guy that walks through that door and slam him down on the couch?"

Amy laughed. "I would like to see that. Especially if the next guy through the door is Grumpy Gates. But how about just having sex with one of the hot escorts you hire?"

Cassie glanced around to make sure no one had slipped into the room without her noticing. "I told you not to talk about that," she whispered.

Amy shrugged. "Why not? It was my idea."

"And a stupid one, at that."

"If you think so, why do you keep hiring them? Especially when all you do is take them to public functions, then go your separate ways."

It was a good question. Why had she gotten into the habit of picking up the phone and ordering a guy just like she would chicken teriyaki from Mr. Tokyo? Maybe that was it. It was just so easy and convenient. And as much as she'd told Amy it was a stupid idea, it had worked out pretty well. Especially for a woman who had a family like hers.

If her brothers and father weren't scaring men off, her sister-in-law and married cousins were trying to fix her up with "the perfect man." The perfect man who always ended up being some imperfect date that she had to suffer through. She either spent the evening searching for conversation starters or fighting off some sex-crazed guy's advances. Hiring a man to escort her was much simpler. The escorts were a little young, usually college students, but nice and well mannered. And because they didn't particularly want anyone to know what they did for a buck, they were discreet. Sometimes she would get the same guy and sometimes she'd get someone different. It didn't matter as long as her family assumed she was happy playing the field.

"So why don't you just have sex with one of them and get it out of your system?" Amy asked.

"Because I could catch some fungus or worse, that's why."

"And you don't think you could've caught something from Mike? If a man is sneaking into your underwear drawer, he's sneaking into other places he doesn't belong. Besides, haven't you ever heard of a condom?"

"Those aren't fail-safe, you know." Cassie walked over to the couch and flopped down.

"Okay, so you don't want to screw the hunka-hunka-burnin'-loves," Amy said. "So stop hiring them and try to find a nice guy to date. Or do you just like the control so much that you're addicted?" Her brown eyes narrowed. "That's it, isn't it? You can't control your dad or your four brothers, but you can control some young sap for money."

Man, the truth hurt.

"Shut up, Amy. Just because some of us have found the man of our dreams doesn't mean the rest of us can be as lucky."

The sparkle faded from Amy's brown eyes, and she seemed to deflate right in front of Cassie. "I wouldn't say I've found the man of my dreams."

"What do you mean? Did you and Derek break up?"

"No." Amy flopped down next to her and smoothed out her wrinkle-free skirt. "I just wouldn't call him the man of my dreams."

"But I thought you said he would make a perfect husband."

"He would—I mean, he will." Amy picked at a piece of lint on the arm of the couch. "He might not be the man of my dreams, but he's dependable and very organized. Besides, I learned a long time ago that dreams don't always come true. It's much better to plan out your life and work toward things that are achievable. Derek is a great guy who loves me and Gabriella. What more could a girl ask for?"

Cassie thought she could ask for a lot more. "So you don't love him?"

There was a long pause before Amy shook her head. "But love isn't everything. I loved Gabby's dad and look where it got me."

It had gotten Amy pregnant and then cast off like a dirty shirt, not only by her high school sweetheart but by her own family. Amy was nineteen when she showed up at M & M with nothing but a GED, a baby girl, and a heart the size of Texas. Since then, she'd worked hard to be a good mom and put herself through college. After all she'd been through, she deserved to be happy. But since Cassie was struggling to find happiness in her own life, she wasn't about to give advice. So she kept her mouth shut and stared down at the scuffed toes of her boots.

After a few minutes, Amy spoke. "Look, I'm sorry for getting on your case. I guess I'm just worried about you. Since your father's heart attack, you've looked so lost."

Cassie wanted to say "you don't know the half of it" but instead she forced a smile and said, "I'm okay, really. I just need a little time off. And possibly some good sex."

"Now you're talking." Amy stood up and forced a smile almost as fake as Cassie's. "I'm going home to eat dinner with Gabby, so I'll see you at the party. The rest of your outfit is on my desk, along with a few little Christmas gifts." Before she closed the door, she issued one last order. "Live a little."

Once Amy was gone, Cassie leaned back on the couch and looked at the tiny garment that lay across her desk. Maybe Amy was right. Maybe she was spending too much time at work. But since her father's heart attack, she felt as if the weight of the company was on her shoulders. Her uncle and brothers helped, but her oldest brother had a family to worry about, Rory had just returned from Chicago, Patrick liked working on site, and Mattie was still in college. Which meant that she was the only one her dad could count on. She wasn't about to let him down.

Getting to her feet, she walked over to the desk and lifted the dress up to her body. But certainly one night wouldn't make a difference.

What the hell; it was almost Christmas.

Maybe it was time to get a little festive.

Chapter Two

A few hours later, Cassie wasn't sure if she looked festive or like a desperate hooker. The dress was a *shirt* with
a hem and neckline that ran at opposite angles, showing
off her right shoulder and a whole lot of left thigh. The
"few little Christmas gifts" Amy had left included a strapless bra that shoved her boobs together and a satiny pair
of panties that covered very little of the front and none of
the back. Then there were the shoes, which weren't shoes
at all, but some kind of torture chambers that imprisoned
her feet in skinny, crisscrossed red straps that ran from
ankle to toes and kept her feet from sliding off the sky-
scraper spiked heels. Mike would have drooled over these
puppies, she thought. Not that his size thirteens would've
fit in them.

The entire ensemble made Cassie feel like a tall, flashing red light that said something like SEX FOR SALE; COME

AND GET IT or DESPERATE, SEX-STARVED WOMAN NEEDS BREAK FROM SHOWER NOZZLE.

But Cassie didn't have much of a choice. Her burgundy dress and shoes had mysteriously disappeared from the executive bathroom. Or not so mysteriously, considering how devious Amy was. Cassie could've gone home and changed, but her escort for the evening was bought and paid for and hopefully on his way to the office to meet her. There was no way she was going to dole out five hundred bucks so some college kid could go home and play video games for the evening.

So Cassie did what she always did in a no-win situation—she went with it, applying more makeup than she normally wore and leaving her hair to fall down her back in long dark waves. The only thing she didn't apply was lipstick. Her lips were full enough without drawing attention to them. She gave her reflection in the mirror one last annoyed look. If this wouldn't degrade and undermine her authority in front of all the employees, nothing would.

On the way back to her office, the phone rang, and since everyone else had left for the night except for Juanita the cleaning lady, Cassie wobbled over to the receptionist's desk and picked up the receiver.

She adjusted it around her dangling diamond earring, the only thing she had planned on wearing, and answered, "M and M Construction."

"Hi, Mama's angel. I'm glad I caught you."

"Hi, Mom. What's up?"

"I wanted to let you know that I'm making your father stay home tonight." In the background, Cassie could hear her father ranting something about how her mother and the damned doctor had ruined all his plans.

"Should I come over?" Cassie sat down on the edge of the desk and examined the last of Amy's gifts, a red beaded clutch purse. She fiddled with the rhinestone latch, trying to figure out how to open it.

"No, sweetheart. He's fine. But if he goes to the party, all he'll do is talk business and Dr. Matheson doesn't think it's a good idea." This time Cassie heard exactly what her father thought of Doc Matheson. "Listen, dear, I need to go and calm him down. I'll talk to you later. Have fun at the party."

"Yeah, Mom. I will." Cassie hung up the phone. Maybe it was best if her father didn't come. If talking business didn't give him another heart attack, her outfit certainly would.

Frustrated with the entire evening so far, she yanked at the latch on the purse. It flipped open, spilling its contents all over the floor. Cassie looked down at the pile of red and black foil-covered condoms surrounding her high heels.

She laughed. "I'll get even with you if it's the last thing I do, Amy Walker." She squatted down and began to scoop the condoms back into her purse, heedless of her unladylike position.

A deep and very masculine cough had her teetering on her heels and almost falling backward on her butt. Grabbing on to the edge of the desk, she regained her balance and got to her feet. Although the sight that greeted her had her reaching out for the desk again.

A man stood by the Christmas tree in the foyer. Not a

man really, more like a vision. The clear lights that twinkled around his dark head made him look like something straight out of a dream. A wet dream. Man, Elite Escorts had outdone themselves this time. This was no gangly college boy in an ill-fitting rental tux, but a mature man in a tuxedo that looked made-to-order for his tall, muscular frame.

Like James Bond right before he bopped a shapely beauty, his bow tie was undone and lay flat against the front pleats of the crisp white shirt that was unbuttoned at his tanned throat. He stood looking at Cassie with a slight smile on his firm lips and one brown brow arched over an eye that was the exact color of her Aunt Wheezie's favorite Scotch.

Cassie forgot to breathe.

"Hi." The smile deepened, along with two dimples. "I didn't mean to spook you." When Cassie still didn't say anything, the smile dropped and both brows lifted. "Are you okay?"

He walked toward her, and she was reminded of the black panther at the Denver Zoo, his movements sleek and predatory. She swallowed and tried to get her mind off his hot body and back in her head. It was difficult, especially when this wonderful eye candy stood so close and when she and Amy had just been discussing how long it had been since she'd had sex. But hot or not, she needed to remember that this man was one of her employees. She dealt with men all day long. Alpha men. She could handle some pretty boy who worked for an escort service.

She plastered on a smile. "Yes, I'm fine. It's just that you're early."

The quizzical look remained, and he tugged up the sleeve of his jacket and glanced at a watch that looked an awful lot like her father's Rolex. "No, I'm right on time."

She waved him off. "It doesn't matter. You're here." She grabbed the car keys from the desk and brushed past him. He smelled really good, like hot spiced cider and primitive lust. Or was the primitive lust her?

"My truck's down in the parking garage." She kept talking as she headed toward the elevator. "We'll take it. The party's at a house about thirty minutes away, so it's probably good you got here early." She pressed the button of the elevator, then turned to steal another peek.

He wasn't there. He still stood at the receptionist's desk, although his head had turned to follow her. Okay, so he looked great, but he was a little slow on the uptake. No wonder he worked for an escort service at his age. The elevator doors opened, and she pointed at them.

"Are you coming?"

He tipped his head to one side. "Who are you?"

Oh, so that was it. She just hadn't introduced herself. She laughed and held the door of the elevator. "I'm Cassie McPherson, your employer for the evening."

He didn't move. "My employer?"

Back to the mental deficiency theory. She tried talking slowly and clearly. "Yes, I called Elite Escorts and hired you for the evening to take me to my office Christmas party. I paid in advance, so I expect a little service here. Like maybe you getting a move on."

His whiskey eyes twinkled, but he still didn't move. "You're Cassie McPherson, the daughter of Al McPherson, and you called for a male escort?"

"Right. So are you coming or do I need to get a refund?"

"Your father's not here, I take it?"

"Not that it makes a difference, but no. He's at home."

He might be a simpleton, but, man, the flash of those white, even teeth and dimples were flat-out sexy. "Then I guess I'm all yours for the evening." He walked over and reached above her head to hold the elevator door. "Here"—he held up a foil-covered condom—"you forgot one."

Cassie jerked the condom out of his hand and then nearly fell flat on her face as she stumbled over her feet on the way into the elevator. He reached out and steadied her.

"Easy there."

The door closed, and he pushed one of the buttons while she rubbed the warm imprint he had left on her arm. Her heart thumped wildly against the tight band of her push-up bra. And suddenly she worried if all her high-cholesterol lunches and lack of exercise were catching up to her and besides inheriting her father's bad disposition, she had also inherited his clogged arteries. She couldn't bring herself to believe that it had anything to do with the man who so casually leaned back against the rail that ran along the wall of the elevator. Cassie McPherson didn't go all weak-kneed over men. Even re-e-e-e-ally good-looking ones who belonged in magazine ads for expensive men's cologne.

She turned away from the hot picture he presented and took two deep breaths, willing her heart to resume its normal cadence. It was hard to do with those eyes pinned on her with such intensity. Hard, but not impossible. She wasn't called Cast-iron Cassie for nothing. She never let emotions get in the way of business. And this was business.

Clearing her throat, she explained the terms of his employment. "So here's what I expect." She opened her clutch and dropped in her car keys and the condom. "Keep a low profile. Be attentive, but not clingy. And try not to talk. If you're asked a question about our relationship, simply say that we've just met."

His eyes narrowed, and one side of his mouth tipped up at the corner. Definitely not a smile, more of a smirk. "How about if I just say that I'm not the kind of man who kisses and tells."

Heat flooded her cheeks, but she held it together. "Just stick to the plan."

"It seems you have a lot of plans." He lifted an eyebrow in the direction of her purse. "I'm not sure I can keep up."

Cassie ignored the innuendo and stayed on track. "The old relatives are the worst. They'll try to get you to commit to family gatherings and such. Decline gracefully. Don't drink with my Aunt Louise. She'll drink you under the table and then interrogate the hell out of you. She looks very sweet, but she's a barracuda."

The elevator doors slid open, but not at the parking garage. He stepped out and held the door.

"You pushed the wrong button." She punched L for the lower level. "I'm parked in the garage."

He took her arm and gently but firmly pulled her out. "I know, but I'm parked right out front. So we can take my car."

"I'd rather drive," she stated as she caught the elevator door before it closed.

"But then you'd be escorting me, and that's not what I'm getting paid for." He caressed the underside of her arm. The tingling sensation caused her to pull away.

She turned on him as the elevator door slid closed. "You're getting paid to follow my orders."

In her heels, Cassie was only a few inches shorter than he was. So she shouldn't feel intimidated by his size, not with four brothers who were just as tall, if not taller. Yet there was something about this man that had her taking a step back. She wasn't frightened, but she was smart enough to be wary.

"And I bet you're pretty good at giving orders." He tucked her hand in the crook of his arm and tugged her toward the glass doors. "But right now, it's my job to get you to a Christmas party, and I intend to do it. After that, you can order me around all you want to."

She tried to dig in her heels, but she wasn't exactly stable in the sky-high shoes. The slippery marble floor of the lobby didn't help.

"I like driving," she stated through clenched teeth as he pulled her along.

"No doubt." He reached for the large gold handle of the glass door. "But I'm kinda old-fashioned about that. When I take a woman out, I like to drive."

"You've got to be kidding."

He glanced down at her. "Nope. Not at all. I don't like women to pay, open doors, or drive." He shrugged. "Call it a character flaw." He pulled open the door.

"Obviously, one among many. Let's not forget arrogance and stubbornness." The toes of her shoes hit the threshold, and he was brought up short. "I want to drive."

"Ms. McPherson?"

They both turned and stared at the worried face of the security guard who had come up behind them. "Is everything all right?"

Cassie thought about saying no and getting her arrogant, stubborn escort tossed out on his ear. But then she wouldn't have a date for the evening and would have to suffer through all the wives feeling sorry for her and trying to hook her up with some desperate relative. Of course, how much more desperate could you get than hiring an escort for the evening?

She stopped pulling away. "Of course. Everything is fine, Scotty. How is that new baby of yours?"

The tension left Scotty's face, and he grinned. "As cute as they come. Although he's not so cute when he keeps me up on my nights off."

"He'll outgrow it. My nieces and nephews all did."

"I hope so." Scotty moved over to the door. "Let me get that for you, sir."

"Thank you." Her escort flashed Scotty one of his megawatt smiles. "Merry Christmas."

"Merry Christmas, sir." Scotty nodded at her. "Ms. McPherson."

The frigid air hit Cassie like an ice-cold fist in the face. With it came the realization that she'd forgotten her coat. She stopped dead in her tracks. And her wallet. And her cell phone. The wallet she could live without, but she never went anywhere without her phone. It was her lifeline. How could she have forgotten it?

She glanced at the man who turned to look at her, and a shiver that had nothing to do with the cold raced through her body. Great! Now, all because of some pretty face, she was freezing her posterior off with nothing in her purse but her car keys and a gross of condoms.

She tried to pull her hand away, and this time he released it. "I forgot my—" Before she could finish her sentence a heat-infused tuxedo jacket slid over her shoulders, along with a very possessive arm. The warmth that enveloped her melted the rest of her resistance.

Maybe she could go one night without her cell phone.

"This way." He led her right out to the street, where a brand-new black Land Rover was parked in the no-parking zone. The locks clicked, and he opened the door and waited for her to slip inside. Once the door closed, Cassie was surrounded by the spicy scent that emanated from his jacket and overcome by a feeling that could be described only as...feminine.

Feminine? Cassie McPherson?

She shook her head to clear it. She needed to be careful. This guy was a bona-fide gigolo who knew how to make a woman feel like a woman. A sexy, feminine woman. Which was why he could afford to drive a new Land Rover. The man probably had every wealthy housewife in Denver lined up with their wallets and legs wide open. Which brought up the next point. She waited until they had pulled away from the curb before broaching it.

"About sex."

The SUV swerved slightly, and she quickly glanced over at him. He didn't look shocked as much as amused.

"What about sex?"

She stared straight ahead and tried to keep her voice steady. "I don't want any."

"Ever?"

She looked back at him. "No, not ever. It's just that I don't have sex with escorts."

"Why not? You're paying for it."

Suddenly, her reasons for not having sex with escorts didn't seem valid anymore. Why shouldn't she have sex with an escort? Not just anyone, but this one. This tall, hot, arrogant, and slightly dumb escort who probably needed no sexual instruction at all, who probably could make her come just by looking at her.

An expert lover.

Which was the main reason she couldn't have sex with him. The guy had probably screwed half the female population of the city.

Lucky bitches.

"Because I don't want some nasty disease." She mentally kicked herself for blurting out the truth. "Not that you have some nasty disease, but just in case."

"Then why all the condoms?"

"Those are a joke."

"Too bad."

Her head swiveled around to look at him, but his gaze was pinned on the road. "So you hire escorts just for the company?"

"No, believe me. With my big family, I have plenty of company. I hire escorts to keep that big, loving—and sometimes smothering—family from matchmaking."

He glanced over at her. "That bad, huh?"

She laughed, relieved to be on a less intimate subject. "You don't know the half of it. I've been on so many blind dates, I could write a book on the dos and don'ts."

"But it must be nice to have a big family."

She sighed. "Yeah, sometimes. No, I take that back, most of the time. But it would be a lot nicer if I were married."

"And why aren't you?"

"I've been told I work too much. And I guess they're right." She turned in her seat and looked at his profile. He really was perfect. His features were strong and masculine, but not too prominent. "And what about you? And please don't tell me you have a wife and five kids at home."

He laughed. "I guess I've been told the same thing."

"You work too much?"

He tipped his head and winked at her. "A true workaholic."

Chapter Three

The fact that the man sitting next to her *had* screwed half the female population of Denver and loved every minute of it should have cooled Cassie down. It didn't. Instead, her pulse shot into overdrive, and she had to clamp her legs together and shut her eyes just to get a grip on her rioting libido.

"Hey, you okay?" he asked.

No, she wasn't. But she would be, just as soon as they got to the party and she could get some space between her workaholic hunka-hunka-burnin'-love and her own quivering, sex-starved body. Or maybe she wouldn't feel better until she got back to her shower. Either way, things weren't looking good.

She opened her eyes and glanced over at him. "Yeah, I'm okay. I just need to eat something." Like a delicious tanned neck. Firm, smiling lips. And whatever else was hidden beneath that crisp white shirt and those black tuxedo pants.

He pulled up at a stoplight, his gaze dropping to her mouth. "Yeah, I'm pretty hungry myself."

It was difficult to swallow when her mouth had suddenly gone dry. Her tongue swept across her lips. It was a mistake. His eyes followed its path. Then his gaze lifted, and she found herself drowning in a swirling pool of amber heat. Every coherent thought melted right out of her brain. All except for one.

Kiss me. Kiss me now.

The car behind them honked and instead of kissing her he pulled away from the stoplight. It took a little longer for her brain to congeal. She sat back against the soft leather seat and closed her eyes.

Man, the guy was good. And she was screwed. Or would be, if she couldn't pull her mind out of the gutter. He cleared his throat, but she refused to open her eyes. Maybe if she kept her eyes closed for the entire ride, she wouldn't find herself with her legs in the air and her morals out the window.

"What kind of music do you like?" He turned on the radio and scanned through the stations. She really didn't care what he chose as long as she didn't have to look at him while he was choosing it.

"This is good," she blurted out when he landed on a Christmas song she recognized. It took only a second to realize it was the Chipmunks singing about huuu-la hoops. That got her eyes open. She glanced over at him.

One eyebrow lifted. "A favorite of yours, I take it?"

Her face heated up, but she refused to let him know

just how much she wanted to open the door and dive out into the snow-packed gutter. She was a McPherson, and a true McPherson would never admit to being wrong. So she cleared her throat and sat up straighter in her seat.

"As a matter of fact, it is. Everyone loves the Chipmunks." To prove her point, she sang along with Alvin in her off-key voice for a full two minutes. After she was finished, she turned and glared at him, daring him to say one word about her performance.

His eyes twinkled, and a huge smile lit his face, but he didn't laugh. Not once. The man had unbelievable self-control. Or he just knew who buttered his bread. Another Chipmunk Christmas song started, but before she could sing one note, he reached over and turned off the radio.

"So tell me about yourself. What do you do at M & M?"

The question surprised her. Not one of the other guys had asked it, which was why she was bluntly truthful. "I do a lot of bookkeeping."

"By the sound of your voice, I would say you don't like bookkeeping."

"You'd be right." She looked out the side window.

"So what do you like doing?"

By the time they reached Mark Hillshire's house, where the party was being held, Cassie had her sex-deprived body under control. Not because of anything she did, but because her date was actually a pretty intelligent guy and a great conversationalist. He engaged her in a discussion about construction that demonstrated a fairly competent knowledge of business and architecture. Somewhere along the line, he had learned a few things besides how to make a woman sizzle. She found herself telling him things she talked about only with her brothers.

"So I don't get it. Why don't you just tell your father that you want to design buildings and work on site?" he asked.

"You don't know Al McPherson."

"I guess I don't." He nodded at the large brick home on the right. "Is this it?"

"Yes. They have parking attendants, so just pull into the drive," she said. He ignored her, bypassing the long driveway, and found a spot down the block.

With his hand gripping her seat, he looked over his shoulder and zipped next to the curb. Her gaze caught on his tanned throat, the knot of his Adam's apple and the shadowy indention at the base.

She swallowed. "You forgot your tie."

He slipped the car in park and turned off the engine. "I didn't forget. I still haven't mastered the bow tie. You wouldn't know how, would you?"

"Face me," she ordered as she turned in the seat. "With four brothers, I've gotten pretty good at it." Of course, that had been with her brothers, not with a man whose amber gaze caused her stomach to flutter and her hands to shake as she slipped the top button into the hole. Beneath the collar, his throat felt hot and smooth.

"Are you cold? Your hands are like ice." He continued to watch her. "What is it they say about cold hands?" His breath was warm and smelled of peppermint. "Cold hands, warm heart." He brushed a piece of her hair back from her eyes. "Is your heart warm, Cassie?"

Luckily, she'd finished with his tie, because her entire

body trembled at his touch. "Most of our employees don't think so."

He ran his fingers along her jawline and tipped up her chin. "Mmmm, I wonder."

Then, just like that, he released her and opened his door. She was so stunned, she didn't even try to get out. Instead, she remained frozen to her seat until he reached her side. Between her trembling knees and spiked heels, she could barely walk. Thank God he held her elbow.

"Where did Cassie come from?" he asked as he slammed the door. "Isn't that more Irish than Scottish?"

Amazed that he knew the difference, it took her a moment to answer. "My mother is Irish and Italian. Mom chose all the first names. Jake, Rory, Cassandra, Patrick, and Matthew. Dad chose the middle names. Douglas, Camran, Catriona, Neill, and Lachlan."

"Ahhh." He studied her dark hair. "Italian. That would explain it, Cassandra Catriona."

"What do you go by?" she asked as they turned and walked down the sidewalk. "I mean, what name do you use when you're working?"

"James."

"James?" She sent him a skeptical look. "Let me guess, your last name is Bond."

He laughed as he guided her around some shrubs. "Exactly."

"Not very original, if you ask me."

"I would imagine that you're used to names with a little more blatant sex appeal like Lance or Rod?"

There had been a Lance and a Rod from the escort service. Ironically, neither one of them had half the sex appeal as this plain James did. But if he was going to work for an escort service, he should come up with a better name.

"How about Dirk?"

"Dirk?" He laughed. "I think James will do."

Before she could ask what his last name was, her oldest brother, Jake, pulled up in his Lexus and hopped out.

"Hey, Cass. Did Mom call and tell you about Dad?" He tossed the keys to an attendant before holding the passenger door for his wife, Melanie. It wasn't until he'd slammed the door that he noticed James. His eyes narrowed briefly; then he held out a hand. "Jake McPherson."

James shook his hand. "James."

Cassie knew Jake was waiting for more, but James didn't appear to notice. Instead, he wrapped his arm around her shoulders and slipped a hand in his pocket. Jake looked like he wanted to say something, but decided against it. Being a tough corporate lawyer, he knew when to push and when to leave things alone.

"Hi, I'm Melanie." Jake's wife stepped forward, her face lit with its usual kind, welcoming smile. Except there was approval in her soft brown eyes that hadn't been there for the other escorts Cassie had introduced. Of course, what woman wouldn't approve of a man who looked like James?

Melanie shivered and took Jake's arm. "Let's get inside before we freeze to death."

"I couldn't agree more," James said, as he allowed them to lead the way up the winding path to the Hillshires' front door.

"You're more confident than the others," Cassie said as

they walked up the path bordered by shrubs mantled in twinkling lights.

He slowed his steps to match her smaller, wobbly ones. "The others?"

"The other escorts."

"How many have there been?" he asked.

She ignored the question. "It probably has to do with age. They were younger than you."

"How young?"

"I think one was nineteen. Although he swore up and down he was twenty-one."

He rolled his eyes. "Good Lord."

A noise came out of her mouth that sounded very much like a giggle. But since Cassie had given up giggling at age ten, she figured her ears had deceived her.

"So you think it's funny to be dating an old man?" he asked.

"You're not that old," she said. "Surely not more than forty."

"Thirty-five. And don't call me Shirley."

Another one of those girlish giggles came out, but this time she clamped her mouth shut and cut it off.

The Hillshires had hidden speakers somewhere on the lawn. The sound of choral voices singing "We Three Kings" filled the air. With his arm tucked securely around her, it was quite easy for Cassie to fantasize that she was walking through this beautiful holiday scene with a man who really cared about her. A man who wasn't being paid for his time. A man who was with her because he chose to be.

Once they got inside, James took his jacket back, but

before he could slip one arm in a sleeve, the rest of the McPherson clan descended. Thank God her father and mother were at home.

"Whoa, Miss Cass, who dressed you tonight?" Mattie, her youngest brother, teased with a wide grin that Cassie wanted to wipe off with her fist when he added, "Hookers R Us?"

"No, Simply Sluts." Patrick spun her around and pulled her into his arms.

He passed her to Rory, who made some comment about a wolf in sheep's clothing. Her face heated up, not because of her brothers' teasing, but because of the pair of whiskey eyes that took in the entire scene.

She hid her embarrassment by socking Rory in the chest. "You guys had better watch out. Amy won't like how you're talking about her handiwork."

Rory scowled and grumbled, "Figures. I don't know why you hang out with that woman. She's a bad influence."

Before she could defend her best friend, a warm hand reached out, and suddenly she wasn't in Rory's arms anymore. Instead, she was flush against James's side. He stared down at her with something that looked a lot like adoration mixed with a small amount of sympathy.

"I think you look stunning," he stated.

She swallowed down the lump that formed in her throat. "James, meet the rest of my brothers."

He shook each one's hand as she made the introductions, then, apparently unconcerned with their censorious stares, turned back to her. "Cassandra, would you like something to drink?"

No one called her Cassandra except her mom. She

liked the way it sounded coming from his firm lips. Feeling a little dazed and confused, especially with all her brothers watching, she could only croak out one word. "Coors."

There was a flicker of surprise, and then he shot her another killer smile before he walked off.

"Oh. My. God. Cassie." Mattie's new college coed, Shelly, released a dramatic sigh. "He's so hot."

"He's a smart-ass," Mattie grumbled.

"Absolutely gorgeous," Melanie chimed in.

"Arrogant," Jake added.

"Deeelish," Patrick's date commented before Patrick whispered something under his breath that was best not repeated.

Cassie watched her tall, dark, and handsome date maneuver through the large room of people, stopping once to ask directions to the bar. The room looked like a boxful of bobbleheads as every person—man and woman—turned to watch him walk by. He might be cocky. And a little arrogant. And even a smart-ass at times. But he was also very hot—absolutely gorgeous—and oh so deeelish.

Unfortunately, she would never find out just how delicious. He was an escort, an expert lover who had probably dipped his wick more times than he could count. Oh Lord, what she wouldn't give to be a puddle of hot wax.

"So where did you meet this one?" Rory asked.

Cassie took her sweet time in answering, probably because she couldn't think of a good lie while her date was still in view. When he disappeared around the corner of the living room, she refocused.

"He's an architect."

"Really?" Rory sounded impressed. "For what firm?"

Crap. What firm? What firm? "No one yet. He's new in town and looking for a job."

Jake snorted, sounding just like their father. "Which is why he's hot after you."

"That's ridiculous, Jake." Melanie took her side. "He's hot after your sister because she's smart, beautiful, and hardworking."

And because she is paying him five hundred dollars. Let's not forget that.

Cassie sent Melanie a smile. "Thanks, Mel. But this is one of our first dates, so I'm really not too worried about whether he's hot after a job—or my body." There was a collective sigh of relief from her brothers just as Amy walked up.

She gave Cassie the once-over. "Just as I thought, you look great." When there was no reply, she looked around. "Doesn't she look great?"

There was a whole lot of grumbling before the McPherson clan dispersed. All except for Rory, who seemed to be more interested in the black dress that Amy wore. If his angry expression was any indication, he didn't like it either.

His reaction wasn't surprising. Since returning from Chicago, he had formed a major aversion to Amy. Which was the complete opposite of how he'd felt when she had first started working for the company. Rory had followed her around like a starry-eyed puppy, and Cassie had hoped that they would get together. Instead, her brother suddenly volunteered to move to the Chicago branch of

M & M and work for Uncle Ryan. Three months later, he'd married Tess, a woman who'd forced Cassie to squeeze into an orange marmalade satin dress with a bow on the back that made her butt look the size of her Aunt Lula's.

Cassie wouldn't have minded the dress so much if she had liked the bride. But Terrible Tess was self-centered and vain and the bitchiest wife anyone could ask for. Fortunately, Rory's life sentence had been cut short when she ran off with her Pilates instructor. Although Cassie was sure her brother didn't see things the same way she did. The man who moved back to Denver didn't come close to being the jovial, easygoing brother she'd grown up with.

"So where's your date?" Amy asked, completely ignoring Rory's glare.

"Getting me a drink."

Amy's eyes widened. "Mr. Tall, Dark, and Hot?"

"How do you know hot?" Rory asked. "You date Derek Terrell."

Amy reached out to adjust the strap of Cassie's dress and brush off a bit of invisible lint. "Derek is hot."

"Yeah, if you like arrogant men with Napoleon complexes." He shot her another nasty look before he turned and strode off.

Cassie started to apologize for her brother's rude behavior when Amy grabbed her arm and pulled her down the hallway to a bathroom. Once inside, she closed the door and turned on Cassie like a rabid dog.

"So?"

"So what?"

"So who is this guy? There's no way he's an escort."

Cassie moved to the cushioned vanity bench and sat

down. Her feet were killing her. She tugged at the straps of the high heels. "What kind of torture devices are these?"

"Cassie!"

"Fine!" She knew Amy wouldn't leave her alone until she had the entire story. She dropped the shoe to the floor and rubbed her abused toes. "He's from the agency, but I think he's more gigolo than escort. He drives a Land Rover."

"You're kidding me."

"Nope."

Amy straightened the towels on the rack before moving to the sink, where she rearranged the white roses in a vase. "So what's his name?"

"James."

"James what?"

The other shoe slipped to the floor, and Cassie sighed in relief. "I don't know; nor do I care. He's just another employee." It really wasn't the truth. He may have started out as just an employee, but after listening to his strong, deep voice, smelling his subtle, spicy scent, and feeling his soft, warm touch, he was fast approaching a status of definite interest. Sexual interest, but interest just the same.

She looked up to see Amy studying her in the mirror.

"You have the condoms I gave you?"

"Real funny, Amy."

She didn't laugh. "It might've been funny to begin with, but after seeing your date for the evening, I think you'll be happy you have them."

Cassie slipped her shoes back on. "Whatever."

"I'm serious. If you're ever going to do something totally irresponsible, it should be with that guy."

"Well, I'm not going to do anything totally irresponsible." She stood, and cringed at her sore toes. "So did you set up a meeting with Sutton?"

"No. Didn't you get the message I left on your cell?" She removed a tube of lipstick from her purse and took off the cap. "Here, put some of this on."

Knowing that Amy wouldn't relent, Cassie took the lipstick. "I left my cell phone at the office."

Amy stared at her. "You never leave your cell phone. This guy must have ruffled your feathers pretty good."

"Not at all." Cassie applied the bright red lipstick. When she was finished, she handed it back to Amy. "As I said before, the man is just another employee."

"Well, that's probably for the best." Amy put the lipstick back in her purse. "I just saw Aunt Wheezie leading him to the greenhouse."

"Did she have a bottle?"

"Two."

Great. Cassie turned to the door. There went her date for the evening. The last escort Aunt Wheezie had commandeered had been carried out feet first.

Chapter Four

James sat at a table in the greenhouse and watched the woman across from him down another shot of Scotch whiskey. He couldn't help but wonder if this would be the one that knocked her out cold. Instead, Louise McPherson blotted her mouth with her handkerchief and sat back in her chair as if she'd just taken a sip of afternoon tea.

"So what did you say you do, Jimmy?"

Stalling, he took a deep drink of the beer that he'd planned on giving Cassandra before this wily woman had abducted him. He didn't know exactly how much to tell Cassie's aunt, especially when Cassandra had given strict orders to say as little as possible. But he couldn't see the harm in telling her a few things. Even if it was more than her niece knew.

"Construction."

Aunt Louise's eyes twinkled, eyes that were the exact

shade of green as her great-niece's. It was an intriguing mixture of deep jade and sparkling emerald. "So you like construction, do you? Don't know a thing about the business myself. I let my nephews handle all that while I just spend their money." She poured herself another shot. "I was in the bar business in Chicago."

Surprise. Surprise.

"My husband—God rest his soul—and I owned a small bar. It wasn't much, but it was a haven to plenty of men and women, I'll tell you that. That was back when people didn't come to a bar because they were horny."

After meeting her niece, James could relate to being horny, so he nodded.

"In my day, people came to a bar to relax and enjoy each other's company," she continued. "When times were hard, they counted on me and Neill to be there with a warm welcome and a stiff drink. And for close to fifty years, we were. There wasn't any need for therapists and antidepressants. All most people need is someone to listen to their problems and let them know that things are going to be all right."

She downed her shot, then scowled at the full shot glass she'd poured for him. "You're not keeping up, Jimmy."

Bluto from *Animal House* couldn't keep up with this pint-sized woman, and James wasn't stupid enough to even try. Still, he might've downed the shot just to be polite if she hadn't been drinking whiskey. He had an aversion to the liquor ever since his mother had passed away and he'd tried to drown his sorrow by drinking an entire bottle. Now just the smell brought back bad memories.

"Humph." Aunt Louise's sharp eyes studied him for a few seconds, before she smiled and pushed the glass and the bottle away. "So you're smarter than the rest." She winked. "Brains and looks. I like that in a man." She leaned forward and rested her wrinkled hands on the glass table. "But if you're planning on catching Cassie, you'll need more than brains and good looks. You'll need the patience of a saint and the endurance of a pack mule. In case you haven't noticed, my niece is a real fireball."

James had noticed. If the daring clothes hadn't given Cassandra away, the escort service certainly had. That and the fact that she was walking around with a purse filled with condoms. Which pretty much made her a fireball and James toast.

As if knowing where his mind wandered, Aunt Louise cackled. "It isn't really her fault. Growing up with four brothers, she had to fight for everything she got— from toys to her daddy's attention. You could say it made her a little aggressive. Which is why she scares a lot of men off."

She studied him. "Of course, in my book, they were all a bunch of candy asses anyway. Every last one of them. Especially that Mike fella. Now, if you ask me, something wasn't quite right in his head. He looked big and capable, but any man who can tell you where to find the best buys on women's shoes has got something out of whack. And him bringing his baked goods to every family function was more than I could take. Although he makes pretty damned good pumpkin bread, I'll give him that."

"When did they break up?" James asked.

"A little over a year ago. No great loss, in my opinion.

And I think Cassandra pretty much feels the same way. She was just killing time with him. Just like all the ones since. Young, good-lookin' group. But not one could hold their booze worth a darn." She lifted one penciled-in brow. "But you, on the other hand…"

James tried not to squirm under those penetrating eyes. The last thing he was looking for right now was a serious relationship. Not when he had a new company to get up and running. He was attracted to Cassandra. No, more than attracted. But what he wanted from her had more to do with the condoms in her little red purse than joining the McPherson family. "But doesn't she work a lot? Maybe she doesn't have time for a serious relationship," he said, in an attempt to dissuade any matchmaking attempts. It didn't work.

"You sound just like Cassandra. But I'll guarantee you that once she discovers the right person, she'll find time to spend with him. Everyone needs to have a reason to quit work and go home. No one wants to go home to an empty house."

He knew exactly what the woman was talking about. He put off getting an office just so he wouldn't have to leave work. Ever. His home seemed less lonely when filled with assistants, fax and copy machines, and computers.

"And Cassandra's long hours are even more pathetic when you consider the fact that she doesn't even like her job," Aunt Louise said. Before James could question her, she leaned closer, her strong whiskey breath almost knocking him out of his chair. "I'll tell you a little secret. I think Albert made one hell of a mistake putting that girl behind a desk. Just like her daddy, she loves to be in the thick of things and doesn't mind getting her hands a little dirty."

The mention of Cassandra's father brought up a question that had been plaguing James for most of the night. "Where is Mr. McPherson?"

Aunt Louise chuckled. "Worried about coming face-to-face with Big Al, are you? Well, don't be. Alby's more bark than bite. Besides, he just had heart surgery, so you won't be running into him tonight. Old Doc Matheson put a stop to that." She got to her feet, and James followed. "Which reminds me. I better be on my way." She picked up the full bottle of whiskey and tucked it under her arm. "I promised Mary Katherine I'd stop by before I go home." She held out a hand. "Jimmy, it was nice meeting you."

"Same here, ma'am. Are you going to be okay to drive?"

She gave his hand a hard shake. "Son, I was just getting warmed up."

James didn't doubt her, but he still couldn't let her drive. Not after an entire bottle of whiskey was almost gone.

"Just the same, I think I'll call you a cab." He pulled his cell phone from the inside pocket of his tux. Since he had turned it on vibrate when he was in the elevator at M & M Construction, he took note of the five calls he'd missed before he started to dial information.

She stopped him, her green eyes sparkling. "You don't have any trouble taking control. I like that, Jimmy. I like that a lot. But there's no need to worry about me. I won't be driving, not when those crazy nephews of mine went and got me a big old Cadillac with a cute, young chauffeur." She patted his arm. "I'll be fine. Besides, what you need to worry about is standing right over there." She tipped her head, and James glanced behind him.

On the other side of the glass wall of the conservatory, Cassandra stood talking with a man.

"That would be Foster," Aunt Louise answered James's unspoken question. "His parents are friends of the family, or like to think they are. Foster's another candy ass, but at least the other candy asses had jobs. He hasn't worked a day in his life. Although he'll tell you different."

"Is Cassandra interested?" he asked as he watched the tall, blond man reach out and take her hand. James's eyes narrowed. He heard Aunt Louise snort, but he kept his gaze pinned on the scene before him.

"I'll let you find that out for yourself," she said. "I think I'll be seeing you, Jimmy."

A sudden draft of cold air pulled his attention away long enough to watch the old woman slip out through the side door. He didn't watch her for long, more interested in what the candy ass was doing with Cassandra's hand. He actually had to fight down a feeling similar to jealousy. It surprised him. He wasn't the jealous type. Yet, for some reason, he felt not only jealous but protective, which was strange considering he and Cassandra didn't have any kind of a relationship.

Except the bizarre escort thing.

After meeting her large, overbearing family, it made more sense. As a fellow workaholic, he understood how difficult it was to maintain a relationship. His ex-girlfriends could attest to that. It looked like Cassandra had found a solution. Not one he would have chosen, but a solution nonetheless.

But understanding her motivation didn't explain why he had gone along with the charade.

As soon as he realized she'd mistaken him for someone else, he should've introduced himself. But she surprised him. He wasn't expecting a beautiful, dark-haired woman. He was expecting Al McPherson, the gruff man who had called him earlier in the day to set up a meeting. James had stepped off the elevator, nervous and excited about meeting one of the most respected men in the business, and was completely sideswiped by long, sexy legs and a tiny patch of red satin. Once his gaze locked on those undies, his curiosity and excitement about meeting Big Al had flown straight out the window. Along with every coherent thought he'd ever had.

Follow sexy underwear with sparkling green eyes and full, luscious lips, and he was lucky that he had remembered his name. He sure didn't give a second thought to her father or to the Christmas party he was supposed to attend. Damn, his mind had been on penis-pilot way before his name even came up. In fact, he was still on penis-pilot, which would explain the sudden intense desire to kill the bastard who had just bent his head for a kiss.

To hell with it.

James pushed his way through the overgrown plants of the greenhouse and headed for the door that led into the house. He shouldn't have bothered. By the time he stepped into the hallway, Cassandra had already taken care of the situation. She didn't slap Foster, but rather punched him right in the face. And from the bunched muscles in her arm and the way Foster's head snapped back, it wasn't a girlie tap.

"Damn it, Cassie." Foster stumbled back with a hand over his eye. "What's your problem?"

"Easy there." James reached out and settled a hand on his shoulder to steady the poor guy. He must've used a little too much pressure because Foster flinched. James completely ignored him as he studied Cassandra.

"You okay?"

"Yeah, I think so," the pompous idiot answered.

James shot him an annoyed look before reaching for Cassandra's hand and examining it. For such a wild-cat, her hands were soft and fragile. He rubbed his thumb over her knuckles. "It doesn't look like you broke anything."

She pulled her hand away and looked up. For a long moment, he got lost in her eyes before his gaze dropped to her mouth. A mouth that was now painted a glossy, sexy-as-hell red. "I'm fine," she said.

Fine? Oh, baby, you don't know the half of it. No wonder the poor bastard tried to kiss you.

James glanced at the poor bastard. "You're lucky."

"How's that?" Foster removed his hand from his eye and studied it as if it might have blood on it.

"I could've gotten to you first." He slipped an arm around Cassandra to make his point. She stiffened, but didn't pull away.

Foster's face turned red, and for a moment, James thought he would actually be stupid enough to say something. Instead, he made a strangled huffing noise, then turned and walked away. As soon as he was gone, Cassandra slipped out from under his arm and walked into the greenhouse. He followed her back to the table.

She lifted the half-full beer. "Mine?"

He shrugged. "I got waylaid."

"Yeah, I know." She took a deep drink, and all he could think about were her lips being on the same spot as his. The tightening in his stomach caused him to reach for the shot glass of whiskey. He downed it so quickly Aunt Louise would've been proud.

Cassandra studied him for a few seconds before she moved over to the fish pond and stared down at the large, colorful koi that were huddled at the bottom. "Are you drunk?"

He felt dizzy, but he wasn't sure the effect was caused by the whiskey. "No."

She turned. "So how much did my aunt get out of you?"

"Not much. She knows I'm interested in construction and that I'm not a candy ass who bakes pumpkin bread."

"A what?" She looked puzzled, but only for a second. "Ahh, you got to hear about Mike."

"A little. So what happened?"

She shrugged, then took another swallow before answering. "I told you—I work too much."

"And?"

"And I'm very controlling."

"With what?"

"With just about everything."

He couldn't help himself. "Sounds like fun."

Cassandra's gaze snapped up. "You're not still thinking about those condoms, are you?"

James laughed. This straightforward woman intrigued

the hell out of him. "As a matter of fact..." He stepped closer.

She held up her hand. "Well, just get them out of your head. Sex is out. Besides, I threw them all in the trash as soon as I got here."

"All of them?"

She smirked. "Every last one."

"Damn." He snapped his fingers before he reached out and pulled her into his arms. "Then I guess I'll just have to settle for a kiss."

"I don't think so."

"You don't?"

"No, I don't. And since I'm the boss..." Her green eyes sparkled with humor.

"What if I told you that I don't take orders well?" He brushed a strand of hair back behind her ear.

"I'd believe you. But your memory can't be that bad." She lifted one delicate fist. "I have a mean right hook. And if that doesn't work, one scream and a horde of possessive brothers will show you theirs."

Leaning closer, James whispered in her ear, "It might be worth it. Wanna see?" He felt her tremble and knew she wouldn't protest if he took a taste of those sexy lips. But he wanted to hear her answer. No, he needed to hear her answer. "Just one," he breathed.

Cassandra's eyes squinted in thought before her arms hooked over his shoulders. "Just one."

His hands tightened on her waist. Part of him craved immediate gratification, but the other part didn't want to rush the moment. So instead of kissing her, he just held her and swayed in time to the music of the string quartet that had set up in the living room. They played some Christmas carol; he wasn't sure which one. He was just thankful it was slow. The trickling water from the fountain added its own music, along with the different tones of people's muted conversation and laughter.

"So are you going to kiss me or what?" Her words were muffled against his shoulder.

He smiled. God, the woman was bossy.

"Or what," he said, as his hands ran over the soft, clingy material of her dress. She talked and acted so tough, he expected her to be more hard muscle than feminine softness. She was a mixture of both. Her body was toned, but her frame delicate and womanly. He bent his head and dropped a kiss on her bare shoulder. It was chilly in the greenhouse, but her skin was warm and feather soft. She smelled good. Not like strong perfume, but like herbal shampoo. His hand skimmed up her spine, pausing at each little bump. At the base of her neck, he spread his fingers and slid them into her thick black hair.

He held her against him for a moment and absorbed the feel of her. In her heels, her body was almost in perfect alignment with his. Her breasts snuggled into the spot beneath his pectoral muscles and her hips cradled the bulge beneath his fly. For his own sanity, he pulled back. Her eyes were closed, those plump lips parted and waiting. Still, he hesitated. He wanted to take as much time as possible, wanted to control every second of the kiss.

It worked for all of a second.

The second right before his lips touched hers. Once they did, he was lost.

James no longer thought. He just felt. Felt the deep pull

of her full, sweet lips as they slid over his. Felt the wet warmth of her mouth as it opened to him. It was everything a kiss should be. Her lips fit against his like a long-lost puzzle piece, filling a space that had been vacant for too long.

She stood on tiptoe, aligning their bodies to perfection before executing a hip movement that rocked his world. If he'd thought he was turned on earlier, he'd been wrong. Now every hormone in his body raced toward the head of his penis, clamoring for release. Which made him think about those condoms. Those damned wasted condoms.

What was he thinking?

He couldn't screw Cassandra McPherson in the corner of a greenhouse, with or without a condom. Especially with her family within moaning distance. And if he wasn't going to be able to have sex with her, he needed to stop.

Now.

It took every ounce of self-control he possessed to pull her arms from around his neck and set her away from him.

With her chin still tipped up, she opened her eyes and blinked at him. Funny, but she no longer looked like a tough McPherson. Instead, she looked all wide-eyed and vulnerable. That should have made him feel just a little triumphant, but it only brought a large lump to the back of his throat and a queer feeling to the pit of his stomach. A vulnerable Cassandra tore at his heart.

James stared into those deep, green eyes that rivaled any of the plants that grew around her and felt intoxicated. Maybe the whiskey had affected him more than he thought. Or maybe he was drunk on something else entirely.

"One more," she whispered, nearly sending him to his knees.

"N-no." He cleared his throat. "I think one was more than enough."

"Not for me," she stated plainly as she tried to move closer.

It took all of his willpower to keep her at a safe distance. She was one determined and strong lady.

"Cassandra, listen to me." He brought her closer, but only so he could pin her arms down. "If I keep on kissing you, I'm going to want more. A lot more."

Her eyes glittered like molten emeralds. "How much?"

God, was the woman numb from the waist down? She had one hell of a raging hard-on prodding her and she had to ask? Or maybe she was as dazed by their kiss as he was?

"Enough to make me wish you hadn't thrown those condoms away and we were somewhere a lot more secluded."

"No, how much money for sex?"

James dropped his arms. "What?"

"Money. How much more do you charge for sex?" She shook her head. "It doesn't matter. Whatever it is, I'll pay it. So how many women have you slept with?"

"Huh?" After the phenomenal kiss, his mind just couldn't keep up with the woman.

Cassandra's eyes narrowed. "Are you sure you're not drunk?"

He wasn't sure of anything. Luckily, she didn't wait for an answer.

"Forget the women. In your business, the number must be staggering. So I guess we can bypass that and go straight to the diseases. Do you have any?" When he continued to stare at her, she added, "STDs?"

After a few dizzy moments, he answered. "No."

She stepped back and a blush covered her face. "Then it's settled." She refused to meet his eyes. "We'll have sex."

The woman was unbelievable.

"Look, Cassandra, there's a few things you need to know about me."

She held up a hand and shook her head. "No, I don't want to know anything about you. This is just about sex."

Oh man, there was a line that every man wanted to hear. Unfortunately, James couldn't bring himself to go along with it. Especially when she had no idea who he was. When he took this woman to bed, he wanted her to know exactly who she was sleeping—or not sleeping—with.

"I thought you didn't have sex with your escorts," he said.

"I don't."

"Thatta girl."

"But I'm ready to start."

This wasn't good. "You don't mean that."

A determined look came into her eyes, and her voice took on a stern tone, as if she were handing out orders to one of her employees. Which she thought she was.

"Don't tell me what I mean. If I say we're having sex, then we're having sex. Now either jump on board or I'll call Elite Escorts and have them send over Lance or Rod. I'm sure they'll know how to do their job."

On that note, she turned and went back inside.

Once Cassandra was gone, James stood there for a moment, completely stunned. *Lance and Rod, my ass.*

They probably used names like that to make up for their deficient equipment. Of course, he didn't really care for the idea of Cassandra seeing their equipment, deficient or otherwise. Probably because his own equipment was still hard and vying for her attention.

Man, he needed some fresh air.

James moved to the side door and stepped out. It was bitter cold, but it felt good. A group of smokers sat in Adirondack chairs on the back patio. He nodded to them, before walking out to a stone bench. There was still snow on the ground from the last storm, so he stayed on the swept path. The cold erased the last of his hard-on and cleared his head enough so he could think.

His mind moved over the last couple hours of his life, settling on the last twenty minutes. *Just who does the little wildcat think she is?* He quickly answered the question. *Cassandra McPherson, that's who.* Obviously, she was more spoiled and headstrong than he'd first thought. Of course, from what he'd seen and heard tonight, she really didn't have much choice. With four brothers and a business filled with hard-ass construction workers, a woman had to be tough. But did she have to be so bullheaded?

Laughter swelled up inside of him, and he chuckled. He liked her. Really liked her. He liked the cocky way she carried herself and her outspoken bossiness. And he liked the fact that she drank Coors and had a mean right hook. He liked that she wasn't caught up in her looks and didn't seem to have a clue how nicely she was packaged. And she was packaged nicely. Long legs. Sweet breasts. Pretty eyes. And great lips. But as much as he liked her physical traits, he liked her personality more.

Which was why he couldn't take her to bed. At least not until she knew who he was. Of course, once that happened, she'd probably dump him flat for carrying on this charade for so long. But he could be persuasive. He'd built a million-dollar company on his ability.

If he could do that, he could tame one very sexy wildcat.

He stood, confident that he had his thoughts in order, his mind made up, and his lower half frozen into submission. As soon as he had Cassandra alone again, he would tell her exactly who he was. But for now, especially while she was with her family and friends, he would bide his time and be as charming as possible. And while he was at it, he might check out a few trash cans.

Just in case.

Unfortunately, before he could take more than a few steps, the McPherson Welcoming Committee came striding down the path, four broad-shouldered-men deep. And it was hard to be charming when you were concerned about getting your ass kicked.

Shoving his hands into the front pockets of his tuxedo pants, he tried to act as nonchalant as possible.

"Nice evening." It was a stupid thing to say considering that it wasn't much over ten degrees outside.

The herd of Cassandra's brothers moved around him, pretty much blocking off all exits. They didn't look happy.

It was Jake who spoke first. "I'm sure you realize that Cassie is our only sister."

James nodded, mostly because he figured he wouldn't get his lights knocked out for a nod.

Jake continued. "That makes her pretty special to the entire family."

Again James nodded.

"We feel very protective over h—"

"Shit, Jake," Matthew jumped in. "Just get to the friggin' point, would ya?"

"Don't interrupt, Mattie," Rory warned.

"He's right," Patrick stated as he glared at James. For being so young, he was already a big man with wide shoulders and a broad chest. With his long golden hair, he looked more Scottish than the other brothers. He also looked meaner. "Jake's beating around the bush," he grumbled.

"What do you want to do, Patrick? Kick his ass and then talk to him?" Rory glared at his brother.

"Leave out the talking part and you got it right," Patrick said.

"That's enough, Paddy," Jake intervened. "No one is kicking anyone's ass." James was relieved, until Jake looked over at him. "Unless you don't understand just how special Cassie is."

Now that it was his turn to speak, James wasn't sure he could. Not with four pairs of intense green eyes pinned to him. He cleared his throat three times before he could get anything out.

"I realize how special Cassandra is. I realized that the first time I met her." The first time he'd met her, he did think she was special. Of course, her satin underwear and purse filled with condoms had helped sway his opinion. But he wasn't about to let that slip. He liked living too much. Living with no cracked ribs or broken arms.

He cleared his throat again. "Not only is she beautiful, but she's intelligent and funny."

"Funny?" Matt looked confused. "Since when has Cass been funny?"

"She was funny when she tried to jump her tricycle over that ramp Jake and I made." Rory laughed. "But you were too young to remember that. You were still clinging to Mom's skirts."

"I never clung to Mom's skirts."

"Yes, you did. You were the biggest Mama's boy I've ever seen," Jake stated. "But Cass breaking her arm wasn't exactly funny, Rory."

"No, but a flying red tricycle was."

"Could we get back to threatening her new boyfriend?" Patrick grumbled.

"Are you her boyfriend?" Rory asked.

"Yes," James said. He wasn't, but he wanted to be.

Jake studied him. "You're older than the others."

Shit. He was starting to get a complex. Lance and Rod might not have better equipment, but from the sound of things it was newer.

"Could we get on with it?" Patrick's scowl had deepened to something close to a snarl.

"Right." Jake nodded at James. "You were saying?"

With all the banter, it took James a second to remember what he'd been saying. "I think Cassandra is special, too. And I have no intention of doing anything to harm her." *Except maybe lie through my teeth so I'll get to hang out with her long enough to eventually get her into bed.* God, he probably did need his ass kicked. Fortunately, her brothers couldn't read minds.

Though he didn't smile, Jake relinquished his pinched look and stuck out a hand. "So I hear you're an architect."

Before James could reply, Matthew butted in. "That's it? You guys made me come all the way out here, freezing my ass off, just to get him to say that he thought Cassie was special?" He turned and trudged back up the path. "What dumbasses."

"Don't mind him." Rory shook his hand. "He just wants to get back inside to all the women." He shivered in the cold. "Which isn't a bad idea."

Jake nodded and rubbed his hands together. "I agree. Let's finish this conversation inside."

James took a step to follow, but was stopped by a hand on his shoulder. A very strong and persuasive hand. It seemed that Patrick wasn't so easily assuaged.

"Let me make things a little clearer for you." Patrick stepped around in front of him. "Mess with my sister and I'll mess with you." Not waiting for a reply, he turned and tromped after his brothers.

James followed, but at a safe distance.

Maybe he should skip looking in the trash cans and take things a little slower.

Chapter Five

Amy Walker finished unloading the last set of glasses from the tray, then grabbed a sponge and quickly wiped the cracker crumbs off the granite countertop. She knew she shouldn't be in the kitchen wiping off counters and cleaning up dirty glasses. Especially when this wasn't even her house. And when there were company employees she should be helping to entertain. And when the Hillshires had hired plenty of caterers and waitstaff.

But she couldn't seem to help herself. When she was upset or nervous, she cleaned, straightened, and organized anything and everything she could get her hands on. During college finals week, she reorganized her entire apartment. From the refrigerator to the closets in her daughter's Barbie Dream House. Those tiny plastic shoes had been a real bitch. Then, armed with one of Gabby's old toothbrushes, she had scrubbed every crack and crevice until the apartment had sparkled. Until her nerves calmed down. Until she got back to being levelheaded Amy.

Except this time, it didn't seem to be working. In the last two months, she could've served soup out of the porcelain toilets in her house, but she didn't feel the least bit better. Her stomach still felt as if it were filled with helium, and her heart still felt like it was being squeezed by a giant fist.

"I can get that, ma'am," one of the caterers said as she moved up behind her. "I don't want you to get that beautiful dress dirty." The woman held her hand out for the sponge.

For a second, Amy thought about refusing her. She needed the sponge much more than the caterer did. It made her feel useful and gave her a place to hide from the one person who was behind her frenzied emotions.

Rory McPherson.

Making one last-ditch effort, she smiled hopefully at the woman. "I thought you might need some help. I used to wait tables."

The caterer glanced around the kitchen at the six or seven people jockeying for position as they filled champagne glasses and serving trays. "Thanks, but I think we have it covered." She lifted a glass of champagne from one of the trays and handed it to her. "Go enjoy yourself."

"Right." Amy took the glass and started to walk away when the woman called after her.

"The sponge."

Shrugging innocently, she handed it back. The woman shook her head before tossing the sponge in the sink and going back to the bowl of peeled shrimp.

Amy turned and walked out of the kitchen. She really needed to get a grip. So what if Rory McPherson was back? And divorced? And gorgeous? What difference did it make? It wasn't like she had any feelings for him.

She stopped in the hall to straighten a painting.

At least, not anymore.

There was a time when she first started working for M & M that Rory McPherson had been her number one fantasy man. He was tall with strawberry-blond hair, deep green eyes, and a smile that could make a woman melt at his feet. He was mature. So much more mature than all the high school boys she was used to. And a heck of a lot more mature than Luke, Gabby's father. After the first few months of being tongue-tied every time he spoke to her, Amy had relaxed and discovered she could talk to Rory about anything and everything.

Especially about Gabby.

Rory didn't look down on Amy for being a single, teen mom. In fact, every time Gabby came to the office, he held her, played with her, and asked all kinds of questions. What did she eat for dinner? Did she sleep the whole night through? Did she love her mom as much as everyone at M & M did? It didn't take long for Amy to start fantasizing about Rory as the hero who would sweep her off her feet and love her daughter as much as she did.

But reality came in the form of Rory's very bitchy and beautiful girlfriend who informed Amy in no uncertain terms that Rory was hers and would never be attracted to some trailer trash secretary with a bastard brat. It had made sense. Why *would* a wealthy, attractive, educated man want to marry someone like her? After that, she'd steered clear of him and spent more time with his little brother, Matthew, whose carefree flirting posed no threat to her emotions. At one point, she actually thought her rejection hurt Rory, but within a month, he had moved to Chicago and was engaged to Tess. Which proved that he wasn't interested in Amy as anything more than a friend.

Amy ran a finger along the picture frame, removing any dust. But that didn't mean Tess was completely right. Amy wasn't trailer trash. She was a hardworking, intelligent woman who deserved a good man.

"There you are."

She turned as Derek stepped out into the hallway from the library.

"I've been looking all over for you," he said.

She wiped her finger off on her dress and held up the glass of champagne. "I went to the kitchen to find another drink and stopped to chat with one of the caterers."

He smiled, his very charming and brilliantly white smile. Derek had a great toothbrush. The kind with big bristles and a smooth handle that would work great for cleaning out tiny little crevices. For a second, she wondered if he carried it with him. The second right before he took her hand and pulled her into his arms.

"I need to talk to you."

It was strange, but she always felt claustrophobic in his arms. Sort of like she wanted to claw her way out. It was ridiculous; Derek was barely taller than she was in heels. She could get away from him anytime she wanted. Couldn't she?

Amy forced her paranoia down and smiled at him. "Talk away."

"Not here." He took her hand and led her down the hallway. "I found a perfect spot."

She followed him through the kitchen. The caterer glanced up, and Amy toasted her with the champagne as if to say, "I took your advice, and I'm enjoying myself." But the woman had obviously put her in the category of the rich and weird. She ignored her and went back to her shrimp.

Derek pulled her into the conservatory, around the fountain, and over to a table and chairs. "Here we are." He pulled out a chair, then waited for her to sit down before taking the chair across from her.

Amy looked around at the large potted plants. She hated the way greenhouses smelled. Like mildew. Could you Clorox a greenhouse or would it kill all the plants?

"Aimers," Derek said.

And she hated that nickname; it sounded like a hunting club. Maybe Lysol would work better. Lysol didn't kill anything except germs. And weren't germs bad for plants?

"I think it's time we got married."

His statement pulled her away from her compulsive behavior.

"What?" She stared at him.

The look on his face was amused and almost superior. "I think it's time we got married."

"Oh," she said.

It was a foolish thing to say. But then she didn't know what else to say. They had talked about marriage, and she had planned on getting married. Eventually. But just not now. Not when her stomach hurt and her heart ached. Not when she couldn't seem to come to grips with the fact Rory McPherson was back and meaner than a rattlesnake. Not when her flatware drawer still needed to be cleaned.

"Oh?" Derek said. "That's all you can say? How do you feel about this?"

She tried to think. "Well, I feel...scared." She hadn't meant to blurt it out, but there it was.

Derek laughed as he took her clammy hand. "I can relate to that. I'm a little scared too. But we've talked about it, and I think it's time to forge ahead. Gabby will be going into third grade next year, and she needs the stability of a father and a home."

He was right. She knew he was right. But why didn't it feel right? And why wasn't she a little more excited about the prospect of becoming his wife?

She smiled because she knew she had a great smile. It was a smile that could sometimes make men forget what they were talking about. Unfortunately, this time it didn't work.

"So what do you say?" he asked.

The smile died. She cleared her throat and then took a deep breath. "Well—I think we should—"

His cell phone chirped out the Texas A & M fight song, which Amy had always thought was a little strange considering he had been out of college for close to ten years. As usual when his phone rang, he excused himself and walked away before he answered it. He either had great cell phone etiquette or another girlfriend. Surprisingly, the latter didn't really bother her. It should, but it didn't. Just like it didn't bother her that he answered the phone at all while proposing. Derek loved his cell phone.

And, at the moment, Amy loved it almost as much as he did.

Derek looked back at her and held up two fingers. It was a pantomime they'd done before. She nodded and watched as he opened the outside door and stepped out to finish his conversation.

Once he was out of sight, Amy released her breath and sagged back in the chair.

"Saved by the bell." A deep voice came from somewhere in the green foliage to her right. She instantly recognized the voice and wasn't surprised when Rory stepped out from behind a bushy plant with bright red flowers.

"Or should I say by a fight song?" He stood there, staring down at her with a look she couldn't read. His mouth was tipped up in an amused smile, but his eyes were dark and angry.

Amy really wanted to come up with a clever reply, but obviously, tonight was just not her night for sterling conversation. Instead, she lowered her eyes and stared at the toes of his black dress shoes. Derek's shoes were Dolce & Gabbana and had probably been picked out by his personal shopper. She would bet Rory had purchased his own without one thought to designer labels.

"You surprise me." He paused, then snidely added, "Aimers. I thought the owner of Terrell Steel would have enough money to satisfy even you. And yet you didn't jump at the chance to get your hands on some of it. Why is that? Hoping Trump will get divorced again?"

She looked up at him. Her insides might be trembling like a scared rabbit's, but she refused to let him know that.

"No, Donald just doesn't do it for me. It's the whole hair thing."

A smile tipped one corner of his mouth. "You could use those big, brown eyes of yours to convince him to cut it."

"Doubtful. If his tall, gorgeous wives haven't been able to do it, I don't think some short ordinary woman could."

"Ahh, but there's nothing ordinary about you, Amy." He slipped into the chair across from her and studied her. "Especially according to my family. Since I've gotten back from Chicago, all I've heard about is how wonderful little Amy is. A true paragon of virtue and strength. Even Patrick loves you, and he's a hard sell." He leaned forward. "But what I can't figure out is why Matt still likes you after you dumped him."

"I didn't dump him." She recapped a bottle of tequila that had been left on the table and lined it up with an empty beer bottle and two shot glasses. "Mattie is like my little brother."

"Really? Somehow I don't think a paragon of virtue passionately kisses their little brother."

She stopped organizing the glassware and looked up at him. "I never—" She hesitated. Wait a minute; there had been that time at the company picnic. Mattie had helped himself to a few beers and was feeling froggy. He'd taken her for a walk and then kissed her. She was too surprised to do anything but stand there and let him. It was only after his tongue dipped into her mouth that she brought it to a halt. Afterward, they'd both laughed about how weird it felt. And it was never repeated. Or witnessed.

Or so she thought.

"How did you know about that?" she asked. Her eyes narrowed. "Were you following us?"

"No," he stated, but his face gave him away. Redheads couldn't hide a blush. He cleared his throat and looked away. "It was stupidity. Plain and simple stupidity. I knew Matt was sneaking beer, and I thought he might get out of hand." He shook his head. "Although I don't know why I felt so protective considering the fact that for the last month you'd treated me like the plague. I guess I was as fooled as everyone else by your little innocent act. It took me seeing you kiss my little brother before the truth sank in. How could a girl who had a baby out of wedlock be innocent?" He looked back at her. "Answer: She couldn't."

"I never pretended to be innocent." She jerked up a cocktail napkin and furiously wiped off the table.

"Bullshit. What would you call all those hot, little blushes and wide-eyed looks you sent me? I have to give it to you. You had the act down cold. But what I never figured out is why you used all your skill on me, then when I fell for it hook, line, and sinker, dropped me for Mattie."

"Dropped you?" She stopped scrubbing and stared at him. "How could I possibly drop you when I never even had you in the first place? You were dating, soon to marry Tess. Or don't you remember? And she made it perfectly clear you weren't about to have anything to do with someone like me."

"She what?"

Amy clamped her mouth shut and went back to wiping off the table. There was one very stubborn spot of plant fungus that refused to come out.

Before she could get it, Rory grabbed her hand. "Answer me. Are you telling me Tess warned you against dating me?"

She stared at the hand that completely covered hers. It was dusted with freckles and there was a scab on one knuckle. Inside the cocoon of his warmth, her hand thawed like a Popsicle on hot pavement.

"It doesn't matter, Rory...not anymore." She tried to pull her hand away, but he refused to let go. Instead, he stood and pulled her to her feet.

"It matters to me."

He was so close she could smell the clean, fresh laundry scent of him. See the laugh lines at the corners of his eyes. Feel the heat that emanated from him like a fire on a cold wintry night. Funny, but even with him being a good head taller, she didn't feel claustrophobic. She felt happy and content. All she wanted to do was wrap her arms around his broad shoulders and melt against his chest. Instead, she lifted her gaze and melted into the green of his eyes.

It took her a moment to find her voice, a moment when she remembered who she was and who he was. "Yes, she warned me against seeing you. She said you would never be interested in someone like me. And she was right. You were never really interested in me, Rory. I was just the new girl at work. Someone to pass the time with."

There was anger, confusion, and a touch of something else in his eyes as he stared down at her. Need? Desire? His mouth opened, then shut. His hands tightened into fists at his sides as the color of his face deepened. She didn't know what she expected him to say, but it certainly wasn't what he ended up saying.

"Shit."

Then he jerked her up to meet his descending mouth.

There were kisses, and then there were kisses. This was a kiss that completely obliterated all other kisses that had come before it. Passion, heat, and urgent need were all communicated through a set of firm, wet, devouring lips. There was no mistaking the message they sent.

Rory wanted her.

Now.

Balanced on the toes of her high heels, Amy absorbed all the heat and need like a dry sponge dunked in hot, soapy water. She slipped her hands beneath his jacket and sent back a message of her own.

Take me. I'm yours.

Except he didn't.

Take her.

Instead, he pulled away.

Slowly she drifted back to earth and opened her eyes.

Rory was no longer looking at her, but at something behind her. His hands tightened convulsively on her arms as if they were having trouble releasing her; then they dropped to his sides, and he took a step back.

"Amy?"

It took a few seconds for her to realize it wasn't Rory saying her name. She turned to see Derek walking toward them with a puzzled look on his face.

"What's going on?" he asked, his voice no longer puzzled. Just angry.

"Nothing," she croaked. It didn't sound very convincing, especially when her hands still rested on Rory's chest.

She removed them. But before she could stop herself, she

straightened his tie, brushed off the shoulders of his jacket, and reached up to smooth back the strand of strawberry-blond hair that fell across his forehead. He caught her hand in his before she finished the task. His gaze fused with hers a second before he released her.

The spot where his hand had touched hers felt branded. No, correction. Everywhere he had touched her felt branded. She jerked her gaze away from him, worried that if she didn't she might just incinerate right there on the floor of the mildewy greenhouse. Which would at least eliminate the need for an explanation.

If Amy thought she was speechless before, it was nothing compared to what she felt as she turned and looked at Derek. But what do you say to a man who just proposed to you and came back for your answer only to find you in the arms of another man?

Oops?

She cleared her throat, prepared to take full responsibility for her actions. But then Rory stepped between her and Derek. He weaved on his feet and waved a hand through the air. "Ssssorry—buddy." His words were heavily slurred. "But…" He pointed to a piece of mistletoe hanging in the doorway a good twenty feet away. "'Tisss the season, ya know."

All the anger drained out of Derek's face, and he laughed. "I thought all you McPhersons could hold your liquor." He shook his head. "Go home and sleep it off, Rory. Just don't grab any more unsuspecting women on the way out. By the looks of things, you've embarrassed Amy to death."

Rory swiveled around, took a few steps closer, and

bowed. "My deepest a-ppologies." When he lifted his head, for just a second, his eyes met hers. In them, she saw something that took her breath away.

His lips moved, forming two words.

Say no.

Then he winked and was gone.

Chapter Six

The world was spinning. A wonderful, giddy world filled with good friends, yummy shrimp hors d'oeuvres, cheerful Christmas carols, and one handsome hunka-hunka-burnin'-love. Snuggling down into the couch cushions, Cassie took another sip of her seventh—or would that be eighth?—glass of champagne. Normally, she didn't drink champagne. Why was that? Oh, yeah, 'cause the bubbles went straight to her head. Beer. She could handle beer. And whiskey. Aunt Louise had taught her all about whiskey. But champagne. Nope, she couldn't handle it at all.

On prom night, she'd thrown up all over poor Todd Birmingham after she'd slipped out of her prom dress in the back of the limo and offered him her virginity. He'd declined, but only because he was worried about the vomit on his rental tux. She looked up at the man who stood right next to the couch. James would look delish in a tuxedo. Wait a minute; he was in a tuxedo, and he did look delish. Crap, she was drunk.

She giggled, and James glanced down at her. She winked at him as she continued to drink her champagne. His brow arched, and he studied her for a few seconds before he turned back to the discussion he was having with Brady Lovelady.

Brady Lovelady. Now, that was funny.

She stifled another giggle and then leaned back against the couch cushions. From that angle, she could really study her delicious escort. Wow, he was hot. She loved his eyes. And that perfectly straight nose. And those lips that had melted her insides like her grandma's grilled cheese. And his hands. She really liked his hands. They were workman hands. Big and rough. But gentle... very gentle.

A shiver ran through her body at the thought of those gentle, rough hands spanning her waist, gliding up over her spine, and running through her hair while his lips devoured her. Yep, she loved those hands. Her gaze wandered down his body and back up. She pretty much liked the entire package. And every sexy inch was hers—all hers. At least for one night. Five hundred dollars for one night. Wow, what a bargain. She giggled again, and Mrs. Applegate stared at her from the other side of the couch.

"Too much to drink, dear?"

"Nope. I'm a McPherson. We can really hold our li-liq-er." She tried to take another sip to prove her point, but one of those big, gentle hands took the glass away from her. She looked up. But his attention had returned to Brady Lovelady.

Okay, so maybe she couldn't hold her liquor worth beans. At least, not champagne. But she figured she had every right. She was going to give the old showerhead a break tonight. Tonight, after eighteen long months, she would get laid. And if the thought of giving her virginity to a skinny, high school boy had wigged her out, the thought of lying naked in a bed with an experienced and very hot manly man really got her jumpy.

That was where the champagne had come in.

What started out as a couple of glasses to relax her nerves, especially after the kiss in the greenhouse, had turned into a few more when he'd followed her back into the house and proceeded to charm the hell out of every man, woman, and family member. The man had an unbelievable wealth of knowledge, along with a quick wit and a good sense of humor. Which was why it hadn't taken him very long to win over her family. He had talked golf with Rory, politics with Jake, and swapped college rugby stories with Patrick and Mattie until they were in tears laughing. He didn't have to talk about much for Melanie and Amy to drool over him. Of course, after her last high-heel-wearing, pumpkin-bread-toting boyfriend, Cassie really couldn't blame them.

So there she sat with her spike heels lost somewhere beneath the couch, her lipstick all licked off, and not a drink in sight, wishing that the guy—her guy—would quit socializing and take her home to bed. What was that line from *Top Gun*? It was one of Jake's all-time favorite movies; she should remember it. If her mind wasn't all fogged up with bubbles, she would have. Meg Ryan had said it to that guy from *ER*. Wait, she had it.

"Hey, Moose, you big stud."

James stopped talking and looked down at her. Both eyebrows lifted.

"Take me to bed or lose me forever," she said. *Or was it Goose, you big moose?*

"Ooookay, then," James said before he turned back to Mr. Lovelady. "It looks like I better get Cassandra home. Nice meeting you, sir." He shook the old guy's hand.

Mr. Lovelady grinned as if he knew something Cassie didn't. "Been there myself, son. More than a few times."

"Can you walk?" The question came from her guy.

"Of course I can walk." She didn't move.

He shook his head. "Where are your shoes?"

"Forget 'em. They are h-horribly painful." She would give them to Mike for one of his smaller-footed friends.

James bent down and reached beneath the couch, bringing his chest against her knees. It was too much to resist. She ran her fingers through his hair, around his ear, down his strong neck to the bow tie she had tied herself. She gave it a tug. Mrs. Applegate coughed. Cassie ignored her and slipped the top button out, then a stud. But before she could get further, James grabbed her hand.

"Enough, princess." He moved back and slid her shoes on her feet.

She sighed. Her Prince Charming for one night. Just one night.

One night? She had to get moving!

She practically knocked her Prince Charming on his butt as she jumped to her feet. The room spun, and she swayed on those damned four-inch heels. Luckily, James was there to steady her.

"Easy there, sailor." His gaze scanned the crowd before he glanced down at Mrs. Applegate. "Would you mind letting Cassandra's brothers know that I took her home?"

"Not at all, dear. Do you need some help?"

Cassie held up a hand. "Nope, I think I've got it."

James chuckled as he led her from the room. In the hallway, he slipped his jacket off and over her shoulders. "Where's your purse?"

"Right here." She held up the purse. She had secured it around her body with the little hidden strap about an hour earlier. She might be drunk, but she was no dummy— just a liar about what she had done with a whole lot of condoms.

A blast of wind and snow flurries greeted them when James opened the front door. He shielded her from most of the snow with his body as he maneuvered her down the steps, which was just fine and dandy with her. The lights on the trees sparkled around them, and she could hear the faint notes of "Silent Night" along with the slow and steady thump of his heart next to her ear.

"Be careful," he said. "The sidewalk's slick."

The warning came about a second too late. Cassie's heels slid out from under her. And instead of being her Prince Charming and rescuing her, James lost his footing and fell along with her. He turned his body to take most of the impact, which wasn't much considering the ground was covered with snow.

"Damn slick shoes," James grumbled, before he leaned over her. "Are you all right?"

He looked so cute with snow capping his dark brown hair and sticking to his long eyelashes. She laughed.

He flashed his dimples. "I'm freezing, you know."

She melted in those whiskey eyes. "I'm not."

"Probably because you have enough alcohol in you to fuel the entire state of Colorado." He brushed snow off her cheeks and chin, his warm fingers a stark contrast to the cold. A chunk of ice slipped into the crease of her lips, and she licked it off. The color of his eyes deepened to a molten gold.

"We probably should get up before your brothers look out and wonder what I'm doing with their sister." He didn't move.

She nodded, but she couldn't find any words. Except maybe, *Oh, James the Flame, come on and kiss me.* He must've heard her silent plea because he bent his head and brushed his lips against hers. Briefly. Way too briefly. Then he was on his feet and lifting her to hers. She quickly sank down into snow up to her knees.

James hesitated for only a second before he dipped a shoulder and hoisted her up over it. All the blood rushed to her head. She bounced against his back and watched the way his butt flexed as he crunched over the snow-covered yard.

"I'm sorry, but I'm a little more stable this way," he said.

"Okeydoke," she grunted, finding it very hard to talk when upside down.

The cold sobered her. At least a little. Enough to where she didn't feel so giddy anymore, just hot and dizzy. When they arrived at his Land Rover, he set her down and reached in his pocket for the keys. The locks clicked up, and before she knew it, she was inside with her seat belt on. The guy was quick. So quick she had barely gotten to enjoy his snowy kiss. But there would be others. She smiled. Before the night was over, she planned on getting a lot more.

He opened the door, then took the time to stomp the snow from his shoes before climbing in. Once inside, he started the truck and cranked up the heat. "Hang in there. It'll be warm in a minute." He popped the gear into drive and pulled away from the curb. "Are you okay?"

"I'm horny." It was one of her great-aunt Wheezie's words, but it pretty much described the way she felt.

The Land Rover swerved, barely missing the bumper of Jake's Lexus. James applied the brakes and looked over at her. "No, Cassie, you're drunk. Now, tell me where you live so I can take you home."

"Okay." She tried to sit up straighter, but somewhere between the house and his truck, her spine had evaporated, and it seemed she no longer had any control over her muscles. Her head flopped over to one side. Fortunately, it was the side he was on. "But when we get there, I want sex. With you."

In the open collar of his white shirt, his Adam's apple bobbed up and down. "Look, Cassandra, believe me there's nothing I'd like more than to have sex with you. But—"

"Good, 'cause it's been eighteen months."

"Eighteen months?" He had some kind of a stranglehold on the steering wheel as he stared at her, and she wondered what it had done to make him so mad. She shook her head to clear her thoughts but succeeded only in making herself dizzier.

"Are you trying to tell me you haven't had sex in eighteen months?" he said.

"Yep." She tried to nod, but couldn't quite pull it off. "Not since Mike tried to squeeze into my undies."

"Your old boyfriend wore your underwear?"

She giggled. "No, silly. Just my Christmas stockings." Or something like that. She was really having a hard time keeping her thoughts organized.

Sighing, James released the brake. "Okay, wildcat, tell me where you live."

"By the office."

"Where by the office?" He stopped at a stop sign.

"So you're going to have sex with me?"

"Eventually."

"Nope. Tonight." She tried to cross her arms, but along with her head, they were too heavy and awkward to move. "I paid for tonight, and I'm ready tonight. Besides, my shower needs a break."

"Your shower?" He scrubbed his hand through his hair, which made it stand straight up in a cute kind of way.

She loved his hair and really wanted to touch it, but all she could do was sit like a puddle in the seat. Which wasn't good. How could she enjoy a night of wild, passionate sex if she couldn't lift her hands? Or her head or her legs? Even her eyeballs had started to have a will of their own.

"Look." He glanced over for a second and then returned his eyes to the road. "I like you, Cassie."

She tried to grin, but her lips had gone numb. Suddenly she didn't feel so good. In fact, she felt just like she had on prom night. Uh-oh. She rolled her head over to the window and rested it against the cold glass. She tried to focus on the houses outside. Tried to remind herself that throwing up in James's SUV wasn't going to help break her eighteen-month dry spell. But then the truck picked up speed, and all those beautiful homes with Christmas lights blazing became one eye-crossing, stomach-swirling blur.

"But there are a few things we need to get straight before we continue," James said. But there was only one thing Cassie wanted to get straight.

"Stop!"

Fortunately, this time he took orders well. The Land Rover slid to a stop by the curb just as Cassie opened the door and leaned out. She wasn't sure how long she bent over the snow-covered gutter, throwing her guts up. It seemed like hours.

Slowly, she sat up and wiped her mouth with the sleeve of his tux. Something was frozen to her lips. She scrubbed it off, then flopped back against the seat, her stomach one tight knot. Her head throbbed from all the blood that had rushed to it, and her mouth tasted fishy. Oh, God, shrimp.

"Get me to a bathroom," she ordered. "Now!"

He chuckled. "Whatever you say." He reached across her and slammed the door before pulling away from the curb.

With her hands clutching her stomach, she stared straight ahead and focused all her attention on keeping the rest of the shrimp in her stomach and not on the floor of his Land Rover. It seemed like it took forever before he pulled into a driveway. Not a driveway she recognized, but at that point, she really didn't care whose it was as long as it had a bathroom.

The garage door took its good, sweet time in opening, and James took almost as much time pulling in. Once they were stopped, Cassie didn't wait for an invitation. She was out the door and into the house before he had even cut the engine.

She didn't have a clue where she was going. She just staggered through the kitchen and down the hallway, dropping his jacket on the way. The master suite loomed at the end. A master bedroom that would, no doubt, have a master bath. She made it to the bathroom in the nick of time, kneeling in front of the toilet and getting rid of the last of the shrimp.

A few moments later, she sat back on the floor and leaned against the wall. A movement had her glancing up to see James standing in the doorway, looking breathtaking in his tuxedo shirt and smile. His eyes twinkled as merrily as any Christmas tree.

"So I'm going to assume that sex is out."

Chapter Seven

James pulled the bathroom door closed behind him and tugged off his tie. The bedroom blinds were open, and he could see the snow falling in the faint glow of the streetlight. It was coming down pretty good, but it didn't concern him. Having grown up in Pittsburgh, he'd had plenty of practice driving in deep snow. He dropped the tie on the dresser, then yawned as he unclasped his watch.

The noise coming from the bathroom sounded a little like a coughing seal and pretty much wiped out the last of his lustful thoughts. James should've been disappointed that the evening hadn't turned out the way he'd planned. He wasn't. Despite the throwing up, he'd thoroughly enjoyed himself. He had expected his biggest competitors to be an arrogant bunch of assholes. Instead, the McPhersons were a group of people he would welcome as friends. There was Jake, the serious businessman who got all misty-eyed when he talked about his wife and four kids. Rory, the easygoing mediator of the family, who kept his hotheaded brothers from killing one another. Patrick, the quiet, watchful one, who seemed more skeptical of James than the others. And Matthew, the jokester and flirt of the group. Like a rambunctious puppy, Matthew raced around vying for attention from all the women. From the look of things, women were more than willing to give it to him.

Still, it was Cassandra who was responsible for the majority of the evening's enjoyment. Just being in the same room with her made him smile. Not that she had spent a lot of time with him.

After the phenomenal kiss in the greenhouse, he had returned to the party to find warm, aggressive Cassandra had turned back into the ice princess. Every time he moved over to a group she was in, she left. He allowed her little cat-and-mouse game, mostly because he enjoyed watching her. The woman knew how to work a crowd. Moving from group to group, she spoke to masons or steelworkers the same way she spoke to wealthy clients, with a natural ease and genuine respect.

Of course, it didn't hurt that she looked as hot as hell in the slinky red dress and high heels. Or that after a couple glasses of champagne, she started to loosen up. If a tightly wound Cassandra was hard to resist, it was nothing compared to a laughing, teasing Cassandra. Her laughter drew men like mosquitoes to a bug light, and before long, she was surrounded by a bunch of horny guys James had to wade through in order to reach her. He thought she might protest when he took her hand and pulled her from the group. Instead, she'd clung to his arm and smiled up at him in a way that had him heading toward the door.

Unfortunately, on their way through the living room, Mr. Lovelady had stopped them to ask James where he'd gotten his tux and then proceeded to give a detailed account of his Mexican cruise plans for the holidays. Meanwhile, Cassandra had dug her grave with the last two glasses of champagne.

James sat down on his king-sized bed and ran a hand through his hair. His plan had been to end the stupid charade he was playing and tell her the truth, in hopes that they could then move on to sex. But he couldn't very well spill his guts when she was spilling hers. Which meant sex would have to wait. For now, he would take her home and tuck her into her bed with only a brief kiss to warm him. Then tomorrow, bright and early, he would arrive at her house and break the news. Hopefully, her hangover wouldn't be so bad that she killed him on the spot. He grinned. She did have a temper. He just had to make sure there were no sharp instruments within reach.

The puking noises from the bathroom stopped, and other noises took their place. The squeak and pump of a shower being turned on. Damn, the woman had balls. He laughed as he flopped back on the bed and tucked a pillow under his head. It didn't matter. He could wait. Hell, he'd waited most of the night. What was another hour?

Staring up at the shadowy ceiling, his mind became consumed with thoughts of a slinky red dress slipping down a firm, gorgeous body. He closed his eyes and let the fantasy play out. Unfortunately, somewhere between the shower spraying over hard nipples and soapy hands gliding over firm round breasts, he fell asleep.

Much later, he awoke. He felt warm and—his brain struggled to shake off the last traces of sleep—oh yeah, and turned on. He felt extremely turned on. It wasn't unusual. He often woke up with a morning erection. He probably just needed to pee. Without much thought, he reached down to make an adjustment and scratch his balls. Unfortunately, someone beat him to it. Not the ball scratching, but the adjusting. Except it didn't compare to any morning adjustments he'd ever done. Like a fantasy straight out of *Penthouse Forum*, a warm hand encased him and stroked up and down his rigid shaft.

His eyes popped open.

Sunlight streamed in through the blinds. He blinked from its brilliance, then tried to focus. It took only a moment. A moment that had him wondering if he was still fantasizing. A woman rested between his legs. And not rested exactly. More like—

A spear of intense pleasure shot through him as he stared past the miles and miles of black, wavy hair pooled over his stomach and into a pair of deep, emerald eyes. But it wasn't her eyes that grabbed his attention as much as her full mouth. A full mouth that was wrapped around his... His eyes slammed shut, and a groan escaped his lips.

Damn, what the hell is she doing? It was a stupid question and one that he answered immediately. *Giving you the best blow job of your life.*

No other woman had treated him as if he were a double-decker ice cream cone and she was enjoying every lick. Cassandra had a technique that was all her own. She moved in a nice, steady rhythm, her lips sliding down before her mouth sucked up. It wasn't the rhythm that had James pressing his head into the pillow and lifting his hips off the mattress as much as the mind-blowing thing she did with her tongue. Every third or fourth stroke, she'd tease the very tip of his cock with a couple of quick flicks. The feeling it created was intense and brought him to orgasm much sooner than he expected.

Just when he was as close as a man could get, she stopped. It took more than a few moments for the sexual haze to clear and his brain to catch up. By that time, she had him suited up and ready to play. He opened his eyes to a naked temptress. A temptress striped with sunlight. She straddled him, her calves tucked under each thigh as her legs gripped his body. Her head fell back, taking the wealth of rich, dark hair with it and exposing her long, graceful neck and sweet breasts. They were small and firm, her nipples dark and large. He reached up and took each perfect orb in his hands and gently squeezed. He wanted to taste them, to put his lips over those distended tips and learn their texture with his tongue. But before he could lean up, she slid down, sheathing him in hot, tight muscle. It took his breath away.

She took his breath away.

Was he dreaming? Somehow he didn't think so.

His mind had never conjured up a fantasy like this one. He could only watch in stunned awe as she undulated above him, all soft body, dark hair, and flashing green eyes. While the erotic picture she presented consumed his mind, her actions controlled his body. Every movement of her hips, every flex of her muscles, pulled him closer and closer to physical release. He tried his best to hold back the tidal wave that rolled toward him. Tried his best to wait for her. But damned if he could do it.

It had to be the longest climax of his life. Then, just when he thought it was over, she pumped out her orgasm with a steady determination that consumed him. It was exciting and completely captivating to watch as she gave herself over to passion like some wild animal. Tossing her head, she arched her back and released a lustful cry of fulfillment. Then, satisfied, she shivered and slipped down to his chest.

James lay there stunned. Here was a woman who knew exactly what she wanted and wasn't afraid to go after it. It was phenomenal. Amazing.

And stupid.

Very, very stupid.

He closed his eyes and took a deep breath. What had he been thinking? He could have gotten away with his little deception if he'd only stolen one kiss before he told the truth. But deception paired with sex was a completely different ball game. Especially to women. While men couldn't care less if their sexual partners turned out to be Mrs. Claus or their mom's best friend, women didn't feel the same way. They took sex much more seriously and could become sensitive as hell over the smallest things. Not that lying about who you were was a small thing.

If it had been another woman, James wouldn't have cared. But he liked Cassie. No, more than liked her. She intrigued him, and he hadn't been intrigued by that many women in his life—if any—so he wanted to play this one out to see where it went. He wanted to spend time with her. A lot of time. He couldn't do that if she wanted to rip out his heart and feed it to her brothers.

While James was contemplating how to go about breaking the news of his identity to Cassandra, the doorbell rang. He glanced over at the clock, wondering who the hell it could be at seven thirty on the Saturday before Christmas. Figuring it was one of the many kids who lived in the neighborhood playing a prank, he ignored it. Unfortunately, whoever was at the door was annoyingly persistent. They rang the bell a good ten times before James could slide Cassie off him and roll to his feet.

He was still completely dressed. Well, not completely. The little minx had managed to undo his trousers and unbutton his shirt. He zipped and fastened his pants on the way to the door, not at all happy about being taken away from the sexy minx who continued to sleep like the dead.

He jerked open the door, intending to let whoever it was have a piece of his mind, but he hesitated when he recognized the woman who lived across the street. He didn't associate with his neighbors. He waved to the guy next door occasionally, but other than that, he kept to himself. He liked things that way. Emotional attachments only complicated life. Which didn't explain why he had allowed his assistant, Sierra, to talk him into buying a house in a neighborhood teeming with kids and grumpy retired people. All he had wanted was a town house that was big enough for his office equipment. It was Sierra who was convinced he needed a house. A house in suburban hell.

Something he should've remembered when he had handed out her Christmas bonus.

"Can I help you?" he said as his gaze drifted down to the mangy-looking cat that brushed against his pants and left behind a thick layer of gray hair. Four of its furry buddies prowled James's porch, rubbing up against his railing and batting at the laces of his snow boots that sat next to the door.

"Yesterday was the payment deadline for the holiday luminarias." The woman lifted the clipboard she carried and pointed at the empty space right next to his address.

James pulled his gaze away from the tabby cat that seemed to be squatting in the corner. The woman looked casual enough with her short gray hair and Eddie Bauer–style clothing, but there was an intensity in her eyes that warned James there was nothing casual about her personality.

"Luminarias?" he asked.

"Candle-lit paper bags. I thought it would be a good fundraiser for the neighborhood association, besides making the block look festive for the holidays. Didn't you get the flyers I sent out?"

If she was talking about the bright red flyers that had been stuck in the handle of his front door, James had gotten them. He just hadn't read them.

"I'm sorry," he said. "But I really don't celebrate Christmas."

It wasn't a lie. Christmas was one of those holidays that James found more annoying than enjoying. Not only did it affect deadlines, due to employee vacation time, but James dreaded a day spent trying to find something other then *It's a Wonderful Life* on television and scrolling his cell phone app for a restaurant that was open.

He wasn't complaining. After all, it was his choice. He could always go home for Christmas. Except home wasn't home anymore. Not after his mother died. And especially not after his father remarried. Now he just didn't feel comfortable there. He barely knew his stepmom and stepbrother. Besides, the old house made him think of his mother. So the only contact he had with his father around Christmas was the box of baked goods Marge sent and the check James sent in return.

James started to close the door, but the woman wasn't about to be gotten rid of that easily.

"The Greenburgs don't celebrate either, but they're still buying the luminarias," she said. "The money will help pay for our brand-new recycling containers." She sent him a censoring look. "Something you should start doing."

James blinked. How did the woman know he didn't recycle? Was she keeping track of his trash? He usually wasn't one to be bulldozed, but he was also a man who prioritized, and he had something much more important waiting in his bed.

"Fine," he said. "What do I owe you?"

"Ten dollars a dozen, but that includes setting them up." She glanced behind her. "I figure you'll need a good four dozen."

"Great." He reached for his back pocket before he remembered that his wallet was in his tuxedo jacket. Good manners dictated that he invite the woman inside to wait, but something told him that wasn't a good idea. "I'll just be a minute," he said. Not wanting to be entirely rude, he left the door open and hurried down the hall.

It was a mistake. By the time he got back with the

money, his neighbor was standing in the foyer checking out all his office equipment in the living room. But she was smart enough to wait until he handed her the money before she spoke.

"The neighborhood isn't zoned for businesses."

James tried not to look back at his huge copy machine. "Who said anything about a business?"

"Then how do you explain the young woman who comes over every weekday and claims she's your assistant?"

James should've known Sierra wasn't the type to keep her mouth shut and go about her business. The girl was a regular chatterbox. Figuring it was best to bring the conversation to an end, he reached for the door.

"Well, thanks for stopping by, Ms. . . . ?"

"Ellis," she said as she attached the money to the clipboard and stepped back outside. "Betty Ellis."

More like Betty Busybody.

James shut the door. But before he could take a step, he noticed the gray cat lying on his gym bag. The cat looked up at him with only one green eye. The other appeared to be sealed closed, giving the cat the appearance of winking. The doorbell rang, and he opened the door only long enough for Ms. Ellis to retrieve her cat.

After it left half of its fur behind on his gym bag.

Having gotten very little sleep the night before, James headed back to the bedroom. But when he got there, he discovered that Cassandra McPherson was a bed hog. She slept on her stomach at an angle, a hand dangling off one side and her toes dangling off the other. He should've been annoyed, but it was hard to be annoyed when looking at her perfect ass and long, toned legs.

Besides, it was probably for the best. If he climbed back in bed, there was no way he could keep his hands off all that luscious bare flesh. And before they had sex again, she needed to know the truth. Now the question was, how did he tell her without pissing her off so much that she never wanted to see him again?

The question rolled around in his head as he walked into the bathroom and turned on the shower. After five minutes of standing under the hot water, he still didn't have an answer. He had just about given up when he remembered a conversation he'd overheard on his last flight from Vegas. Two women had been discussing what they wanted from a man. The consensus had been romance. At the time, it had seemed funny to James, and he'd wanted to lean forward and tell them that men who were into romance were the same men who arranged flowers and used more than one type of styling gel. But now that he thought about it, maybe the women were on to something. Maybe romance was exactly the way to handle his situation with Cassandra.

With Christmas on Monday, he had a couple days to kill. Why not spend them romancing a beautiful woman? Wining and dining worked on clients, so why wouldn't it work on Cassandra? He would romance the hell out of her, and then after she got to know him, he would gently break the news that he wasn't an escort. How mad could she be? Instead of a lame escort, she would be getting a businessman who loved the same things she did.

Beer, sex, and construction.

It all made perfect sense. He picked up his shaving cream and gave it a shake before lathering his face. It probably wouldn't take more than a few days to win her over, but he had little doubt that he'd have her back in bed by New Year's.

As he drew the razor across his jaw, James started to hum. Interestingly enough, it was a Christmas carol, and he had never much cared for Christmas carols. Unfortunately, he couldn't shake the tune. Sierra had been singing the song for the last few weeks, and it seemed to be stuck in his head. In fact, once he started soaping up his body, the words would no longer be contained.

"All I want for Christmas is yoooou, baby."

Chapter Eight

Something smelled extremely good. Like Sunday mornings at home. Cassie stretched her arms up and released a long, heavy yawn. Besides the fuzziness in her head, she felt wonderful. Simply wonderful. Wonderful and totally relaxed. Something she hadn't felt in a very long time.

With her eyes still closed, she burrowed down in the expensive sheets and wondered if her mother was making pancakes or waffles to go with the delicious scent of bacon. She smiled at the thought of her mom busy in the kitchen preparing Saturday-morning breakfast while her father sat at the kitchen table reading the newspaper. Of course, once she hit the room he would stop reading and want to talk about business.

Most likely James Sutton.

Cassie yawned again. Screw James Sutton. She didn't

want to think about the man who was responsible for most of her stress. Not today. Today all she wanted to think about was . . .

Screwing James?

Her eyes popped open, and she stared up at the ceiling that wasn't the ceiling of her room at her parents' house. This ceiling wasn't lavender with little tiny stars glued on it. This ceiling was pure white with a gold-trimmed light fixture.

She glanced around, then blinked a few times to clear her vision. But the ceiling and room stayed the same.

Okay, so this wasn't her parents' house. It was somewhere she had never been before. Somewhere with no pictures or photographs or knickknacks or scented candles. Just a bunch of huge furniture. An oak chest of drawers, the big bed, and a nightstand with a lamp—her eyes widened. A lamp with a red strapless bra hung over the shade.

Just that quickly, it all came back to her.

Cassie squeezed her eyes shut and moaned as the bits and pieces of the night before flashed across the back of her eyelids. A slinky red dress—a pile of condoms—a hunk in a tux—a flash of white teeth—whiskey-colored eyes—soft, warm kisses—a muscular chest beneath a crisp white shirt—the deep satisfaction of having a hard, sexy man beneath her.

Her eyes slowly opened.

Good Lord, what had she done?

She vaguely remembered stumbling out of the bathroom in a towel and staring down at a sleeping man before falling facedown on the mattress next to him and passing out. Obviously, an eighteen-month dry spell was no match for eight glasses of champagne and a good thirty minutes of puking. But a few hours of sleep had changed all that. Waking up to a phenomenal body in a sexy tux was hard to resist for any woman, but when compared to a pulsing showerhead it was impossible. Within minutes, she'd had his shirt unbuttoned and her fingers skating over his chest and abdomen. There wasn't an ounce of body fat on him. Just smooth, tanned skin covering lean, sculptured muscles. It had been so easy to unhook the waistband of his pants. Easier still to slip a hand down the front of his boxer briefs.

Her actions had surprised her. She was aggressive and bossy in bed, but never that aggressive. She liked to be in charge and give the orders, but usually the orders were all based on what she wanted done to her. She had never been overly concerned about pleasing a man. Of course, she hadn't been overly concerned this morning either. The oral sex wasn't about him. It was more about her desire. Like an Atkins dieter in a bakery, she tried to make up for what was lacking in her life by gorging herself while she had the chance. Once satisfied, she'd fallen fast asleep, unconcerned with the carnage she left behind. Or whether or not her partner was as satisfied as she was. She thought he had been. But she really couldn't say.

From the kitchen came the sound of breaking glass followed by a mumbled curse. Cassie jerked the covers closer to her neck, suddenly feeling very naked. And extremely embarrassed. She didn't want to confront the man she'd acted like such a sex-crazed slut with. She wanted to slip unnoticed out the front door and never have to see him again.

Unfortunately, James didn't seem like the type of guy who would let a woman walk out his door without a good-bye. Especially after sex. Goodbyes after sex probably went hand in hand with door opening and driving.

Damn. Why couldn't she have gotten turned on by one of the younger escorts who probably wouldn't have cared less if she ducked out after sex? In fact, they probably would've beaten her to it.

A cheerful whistling started. It sounded like that Christmas song by Mariah Carey. She sat up and stared fearfully at the open bedroom door.

Get a grip, Cassie. Obviously, he isn't feeling embarrassed, so stop acting like you're in high school and pull yourself together. So you jumped him and screwed his brains out. With his profession and looks, it can't be the first time.

All she needed to do was act nonchalant, as if nothing special had taken place. Especially hot and heavy sex that had nearly set her hair on fire. She would get up and get dressed and ask for a ride back to her car. Then she would never have to see his face again.

It was a shame.

Timidly, she removed the sheet and placed her feet to the floor. The microwave beeped above the whistling, and she almost jumped through her skin. The bacon now smelled a little burnt, but the other smell was heavenly. Coffee. Strong, wonderful coffee. How she would love a cup right about then.

But the coffee would have to wait.

She looked around the room for her dress. It rested on the back of a blue chair along with her underwear.

She hurried across the room and grabbed her panties. A sound in the kitchen caused her to pause. With only one leg in the skinny little scrap, she glanced back at the bedroom door. Crap, she should've closed it. Too late now. She would just have to be quick, which wasn't easy after a night with eight glasses of champagne and strenuous sexual activity. She moved like her mother had after hemorrhoid surgery.

Getting the piece of dental-floss panties on wasn't too bad, but the strapless bra was a different story. Why hadn't Amy gotten her one that clasped in the front? And who had invented the hooks from hell?

A throat cleared, and she froze with her back and bare butt to the door and her hands gripping both sides of her bra.

"You need some help?"

Acting nonchalant was a lot harder than it had seemed a few minutes earlier.

"No, I think I've got it." She continued to fumble with the hooks while wondering if her blush covered both sets of cheeks.

"Here." Suddenly James was right there behind her, smelling like clean, spicy soap and fragrant coffee. He took the bra out of her hands and handed her a steaming mug. She stood like Lot's solidified wife with the mug in her hand while he slipped the bra over her breasts and, with very little effort, hooked it together.

"There," he said, acting as if it was something he did every day.

It probably was. *Earth to Cassie; he's an escort.* Considering the nice house he lived in, the man had probably clasped and unclasped thousands of bras. The thought pulled her out of her embarrassed trance, and she handed the mug back to him, picked up her dress, and slipped it over her head. It was backward, but she wasn't about to take it off again.

"Thanks," she said as she took the mug back.

Those golden eyes of his looked a little hot and glassy as he smiled down at her. "Anytime."

She took a sip of coffee, burned her tongue, and grimaced.

"It's hot," he said.

"Right." She ran her teeth over her scalded tongue and glared at him.

He studied her, and those eyes turned hotter. "You want me to kiss it and make it better?"

Everything inside of her pooled together into one simmering mass. She felt limp and warm and dizzy. God, the man looked even more delicious in full daylight. He wore a cream cable-knit sweater with a turtleneck that framed his smooth, strong jaw and brushed the curls of brown hair at the nape of his neck. Last night his hair had been slicked back and styled. Today, it was mussed and sexy. A lock fell over his forehead. Her fingers tingled with the need to reach up and brush it back.

And her fingers weren't the only thing tingling. No wonder the man had such nice things. Women probably spent their life savings just to have the pleasure of looking at him. She had to admit that he was one fine piece of art.

She pulled her gaze away from him and looked around for her purse. She spotted it on the dresser and walked over to pick it up. "I really need to be going."

"What's your hurry?" he asked, then nodded at the purse with a knowing grin. "I thought you threw all the condoms away."

For the second time that morning, Cassie's face heated up. "I lied."

James tipped his head back and laughed. It was a hearty laugh, one that came straight from a man's gut. She couldn't help but smile. Looking at him, she thought that maybe losing her entire life savings would be well worth keeping this man around for a while.

"A while" was the key word. After her money ran out, so would he.

He winked at her. "I'm glad you lied."

Cassie opened her mouth to say something, but she didn't know what. "I'm glad I lied too" just didn't seem like enough. Or maybe too much. So instead she nodded and looked around for a place to set down the coffee that was still too hot. With the top of the dresser covered by his tuxedo shirt and tie, she couldn't find a spot. So she handed it back to him.

"Look, I need to be going."

A look of disbelief came into his eyes. "So that's it?" James sounded extremely offended. It took a moment to figure out why.

The tip.

Of course he was offended. He had endured a puking nympho and he expected to be compensated for it. She couldn't blame him. She gave her masseuse a huge tip, and all the guy did was rub her muscles. This man had rubbed a whole lot more. Unfortunately, she didn't have anything in her purse but a pile of condoms. Which he probably could use, but wouldn't appreciate as much as money. Besides, she couldn't stand the thought of him using them on another woman.

Which brought up a good question: How many clients did James have in one day? As soon as he dropped off Cassie, would he be on his way to another desperate woman who was tired of her showerhead? A woman who wasn't as bossy, could hold her champagne, and knew how to tip.

Cassie knew how to tip too. Just not for sex. If she gave twenty percent for a hot wax, should she give the same for hot sex? Of course, a wax job took no more than an hour and hurt like hell. She had been with James for a lot longer than that and enjoyed every minute of it. Did escorts charge overtime? And if they did, when did it start? Midnight? Two a.m.?

There was no use worrying about it now. She would have to wait until he took her back to the office. Unfortunately, all she had at the office were credit cards. And she was pretty sure he didn't take those. She kept a couple hundred in her underwear drawer at her apartment, but that meant she'd have to tell him where she lived. Surprisingly, the thought didn't bother her as much as it had with the other escorts. James just didn't seem like the stalker type.

He probably had women stalking him.

Cassie cleared her throat. So how did one broach an indelicate and embarrassing subject? Straight on, she guessed.

"I don't have any money with me."

He went from looking offended to looking confused.

She swallowed. "So if you could take me home…"

The offended look came back with a touch of anger. "Oh, right, you don't have any money for the cab." He crossed his arms. "As if I'd let you take a cab."

The entire cab thing threw her, but she just couldn't bring herself to explain that she wasn't worried about the money for a cab as much as the money for hot sex. So she kept her mouth shut and decided he would have to be angry for a little while longer. At least, until he got her home.

After what seemed like a good five minutes, James took a deep breath and slowly released it as if he had come to terms with the fact that he wasn't going to get one extra penny for their sexual encounter. It had to be a real blow to his ego.

"Okay, Ms. McPherson." He held out a hand for her to precede him to the door. "Your wish is my command."

Cassie did have a wish. A wish that wasn't likely to be granted. Especially when it concerned a certain sexy escort not being an escort at all, but rather, being just a regular guy who happened to like her as much as she liked him.

Chapter Nine

The side streets were slick and icy, but James maneuvered through them without any problems, which was pretty good since he drove with one hand. In the other, he held a scrambled egg and burnt bacon sandwich. Cassie had declined breakfast. Not because she didn't like her bacon a little overcooked, but because her stomach still felt queasy and she didn't think she or James could go through another puking session.

Although she felt a lot better than she had the night before. At least today she could move. She snuggled down in the shearling jacket James had loaned her and took another sip of coffee from the travel mug. She had watched him prepare it in the kitchen and learned he liked his coffee black, exactly like she did. She also discovered he worked out of his home and took the job of escort very seriously. The only rooms that were furnished were the den, his bedroom, and one small guest room. The other rooms had desks with computers, copy and fax machines, and a lot of paper.

There was much more involved with being an escort than Cassie realized.

They didn't talk much on the ride to her condo. James ate, and she sipped her coffee and listened to the Christmas carols on the radio. The freeway had been sanded so it didn't take them long to reach lower downtown, or LoDo as the locals called it.

Her condo was located in a converted warehouse. Patrick lived on one side of her and Mattie on the other. Converting the warehouse had been her father's idea. Obviously, he'd thought that tucking her between her two brothers would keep her safe from all the big bad wolves in the world.

She shot a glance at James. He had finished his sandwich and now sipped his coffee. He looked over at her, and she saw her reflection in the dark lenses of his sunglasses. She looked like hell.

"You live here?" he asked.

Cassie knew it didn't look like a residential building. The outside still looked like a three-story warehouse. It was all brick with shops on the ground floor that were rented out by a Realtor, a flower shop, and an insurance agent. It had been built in the late 1800s as a warehouse for a cigar company. There were times that Cassie could swear she smelled the strong, sweet tobacco.

As they pulled around back, James commented on the row of steel garage doors. "Are those the only way in?"

Cassie laughed. "If you don't count the fire escape on the third floor."

"Well, it's secure. I'll give it that."

She directed him into the first parking space and wondered how a person ended a date with an escort. It had been easy with the other ones. They usually hopped out of her car and ran for the hills. Of course, she hadn't had sex with them. Or owed them a tip.

"If you'll wait here for just a minute—" She hesitated, because the words sounded so rude and pompous, especially after the man had offered her his home and the use of his toilet and shower. Not to mention the use of his gorgeous body. The least she could do was ask him inside, instead of making him wait in the car like the hired help. Which he was. But she didn't have to treat him like that.

"On second thought," she said, "would you like to come in for a minute? I have something for you."

James looked surprised before he flashed that wonderful smile. Obviously, the promise of a tip brought out the best in him. "Sure. Besides, I really want to see the inside of this fort."

She got out of the car before he had time to walk around to her side. But that didn't stop him from holding her elbow and helping her over the slick asphalt. Her high heels still hurt like hell, and she couldn't wait to get inside and take them off. Taking the keys out of her purse, she unlocked the small box that was located to the left of the garage and punched in her security code.

The garage door rumbled and slowly slid up. The spot for her truck was empty, reminding her that she'd need to go pick it up from the office later. On the other side of the garage sat her gun-metal-gray Harley-Davidson. It brought a low whistle from James as he circled it and ran a hand over the leather seat.

"Whose is this? One of your brothers'?"

"Mine." She loved the reaction her bike always got from men.

James's eyebrows shot up. "A Fat Boy? This is a pretty big bike for a girl."

"If you think that's big, you should see my half-ton truck." She pulled open the door at the left of the garage. "You coming, or do you want to stay here and drool over my bike?"

"I'm coming. I wouldn't want to miss any other surprises."

Cassie led James up the set of stairs to the first floor of her condo. At the top, she paused and scanned her living room looking for anything that might be embarrassing. Luckily, Elma, her cleaning lady, had come on Friday, so things were a lot cleaner than they usually were. Her mother had decorated the entire apartment, simply because Cassie had no patience with that kind of thing, which was why it reflected more of her mother's feminine personality than it did her own taste.

The sofa and love seat were floral with numerous pillows of various pastel shades. The coffee table and end tables were some kind of antiqued white. They looked old and chipped to Cassie, but she knew her mother had bought them new at some shabby-chic store she liked to frequent. The only thing that Cassie really liked about the furnishings was the window seat. The window was large and looked out onto the street and the downtown area. After a long day at work, she liked to stretch out on the soft cushion and look at the city lights and the traffic below.

"This is great." James moved up the stairs while she slipped out of her shoes and took off his jacket, placing it and her purse on the sofa. She watched him look around, but he didn't seem to be as interested in the furniture as he was with the high ceiling and wide-planked oak floors.

"Is the floor original?" he asked.

The remodel had been one of her first jobs. She had designed the renovation and overseen every aspect of construction, so she couldn't keep the pride from her voice. "Yes."

He moved over to the multipaned front window. "You've got a great view from here." He laughed. "I can even see your neighbor across the way decorating his Christmas tree in his underwear." He glanced around the living room. "Where's your tree?"

"I haven't had time to get one. Besides, a tree isn't a Christmas tree unless you have someone to share it with." She wanted to bite her tongue for saying something so personal and stupid.

James studied her for a moment before he nodded. "I know what you mean." He glanced up the stairs. "May I?"

He didn't wait for a reply. Instead he climbed the stairs and disappeared from sight. She probably should have yelled a warning. Her room was the only room she didn't allow the cleaning lady in, and it usually resembled a construction site minus the heavy equipment and workers. Today was no different. Her clothes were scattered across her king-sized bed and floor, along with shoes, hair clips, towels, and half-empty water bottles. Fortunately, there was no leftover food lying around, but only because she hated bugs more than cleaning.

James didn't appear to be bothered by the mess. He stepped over the piles of clothes to get to the exposed brick wall behind her brass headboard.

He ran his hand over the brick. "What year?"

"Eighteen ninety-six." She jerked a bra up off the floor and shoved it into an empty vase on her dresser.

"They could really build them back then." He took his time studying the brick before he glanced at her messy bed. "A half-ton truck, a Fat Boy, and a king-sized bed. If you were a man, I would think that you were trying to compensate for something." He winked at her before he moved over to the French doors that led out to the balcony. "Whoever designed this did a great job of complementing the old with the new. Who was the architect?" When she didn't answer right away, he glanced back over his shoulder.

For some reason, she felt her face heat up.

"You did this, didn't you?" He turned to face her. "You designed it."

The admiration in his eyes caused a lump to form in Cassie's throat the size of a Colorado Rockies' baseball. All her life, she had waited for a man to look at her like this. It hadn't come from rough and tough Big Al or any of her brothers. Or even Mike, who had been too concerned with his own fragile ego to pay attention to her accomplishments. Instead, it came from a most unlikely source. It came from a sexy escort who seemed not only to love women but brick and wood and architecture. It touched something deep inside her. Something that had needed to be touched for a very long time.

Cassie felt exposed and completely vulnerable. For the first time in a long time, she just wanted to sit down and cry. Correction, she wanted to step into a pair of strong arms and bury her face against a thick sweater and then cry. But McPhersons didn't cry. At least not where people could see them. And especially over something as stupid as a man praising her for designing a condo.

Unfortunately, her mind might understand that, but her heart refused to listen. The lump grew until tears filled her eyes. James's eyes widened with concern and a small amount of fear. "Cassandra?"

She tried swallowing, but there wasn't enough saliva to wash down a pebble, much less a baseball. She blinked twice and cleared her throat, scrambling for anything to say.

"I can s-sit out there in the summer and see the f-fireworks at Coors Field." She hated the way her voice shook.

The look of fear deepened, and he moved around her bed. "Cassandra, what's wrong?"

Realizing she needed a minute away from his penetrating gaze, she turned and walked over to her chest of drawers. Things were a little bit blurry, but she was still able to pull open the top drawer and take out the money. She stared down at the two hundred-dollar bills and tried to take deep breaths. They came out short and quivery.

He moved behind her and gently ran a hand up and down her bare arm. "He-e-ey, what's going on?"

"Here." She turned and shoved the money into his chest. "I think you should go."

The money was ignored as his fingers slipped under

her chin and tipped it up. She refused to look at him and instead stared at the turtleneck of his sweater.

"Damn it, Cassandra." His hand gave her chin a little shake. "You don't get it, do you? It's not about the money. It's about me liking you—about me wanting to be with you."

She tried to say something, but she couldn't. She was too busy trying to keep the tears from falling. Unfortunately, one unruly tear escaped and trickled down her cheek.

"Oh, baby, don't cry." He pulled her into his arms and tucked her under his chin. "If you want me to, I'll go. Just don't cry."

That was pretty much all it took. The dam broke. Cassie hadn't cried very much in her life, but the times that she had, it wasn't pretty. Her brother Mattie said she sounded like a baby calf calling for its mother and looked like a red-faced monkey he had seen on the Discovery Channel. But James didn't seem to care.

He just sat down on the end of the bed and pulled her onto his lap. His hands caressed her back while he spoke to her in soft, soothing words, words that could barely be heard over her loud, racking sobs. Finally, he stopped speaking and just held her, planting small kisses on the top of her head.

The tears that started out from a man appreciating her talent soon turned into a release of all the stress she'd been under since her father's heart attack. Add lack of sleep and an empty stomach to the mix, and you had one weepy woman who might've continued to cry until New Year's if her little brother hadn't shown up.

"What the hell are you doing to my sister?"

Patrick's angry, booming voice could've been heard over a jackhammer. He stood in the doorway of her bedroom dressed in his running clothes with his hands clenched in fists and his green eyes snapping. She had witnessed this posture a few times in her life and knew that the outcome wouldn't be pretty.

Taking a deep, trembling breath, she prepared to soothe her brother's fiery temper. James beat her to it.

"Hey, Patrick." He slipped Cassie off his lap and stood.

She wondered if the man had a death wish. Without her between them, Patrick had a clear shot. Obviously, he didn't understand that her brother broke noses first and asked questions later. She jumped to her feet and tried to step between them, but James moved her aside with a firm but gentle hand.

Patrick glared at that hand and took two steps closer. "So you want to explain why my sister's crying? And while you're at it, you can also explain why you didn't bring her home last night."

"Paddy!" Cassie gasped, then ruined it all with a hiccup. Neither man spared her a glance. They just stood there mad-dogging each other. So she tried again. "Patrick McPherson, it is none of your business what I do—"

"Let me handle this, Cassie," James said.

"Don't tell my sister what to do," Patrick grumbled.

"He can tell me what to do if he wants, Patrick." She wasn't sure why she defended James, especially when she was about to tell him the same thing. She just wanted to be the one to do it. Not her little brother.

"It's all right, Cassandra," James said. "I understand perfectly why Patrick is so upset. If I had a sister and discovered her crying her eyes out with some guy I barely knew, I wouldn't be so happy about it either. All kinds of questions would be going through my head. Had the jerk hurt her physically? Verbally? And which of his limbs did I want to rip off first?"

Patrick's eyes darkened. "That about sums it up. Except I wasn't thinking of limbs as much as your head."

Cassie cringed, but James only nodded. "Well, before you do, I have a few things I want to make clear. First, I'm just as upset about your sister's tears as you are. A woman's tears scare the hell out of me." He glanced at Cassie. "But it appears the worst is over." She smiled at Patrick to show she wasn't upset anymore, then at James to show him how well she thought he was handling the volatile situation. But the smile dropped when he got to his next point. "And secondly, what we did or didn't do last night is really none of your damned business."

Cassie was sure that the shit was going to hit the fan. But even after having four brothers as playmates, she still didn't understand men. One second, her brothers would be beating one another senseless for no apparent reason, and the next, they'd be slapping one another on the back. If Patrick's smirk was any indication, this was a slap on the back kind of moment.

He nodded his head. "Fair enough." His green eyes examined her for a minute before he chucked her under the chin. "Sis, did you realize that your dress is on backward and you look like hell?"

"Patrick McPherson, shut up." She sniffed and wiped at her eyes, then jerked her hand behind her back when she realized she still held the money in her fist.

Her brother's eyes narrowed, but he didn't say a word. "I'll call you later." He turned and left the room.

After Patrick was gone, James didn't waste any time pulling her back into his arms. "Are all the McPhersons so unpredictable?"

Cassie smiled up at him. "Pretty much."

"Hmmm? At least there's never a dull moment." His eyes grew serious. "Are you okay?"

No, she wasn't. A man had walked into her life and turned everything upside down. She wasn't okay. She was dazed. Breathless. And happy for the first time in a long time.

"What brought on the tears, Cassandra?" he asked.

She lowered her gaze and scrambled through her mind for an answer. When she didn't find one, she told the truth. "You liked my bricks."

She felt the rumbling in his chest before she heard his laughter. "You are the most intriguing woman I have ever met. And I want to spend the entire day making you smile. What do you say, Cassandra McPherson? You want to hang out with me?" When she looked up, James winked. "This time it won't cost you a dime."

"Yes," she whispered, right before his lips covered hers.

Cassie might be stubborn, but she wasn't stupid. She knew a bargain when she saw one.

Chapter Ten

"Cassandra's still not answering." Mary Katherine hung up the phone and set it back on the kitchen counter next to the egg carton and huge mixing bowl. "Where do you think she is, Wheezie?"

Louise McPherson Douglas didn't know for sure where her great-niece was, but she had her hopes. She just couldn't tell the girl's mother that she hoped her daughter was in bed with Jimmy, making Mary Katherine more grandchildren and Wheezie more great-nieces and nephews.

"She's probably still in bed," Wheezie said. "I hear the party ran a little late last night."

"Which is exactly why I'm worried about Cassandra." Mary cracked an egg into the bowl. "Gladys Applegate couldn't wait to call me this morning and tell me about Cassie drinking too much last night."

"Gladys Applegate is a busy butt who should mind her own business." Wheezie poured some more rum into the saucepan and tried to act nonchalant. "So what did Gladys have to say?"

"Just that Cassandra drank too much champagne and almost had to be carried out by 'her nice young man.' What nice young man? I thought she had broken it off with Lance."

Wheezie squinted. "If that's the one who passed out after just a few drinks, I say good riddance. Who wants a man who can't hold his liquor?"

Mary Katherine sent her one of those looks that only a woman who spent too much time in church could send. "I'm sure you gave him more than a few drinks, Wheezie." She nodded at the saucepan. "And that recipe calls for one-fourth cup of rum, not half a bottle."

"What's a holiday without a little spirit?" she huffed. "Besides, the alcohol will burn off."

"Why don't you let me finish the rum sauce?" Mary said. "You need to sit down and take it easy."

Take it easy.

That was the problem with being ninety; everyone treated you like you were at death's door. They probably had a point. Recently, Wheezie had woken up in the middle of the night with a chilled feeling like the grim reaper was only a breath away. She wasn't scared of death. In fact, she looked forward to it. She didn't doubt for a second that her husband, Neill, would be waiting on the other side with a sweet smile and a glass of good Scottish whiskey. But as much as she longed to see her soul mate, she wasn't quite ready to leave this world behind. At least, not yet. Not until her great-niece and nephews were as happily married as she had been.

She ignored Mary and kept stirring the sauce. Mary heaved a heavy sigh, but didn't say a word. After being married to Big Al for close to forty years, she was used to stubborn McPhersons.

"So did you meet this man Cassandra brought to the party?" she asked. "What's he like?"

"Jimmy's older than the rest of the youngsters she's been dating, twice as intelligent, and three times as good-lookin'." Wheezie tasted the sauce and had to admit that she was still one damned good cook.

"Do you think Cassandra is really interested in this one?" Mary asked.

"If she isn't, she should be."

Having been in the bar business for years, Wheezie prided herself on knowing what relationships would work and what relationships wouldn't. Some might call it matchmaking. She didn't much care for the word. Matchmakers were busybodies like Gladys Applegate. Women who had nothing better to do with their time than try to make people's lives as miserable as theirs were. They would willy-nilly set up relatives and friends without any thought of how they would actually get along.

Wheezie preferred to call what she did soul-mating. Anyone could randomly throw single people together. Soul-mating took a lot more thought and intuition. And Wheezie had intuition in spades. She knew after only five minutes with Cassie's new boyfriend that he was the one for her niece. With five headstrong men in the family, Cassie thought she wanted a man that she could boss around. When in truth, what she needed was a man with a firm, but gentle, hand. Jimmy had those hands. And Wheezie intended for them to catch her great-niece. Even if Wheezie had to set up a few roadblocks.

But first she had another McPherson to take care of.

She glanced out the window at Rory, who was shoveling the side walkway. While Cassie's unmarried state had just recently drawn Wheezie's attention, Rory's had occupied her thoughts for the last five years. The stubborn man would've been happily married by now if he hadn't run off to Chicago and married a woman he had no business being with.

Wheezie wasn't about to let that happen again.

"So did you talk to Amy this morning?" she said, then waited until Mary turned her back to get something out of a cupboard before she added some more rum to the sauce. "I was thinking about stopping by today to drop off their presents."

"You'll have to do it later in the afternoon. Amy and Derek are taking Gabby to see Santa at Gruber's Toy Store."

Wheezie snorted. "Derek. Now there's a putz if ever I've seen one. The man uses his telephone more than Alexander Graham Bell. When he's not talking on it, he's tapping and scrolling like a blame idiot. You can't even hold down a decent conversation with him."

Mary poured the oil into the cake batter. "Well, it doesn't matter how we feel. Amy loves him, and I wouldn't be too surprised if wedding bells are in the near future."

"Over my dead body," Wheezie mumbled under her breath, just as Big Al's voice boomed from the other room. He released a string of cusswords that had Mary Katherine reaching for a towel.

"No more rum, Wheezie," she said as she wiped off her hands and hurried from the room.

Once she was gone, Wheezie picked up the bottle of rum and splashed some in the saucepan, then shuffled over and splashed some more in the mixing bowl. She was just giving it a stir to mix it in when the side door opened.

"What's Dad yelling at this time?" Rory asked as he stomped off his boots and stepped inside. "The neighbors can probably hear him all the way down the street."

"Close the blasted door, Rory. My arthritis can't take the cold." She tossed the empty fifth into the trash.

After closing the door, Rory pulled off his gloves and then his jacket as he sniffed the air. "You making rum cake?"

"It wouldn't be Christmas without it." But instead of continuing to cook, she turned off the burner and moved over to one of the stools at the breakfast bar. She slid onto the leather seat, liking the way her feet felt against the bottom rung. Not a day went by that she didn't miss Neill's Bar. Or her late husband.

Maybe it was only her wishful thinking, but Rory looked like Neill. Same strong features. Same sweet smile.

"You're looking awfully beautiful today, Wheeze." He kissed her head on his way over to pour himself a cup of coffee.

"Don't brownnose me, you rascal. I look exactly like what I am—an old broad whose days are numbered. I'll be lucky if I live past New Year's."

Rory chuckled. "You'll probably outlive us all, Wheezie."

He filled his cup while she tried to figure out how to best go about getting what she wanted without Rory catching on. And using the old deathbed routine didn't look like it was going to work. But maybe a little reverse psychology would.

"You're right," she said. "I'm not planning on going anywhere until you kids are all settled down."

Turning back around, he shot her a quizzical look. "Thinking about doing a little matchmaking, are you, Wheeze?"

She shrugged. "Since all my bridge partners are dead and buried, I need something to keep me occupied." She tipped her head in thought. "Of course, Mattie needs a couple years to grow out of his wild stage. Cassandra is too busy with work. And you've just gotten divorced and need some time." She released her breath in a long sigh. "Which leaves Patrick."

Rory's grin got even bigger. "I think that's a great idea. So just who do you have in mind for my volatile younger brother?"

"Oh, I don't know." She paused and shot him an inno-cent look. "Amy Walker?"

The coffee mug halted inches from Rory's mouth as he stared at her in shock. It was just the reaction Wheezie was hoping for. She bit back her smile and went in for the kill.

"It makes perfect sense. Amy and Gabby are practi-cally family. And I think Patrick already has a little crush on her."

Rory lowered the cup. "And what about Derek Terrell?"

"Do you actually think Amy will choose Derek once she finds out how Patrick feels? Patrick is taller, handsomer, and isn't constantly on his damned cell phone. Not to mention that your brother is much better with Gabby." She paused and squinted. "In fact, there are times when I don't even think that Derek likes children. Which would be a crying shame if he ended up being Gabs's father. That child needs a daddy who will love her and treat her like the angel she is."

While Rory stood in stunned silence, she continued. "Yes, I think that's the best plan. I'm going to call Patrick right now and have him go over to Gruber's Toy Store where Amy is taking Gabby to see Santa. Christmas is the perfect time to declare your love for someone."

"Rory." Mary Katherine came back into the kitchen. "I'm glad you're still here. Your father's about to blow a gasket. From what I can get out of him, it has to do with Slumber Suites. He tried to get ahold of your sister, but she's not answering. So why don't you go into his study and see if you can't calm him down."

For a moment, Rory looked like he was going to listen to his mother. He set the mug down and turned in the direction of Big Al's study. Wheezie had to do some quick thinking to get him back on track.

She reached out and picked up the phone. "What's Patrick's number again, Mary Katherine?" Less than a moment later, Rory had his jacket and gloves and was slamming out the door.

"What in the world?" Mary Katherine turned to her.

Wheezie shrugged. "It beats me. Who can figure out young kids?" She slipped off the stool. "If you'll excuse me, I need to make a phone call."

Mary Katherine rattled off Patrick's phone number, but

it wasn't her nephew's house that Wheezie dialed as she walked into the living room. If things were going to work out between Rory and Amy, she needed some backup. God must've agreed because the person who answered was exactly the person she wanted to speak with.

"This is Aunt Wheezie," she whispered. "You know that Christmas gift you've been wanting? Well, I think I just figured out how to get it for you."

Chapter Eleven

Rory McPherson could not remember the last time he'd been in a toy store—not that he didn't buy toys for his nieces and nephews. He just didn't buy them at a store. He bought them, like most childless men, on the Internet, where he could have them wrapped and delivered with very little effort.

Which explained his stunned shock when he stepped out of the revolving doors and into the mayhem of a toy store two days before Christmas. Hordes of adults and children swarmed around the aisles of stuffed animals, games, dolls, and action figures like roaches around a restaurant Dumpster. Except roaches went about their scavenging quietly. The noise level in the store was deafening.

Stressed-out parents yelled at dazed salesclerks. Babies in strollers screamed in exhaustion. The Christmas cartoon that played on the television monitors competed with a high-pitched version of "Santa Claus Is Coming to Town." And mixed into the cacophony were the sirens, beeps, and screeches of every electronic toy the hyped-up kids could get their hands on.

Rory froze. *What in the hell am I doing here?*

The answer came only seconds later, when his gaze shifted down to the lower level of the store, where a long line of people waited to see Santa. Amid all the frazzled Christmas shoppers, the petite blonde stood out like a beacon of light on a dark, cold night. And Rory found himself moving closer to the railing.

Today, Amy wore a fuzzy pink sweater that accented her small, perfect breasts and pointy-toe high heels that stuck out beneath the hem of her form-fitting jeans. High heels that drove Rory crazy every time they strutted past him in the hallways of M & M. He spent many a lunch break picturing that cute, compact body in nothing but heels and fantasizing about them being wrapped around his hips.

But it wasn't the heels that had sealed his fate the night before. It was the rosebud mouth. All it had taken was one mind-blowing kiss from those lips for the truth to come out.

Rory McPherson loved Amy Walker.

And time, distance, and marriage hadn't changed the truth.

For five long years, Rory had tried to hide it from his family, his wife, and mostly, from Amy. He'd tried to hide it behind a veneer of hateful words and indifference. It had worked as long as he didn't see her. Or touch her. Or taste her. Okay, so it hadn't worked at all. All he'd succeeded in doing was hurting a lot of people who hadn't deserved to be hurt.

Like his ex-wife. Poor Tess. She was arrogant and self-absorbed, but she hadn't deserved to be saddled with a man who didn't love her. A man who lost himself in work just so he could forget about a nineteen-year-old blonde in sexy high heels. Rory wasn't at all shocked when Tess left him for some exercise dude. If he'd been her, he would've left a lot sooner. He'd been the worst sort of husband.

He worked fifteen-to-sixteen-hour days and most Saturdays and Sundays. The only time he took off was when his family flew in and, even then, most of their conversations revolved around work. There had been nothing for Tess except money. And since her father had passed away, she had plenty of her own. Of course, he couldn't take all the blame for their rotten marriage. If Tess hadn't claimed she was pregnant, he wouldn't have married her in the first place.

Still, he should've divorced her right after their first marital fight, when Tess had screamed the truth at him. Why hadn't he? Maybe because Tess was convenient. She wasn't blond and she wasn't brown-eyed, but she had loved him. Something he believed Amy would never do. So he stayed married to her because it was easier than getting a divorce. And because he could never have Amy.

Or so he thought.

Now he wasn't so sure. The only woman who could help him figure it all out was the same woman who had just turned to say something to the man behind her. A man who had all of Rory's dreams tumbling down like the boxes of remote control cars a kid had just knocked over. Obviously, Rory had read more into his kiss with Amy than there was.

If Derek Terrell was here, nothing had changed. Except Amy's status. She was now engaged. Which meant Rory had made a fool of himself again. He had no business being there. None whatsoever.

Damn Aunt Wheezie.

He turned to leave and almost fell over a pint-sized kid in a Broncos' cap.

"Hey! Watch it, knucklehead."

Big Al's words coming out of a little girl's mouth had Rory stepping back and taking a closer look. A pair of big brown eyes flashed up at him with annoyance before recognition settled in.

"Hey, Uncle Rory. I've been looking for"—she stopped and smiled brightly—"what I want Santa to bring me."

No matter how battered his heart felt at the moment, Rory couldn't help grinning at the little girl in the tattered jeans and Transformers hoodie. Gabriella Lynn Walker had stolen his heart the moment he first held her in his arms. But she wasn't the chubby toddler who nestled against his shoulder anymore. Five years had gone by, and she had grown into a sassy tomboy who talked even louder than Big Al McPherson.

"You want to keep it down, Gabs?" he said as he glanced back over his shoulder. Amy was craning her neck, no doubt looking for her daughter.

"You hidin' from Mom or Dodo Derek?" Gabriella asked when Rory jumped behind the life-sized giraffe.

It lightened Rory's mood considerably to hear the nickname. "I thought you liked Derek."

"Nah." Gabriella set down the Lightsaber she'd been playing with and moved over to the Lego table. Most girls would've started working on the pink castle. Gabriella went straight to the pirate ship. "That's only a game we play. I act like I like him and he acts like he likes me."

"And what makes you think he doesn't?"

She shot him one of those kid looks that pretty much called him a dodo before she picked up a miniature cannon and snapped it onto the side of the ship. Rory had always been the peacekeeper of the family, the one who calmed tempers and kept fists from flying, but at the moment he felt like hitting something. Preferably Derek's face. It looked like Wheezie was right. Derek didn't like Gabby. And what kind of person wouldn't like a kid like Gabriella? Sure she was outspoken and loud, but that's what made her so cute.

He handed her another cannon. "So I take it that you don't want your mom marrying Derek?"

Gabriella glanced up, and her eyes squinted. "Who said she's marrying Derek?"

Realizing his mistake, Rory tried to backpedal. "I guess I just assumed that they were getting married since they've been dating for so long."

"Well, you assumed wrong." Obviously upset, Gabriella tried to ram the cannon Lego into a spot it didn't fit. "My mom is going to marry a McPherson. Aunt Wheezie said so."

The information didn't surprise Rory. Obviously, Wheezie had already started her matchmaking attempts with Gabby. Which didn't explain why his aunt had laid it on so thick that morning. Not unless...

"Why, that devious old bird," he whispered.

Gabby heard him and didn't hesitate to stand up for his great-aunt. "She's not an old bird." She scowled at Rory. "She just wants you to poop or get off the pot." When she slapped a hand over her mouth, his suspicions were confirmed. Patrick wasn't his great-aunt's target.

He was.

A smile broke out on his face, followed by laughter. He laughed so hard and so long that he scared off most of the kids from the Lego table. Only Gabriella remained. She dropped her hand from her mouth and got to the point as only a kid can do.

"So do you love my mom or not?" she asked. "Because if you love her, you need to tell her before she marries Dodo Derek."

Her serious brown eyes caused him to sober, and he squatted down next to her. "It's not that easy, Gabs. There are a lot of things to consider. Like what your mother wants. She might love Derek." Just the thought made his stomach hurt.

"But if she loves him, then why does she keep that picture of you in her drawer?"

For a man who kickboxed and had always prided himself on his balance and agility, all it took were those words to make him lose his balance and fall on his ass behind the Lego table. Amy kept a picture of him in her drawer? The information had him reevaluating the reason she had brought Derek to the store. And if she'd said yes to marrying Derek, why hadn't she told her daughter? According to his sister and mother, Amy never kept anything of importance from Gabriella.

"Uh-oh." Gabriella glanced over her shoulder. "Here comes Dodo." She looked back at Rory, her eyes pleading. "Please, Uncle Rory, just tell her how you feel. I'll keep Derek away so you can talk to her."

Before Rory could say anything, she hurried off toward the escalator, disappearing behind the huge giraffe.

"Hi, Derek," she said in the sweetest voice Rory had ever heard come out of her mouth.

"Your mother is very upset, young lady," Derek said in a way that got Rory's temper up. "You can't just run around like some wild, unsupervised heathen."

"Sorry," Gabriella wheedled, "but I found exactly what I want Santa to bring me."

"I told you before that I'm not buying you a dirt bike. Why can't you act more like a little girl and ask for a doll?"

"Actually," Gabriella poured it on. "That's exactly what I was going to show you. It's the cutest little pink dollhouse I've ever seen. Let's stop by and tell Mom before we..." Her voice trailed off.

Once they were gone, Rory got up from the floor. He was still confused about what Gabriella had told him. Amy having a picture of him in her drawer could mean absolutely nothing. He paused in the middle of brushing off the back of his jeans. Or it could mean absolutely everything.

There was only one way to find out.

By the time Rory stepped off the escalator, Amy was only about ten people away from Santa. Rory's gaze ran over the sweet curve of her behind before he stepped over the partition and touched her arm.

She whirled around so quickly, her purse slipped off her shoulder and landed on the floor. Cosmetics, keys, and loose change spilled out. People in line scrambled to help pick up the items while Amy stood frozen in place and stared at him with a look of complete horror. A woman nudged her arm with the brush she'd picked up, but Amy didn't even glance at her.

Happy for something to do, Rory took the brush from the woman and thanked her. Then he leaned down to pick up the purse and started collecting the other items people had retrieved from the floor. By the time he was finished, Amy had come out of her trance.

"Thank you," she said as she took the purse from his hand. "What are you doing here?"

For a second, his pride took over and he almost said he was shopping for his nieces and nephews. But then Gabby's innocent face popped into his head, forcing him to speak the truth. "Wheezie told me that you were here and I wanted to see you. We need to talk."

Amy glanced around. "Now isn't exactly the time, Rory."

She was probably right. After the incident with the purse, every eye in line was trained on them. But it didn't matter anymore. He'd kept his feelings bottled up for five years. It was time to let them out. No matter what the outcome. Of course, being a typical insecure male, he needed just a little reassurance.

"Do you have a picture of me in your drawer?"

Her mouth dropped open as her face flamed a pink almost as bright as her sweater. With a stuttered gasp, she turned her back to him. Rory's grin felt like it went from ear to ear, and suddenly the words came much easier than he'd expected.

"I'm sorry, Amy, for the way I've treated you since I got back. Jealousy can make a man do some pretty stupid things, and I'll admit that I was pretty jealous. First about Mattie and then Derek."

He stepped closer, savoring the scent of strawberries that was uniquely Amy. He wanted to touch her. To place a hand on her trim waist and pull her back against him. But it was probably better if he didn't. Touching Amy screwed with his head, and he wasn't sure how long Gabriella would give him. He cleared his throat and tried to place his thoughts in some kind of order.

"From the moment you walked into M & M looking for a job, I knew you were special. And I looked for any excuse to walk past your desk or hang out in the copy room." He paused before he continued. "I don't know why I didn't ask you out. Maybe I thought you were too young for me. Or maybe dating a mother scared me. Anyway, by the time I figured out what I wanted and finally broke it off with Tess, you started avoiding me and hanging out with Mattie." He ran a hand through his hair and followed behind her as the line moved up. "Now I realize I should've talked to you before I ran off to Chicago like some immature idiot."

The woman who stood behind them butted in. "Men." She shot a mean glance at her husband, who stood next to her holding a little girl with chocolate on her face. "You're always running off when the going gets tough."

The man glanced around. "But what happened to the other dude she was with?"

The woman shushed him. "Let him finish."

Rory rolled his eyes and turned back to Amy. It might have been his imagination, but her shoulders looked less stiff. He took this as a positive sign and forged on.

"After the divorce, I told everyone I wanted to move back here to be close to my family. But the truth is that I wanted to move back here to be close to you. I've missed you more than I can ever put in words. I'm not going to tell you not to marry Derek—if that's what you want. But before you make that decision, I think we need to give what we have a chance."

The little boy and father in front of Amy finally reached Santa. The kid took two steps toward the elderly man with the full white beard and let out a bloodcurdling scream that sent his father into panic mode. It took two elves and a handful of candy canes to quiet the kid down.

The boy was still whimpering in his father's arms when they walked past.

"Just say it already." The man looked more harassed by Rory than he did by his son's crying. "You love her."

"Of course he does," another woman in line said as she swiped at her eyes with a tissue.

"Geez, Mister, even I know that," a freckle-faced kid said as he cut in front of two little girls.

It was the final straw. It was bad enough that Rory was standing there spilling his guts for the entire line like some hormonal teenager. He refused to talk to Amy's back. Taking her arm, he pulled her around. Her head was bent so he couldn't see her face, but he could see what she held in her hands.

A pen and a checkbook.

He blinked, wondering if his eyes were deceiving him.

But the checkbook remained. Amy's concise numbers neatly written in the lined columns.

"You were balancing your checkbook?" he asked in disbelief. "Here I was spilling my guts and you were busy calculating how much money you have in the bank?"

She looked up at him. If he hadn't been so blinded by anger and humiliation, he might've noticed the tears in her eyes. But he was more concerned with her inability to deny the accusation. Completely demoralized, he turned and pushed his way through the line. As he passed the family with the chocolate-smeared little girl, the father spoke.

"I don't know what he's so upset about. A woman who can balance her checkbook is worth her weight in gold."

Chapter Twelve

Please tell me this is the end of it." James readjusted the numerous shopping bags he already held so he could take the most recently filled bag from Cassandra.

She pulled a list out of her purse and studied it. "I need to get something for two more cousins. Oh, and Aunt Wheezie." She turned and weaved her way through the crowded department store.

James followed, taking note of the way she filled out her jeans. The blue denim tapered up long legs and clung to her perfect ass like a second skin. With every step she took, those sweet cheeks twitched. First to one side and then the other. Enthralled by the hypnotic wiggle, he didn't notice she'd stopped until he ran into her from behind. A curtain of dark, silky hair whipped across his face, and she shot him a questioning look.

He shrugged. "Sorry."

"If you weren't such an arrogant control freak, you wouldn't be staggering around with all the bags." She took a red scarf off a rack.

"Control freak?" He laughed. "Look who's calling the kettle black. Just what would you call your personality? Reserved? Easygoing? Since the moment I met you, you've done nothing but give me orders."

She turned on him. "And you haven't listened once. I wanted to drive; you drove. I wanted to wear my hair up; you took my hairclip. I wanted to eat brats for lunch, and I ended up at a place that served dry fish tacos. I wanted to pay for those tacos, and you convinced the cashier not to take my money." She jabbed a finger at his chest. "Now I ask you, who's the worse control freak?"

He grinned, liking the way her eyes sparkled when she got angry. "You might have a point." He reached out and smoothed a soft strand of hair back behind her shell-shaped ear. "But your hair's too beautiful to hide in that clippie thing. And you just got finished telling me your father had triple-bypass surgery, so you should eat healthier. And you can't blame me for the dinner tabs and driving. My mother drilled proper etiquette into my head from day one."

"Let me guess, your mother is one of those perfect ladies who doesn't burp, cuss, or open her own doors." She flipped the scarf back and sorted through the other ones.

"Actually, she used to have burping contests with me and my friends and always won. I think it had something to do with her Diet Coke. And she cussed a blue streak when something set her off, but that wasn't very often."

He paused as a familiar pressure built in his chest. "As for doors...she had a husband who worked a lot and a son who didn't think of his mother as a woman. So she had to open doors for herself."

Once the words were out, he wanted them back. He didn't like to talk about his mother. A therapist he had dated once told him that he suffered from repressed emotions. But repressed emotions were better than released pain, so he planned to continue to repress them for as long as he could.

Hopefully forever.

"So?" He tried to change the subject in hopes that Cassandra hadn't caught his use of past tense. "What are you going to get your Aunt Wheezie? A case of whiskey?"

Unfortunately, nothing got past Cassandra McPherson. She turned away from the rack of scarves, her eyes concerned. "Is your mother still alive?"

"No." Not wanting to look in her perceptive eyes, he studied the scarves. If he weren't so weighted down with bags, he might've even tried one on. Anything to get on a different topic.

"I'm sorry," she whispered. "I—I..." She fell silent.

"It doesn't matter. It happened a long time ago." Except it didn't feel like a long time ago. It felt like only yesterday. The loss. The pain. Especially with Cassandra standing so close.

"How old were you?" She reached out and touched his sleeve. The heat that sizzled through his body was immediate and reminded him it had been hours since he'd touched her. Early that morning, to be exact. It was all part of his plan to get her back to bed. Charm her first.

Tell her who he was. Then touch the hell out of her. The plan had been working well until he had put a damper on things by bringing up his mother.

"I had just started high school," he said.

"So that explains it."

Thinking she was still on the subject of etiquette, he nodded in agreement. "You're probably right. Maybe most of my door opening and package toting has to do with trying to make up for all those doors I never opened for my mom."

"True, but I was referring to your choice of careers." She walked up to the sales counter and handed the red scarf to the clerk. While she rang it up, Cassandra turned back to him. "My friend Amy read this magazine article that said that men who lose their mothers early can be so traumatized that they hate women or, the opposite, end up dating a lot of them. It makes sense that your desire to be an escort stems from wanting to replace your mother."

Cassandra had just handed him the perfect opportunity to set things straight. Unfortunately, the timing was all wrong. He didn't want to tell her the truth in the middle of a department store with Burl Ives singing "A Holly Jolly Christmas" over the grumblings of frustrated shoppers. He wanted to tell her in a quiet restaurant after five or six drinks—and after all the eating utensils had been removed from the table. He wanted to tell her when her green eyes weren't misted with understanding and compassion for a motherless escort.

Of course, now he didn't have a choice. If he kept lying, he would really be an asshole.

"Actually." He fidgeted with the handles of the bags as she handed the clerk her credit card. He waited for the woman to walk back over to the cash register before he continued. "There's something I need to tell you." He cleared his throat. "I'm not trying to replace my mother with women. You see . . . I'm really—"

"Oh. My. God." Cassandra's eyes widened. "You're gay."

The saleswoman stopped in midstride on her way back to the counter, confirming the fact that James had heard what he thought he'd heard.

"Gay?" A shopping bag slipped off his arm and hit the floor with a thud. By the time he bent to pick it up, Cassandra was already heading for the door.

"She forgot her scarf." The salesclerk held the small bag out to him as she sent him a sympathetic look. "My brother-in-law is gay. Do you want his number?"

Ignoring the question, James grabbed the bag and chased after Cassandra. Once outside, he stepped around the Salvation Army Santa and his kettle and looked up and down the street. Cassandra was a good half a block away, heading for her condo instead of the parking garage where he'd parked his SUV. Obviously, she'd rather walk than be stuck in a car with her gay lover.

He turned and headed for the garage.

Gay? Where in the hell had she gotten gay? Had he fingered the scarves too much? Crossed his legs at lunch? Put on too much cologne? Shown too much enthusiasm over the black stilettos she'd stopped to look at? Of course, he had only himself to blame. If he'd been truthful from the beginning, she wouldn't have jumped to the wrong conclusion.

It was something he needed to remedy as soon as possible.

After jogging to the parking garage, he beat her back to the condo. He parked the Land Rover in the lot in back and met her as she walked around the corner of the building.

"We need to clear some things up." He stepped in front of her.

"I don't want to talk right now." She skirted around him.

"Stop, Cassandra." He reached for her arm, but then thought better of it. "Please."

The word "please" worked. She froze, then slowly turned back around. "It's all right. Really, it is. I mean, you can't help who you are. And you certainly couldn't help what happened last night." She blushed and looked away. "I mean, I practically—" Her hand fell limply to her side. "I just wish you'd told me sooner. And I really wish I would stop attracting guys who like my underwear better than I do."

"Your underwear?"

"I realize I'm kind of a tomboy." She tipped her head back and stared up at the cloudy sky. "But for God's sake, can't I, for once, attract an alpha man?"

"Would you listen to me, Cassandra? I'm not gay." But it appeared she was no longer in any mood to listen. Since words weren't working, he decided on action.

Slipping his hands around her waist, he pushed her up against the first garage door and lowered his mouth to hers. It was something he'd wanted to do for the last five hours. Kissing Cassandra was like diving headfirst into heaven. Or a place much warmer. Her lips were hot and wet and devilishly delicious. Her tongue brushed against his, all slick and tempting. For a moment, he allowed himself to get lost in the kiss. Allowed the heat of her mouth and the warmth of her fingers in his hair to stoke his desire before he pulled her closer. Close enough to feel the aching hardness beneath the fly of his jeans. Close enough to demonstrate his sexual preference.

At the feel of his hard evidence, she pulled back and looked up at him, all dazed and cute. "You're not gay."

"Nope." He nipped at her bottom lip.

The garage door rumbled, and James quickly moved Cassandra out of the way as the door rolled up. Matthew stood on the other side in a pair of holey jeans and a Colorado State sweatshirt.

"What's up?" he asked, although, by the smirk on his face, James figured he knew exactly what was up. And exactly what he had interrupted. But it was hard to be annoyed with Matthew when he was so friendly. "Hey, James. I'm glad to see you're still around. I was just headed over to Patrick's to shoot some pool. Why don't you join us? Patrick's ordering pizza."

Any other time, James would've accepted the offer. He liked pool and pizza and enjoyed hanging out with the McPherson brothers. But tonight he had different plans. Plans that included only one other person—the woman who was still tucked beneath his arm, looking at him as if he were a big slice of pepperoni.

"Thanks, Matt," he said, "but I've got other plans."

But for all his boyish charm, Matthew turned out to be just as hardheaded and manipulative as the rest of the McPhersons.

"Suit yourself." Matthew shrugged. "I'll just tell Patrick that you'd rather have sex in the parking lot with our sister."

"Matthew McPherson!" Cassandra finally snapped out of her daze. "Don't you dare!"

Matthew looked over at James and innocently cocked his head. "So you want pepperoni or sausage?"

Four slices of pizza and what felt like fifteen games of pool later, James finally had Cassandra alone. Not exactly as alone as he'd like, but being in a park in the middle of downtown Denver was better than being in a small condo with her two brothers.

"You had better think twice before you throw that," he warned, as he stood calf-deep in the snow.

The dark-haired beauty in the green parka didn't blink as she pulled back her arm and launched a snowball straight at his head. He ducked, but not fast enough to completely escape. The ball smacked him on the forehead, dusting him with icy powder. He shook his head and growled a warning before he charged after the giggling woman who had decided escape was the better part of valor.

James caught Cassandra beneath a large evergreen and easily pulled her down. The striped knit hat she wore had slipped down to her nose. She pushed it back and looked up at him with laughing eyes that melted everything inside of him. Including any thought of revenge.

"Did you realize we keep ending up in the snow?" He brushed the icy chunks off her cheeks.

"And I seem to always be on the bottom." She narrowed her eyes. "Why is that?"

He rolled with her until she was smiling down at him, framing them both in miles of thick black hair. "Better?"

"Much." She leaned down and kissed him. Not a quick peck like the one he'd given her the first time they'd ended up in the snow, but a long, deep kiss that ended with heavy breathing and two very aroused bodies.

"I'm beginning to believe that you have a thing about being on top," James rasped.

"Maybe." She ran her tongue over his bottom lip and nibbled on it. "Do you have a problem with that?"

"God, no," he groaned. "But the people walking by may have a problem with it. Especially if you keep looking at me like that."

"Like what?" she teased, her gaze giving him the exact come-and-fuck-me look he was talking about.

His plan of holding off on sex until he could tell her who he was didn't seem like such a good one anymore. He should've told the truth when he'd had the chance. But the entire gay thing had screwed him up and then her brother had shown up—shit, who was he fooling? The truth was that he was too scared to tell her. Scared that when she found out he'd been lying to her she would send him packing and he would never get to see her naked again.

Or even clothed.

"You're going to be the death of me, woman." He rolled her back over, then got to his feet and pulled her up. "I'm freezing. Let's go find something hot to drink."

"I have coffee and hot chocolate at my place." She tugged on his jacket until her lips were inches from his. "Let's go back there."

"How about Starbucks?" he suggested, thinking a

public place would be much better for springing the truth on her. If she was going to react the way he thought she would, he might need witnesses.

"Are you afraid I'll take advantage of you if we're alone?"

He closed his eyes for a second, reliving exactly how well she took advantage. Unfortunately, there was the little problem of the truth that needed to be brought up before anyone took advantage of anyone.

He took her hand and led her down the path toward the street. "I think Starbucks is better."

"My place." She leaned in to him and dropped her head to his shoulder. The soft yarn of the hat tickled his chin. The woman knew how to get her way.

"Okay, your place."

They walked without talking, which was another thing James liked about her. Unlike most women he knew, Cassandra didn't have a problem with silence. If she didn't have anything important or pertinent to say, she didn't say anything.

The night was cold but clear. The sidewalks had been shoveled, but were still slick in spots. James knew the area. He had dined at the restaurants, had gone to a Colorado Rockies game, and had been to the Performing Arts Center with some woman whose name he couldn't remember. But tonight trumped all those other nights. For the first time in his life, he felt as if he was in the right place at the right time.

As they came around the corner of Cassandra's condo, two drunk college-age men stumbled down the side street, singing a raunchy rendition of the "The Twelve Days of Christmas."

"Eight maids were doing what?" James asked.

"Never you mind." Cassandra punched in the security code to her garage, then took his hand and pulled him under the opening garage door. "The only maid you need to worry about is me."

They had barely reached the top of the stairs when her phone began to ring. She ignored it and turned to kiss him. James had just slipped a hand over her breast when the answering machine clicked on.

"We lost Slumber Suites!" a booming voice came through the speaker.

Both James and Cassandra pulled back at the same time. She sent him an apologetic look before she hurried across the room and picked up the phone.

"What's going on?" she asked. "There's got to be a mistake, Dad." There was a string of muffled words before she spoke again. "So did Steve say who they plan to go with?"

It was hard for James to keep from butting into the conversation. He had been working on getting the contract for Slumber Suites for the last six months, even though he knew it was unlikely that Steve Mitchell would leave M & M Construction. Of course, just because Slumber Suites left M & M didn't mean that Sutton Construction had gotten the job. But there was a distinct possibility.

A surge of adrenaline shot through him. For a moment, he felt like jumping up and punching the air. The moment right before Cassandra turned on the lamp and he noticed her face. All the flushed happiness had drained out of it and been replaced by disbelief and something that looked a lot like fear.

"I don't want you upset, Dad. I'll call Steve tomorrow," she said. "I'll make this right. I promise."

She hung up, then stood there staring at the phone, stunned. Suddenly James realized that the stakes of the game he was playing had changed. If it was true, and Slumber Suites had left M & M to go with his company, it was just one more thing Cassandra would hold against him. But how could she fault him for just doing his job? Business was business; pleasure something else entirely. Besides, he didn't even know for sure if he'd gotten the contract. Until he found out, why not take baby steps? Deal with one lie at a time.

"Cassandra," he said, "we need to talk."

His words snapped her out of her thoughts, and she looked at him as if just realizing he was there. Then the strangest thing happened. The disappointment melted from her eyes and was replaced with something that made James feel as drunk as the two college boys.

"No," she said as she walked over and took his hand. "I don't want to talk. Not tonight." She took off her hat and tossed it to the couch before leading him up the stairs. Once in her bedroom, she didn't waste any time taking off her coat and sweater. Moonlight filtered in through the French doors, revealing a lace bra that took all the moisture from his mouth.

He squeezed his eyes closed. "You need to listen to me, Cassandra. I don't work for Elite Escorts."

"You're right." She walked over and unzipped his jacket, pushing it off his shoulders. Her hands slid down his chest to the fly of his jeans. She caressed him through the denim, and her breath fell hot against his ear. "Tonight you're just a man, and I'm just a woman. Your woman."

Chapter Thirteen

It was the second day in a row that Cassie woke up feeling rested. But this time she knew exactly where she was and who nestled against her back with his hand resting over her bare breast.

James.

Gorgeous, wonderful James.

She still didn't know his last name. And at this point, she really didn't care. All she cared about was staying right where she was. For a whole day. Or maybe a week. Or even a month.

She wondered what her family would say if she didn't come in to work for a month. Her dad wouldn't be happy, but her mother would be ecstatic—until she found out what her daughter's new boyfriend did for a living. Cassie wasn't exactly ecstatic about that part either.

Of course, James had denied being an escort. Who

wouldn't? It was like a stripper saying the only reason she danced was to put herself through college. James didn't want her to think he was cheap. Surprisingly, she didn't. Nowadays, most people had multiple partners. Her sweet little Mattie had probably gone to bed with as many women as James had. He just hadn't gotten paid for it. Still, she wasn't willing to date a man who continued to have multiple sexual encounters for money.

Cassie quietly nibbled on her thumbnail.

Maybe she could convince him to get another job. After all, she just happened to own a construction company, and he seemed to know a lot about construction. Unfortunately, he didn't act like the type who would take handouts from women. He'd refused to let her pay for one thing since they'd met.

She stopped biting her nail.

Come to think of it, his personality didn't go with his career choice. He was nothing like the other escorts. He wasn't vapid or cocky about his looks. Or immature, with more brawn than brains. While the others had fawned over her, catering to her every whim, James was mannerly but had no trouble taking charge. The night before was a perfect example. She had started out on top, calling all the shots, but somehow had ended up on the bottom with James in control.

Which made him more of a leader than a follower.

Maybe that was what he'd been trying to tell her. Maybe James wasn't just an escort. Maybe he was *the* escort. The top dog and owner of Elite. It made sense. With the way he knew how to push a woman's buttons, he had to be in charge of Elite Escorts' School of Drool. That would explain why he was so much more cultured and mature than the rest of the men had been. It would also explain all the office equipment in his house.

James owned the business. A business that prostituted men for money.

A light went on in her head.

Sweet Jesus, Mary, and Joseph.

What dream world had she been living in? Obviously, one where the little rich girl thought she could justify ordering men just like she ordered her chicken teriyaki all because it suited her needs. And what if he didn't just handle prostitutes? What if he was into other illegal things? Like drugs or human trafficking? Cassie could very well end up in jail for the rest of her life all because she couldn't keep her hands off the escort she'd hired. And not just any escort, but the big pimp daddy of them all.

Oh, God, her head hurt. She squeezed her eyes shut and moaned.

"Hey, baby," James the Pimp whispered into her ear, sending a rush of warm heat through her body and tightening her nipple against his palm. He rubbed his extremely hard erection against her bottom. "Mmmm, you feel good."

Cassie kept her eyes closed for a second more, wishing her brain hadn't woken up from its phenomenal-sex stupor. But it had, and she needed to face reality. As her mother liked to say, "You made your bed; now you have to lie in it."

Or get the heck out of it as quickly as possible.

"James?" Her voice cracked. "What do you do for a living?"

He sighed deeply. "Look, we need to talk."

Those five words clinched it. What he was about to say wouldn't be good.

She pulled away and sat up on the edge of the bed, her back to him. "No, forget it. I don't want to know what you do for a living. Just pretend I never asked. But I think you need to leave. The sooner, the better."

He reached out and ran the tips of his fingers along her spine, sending hot tingles skittering through her body. "Cassie, what's wrong?"

"Do you own Elite Escorts?" she whispered.

James laughed, a deep, hearty chuckle that shook the bed. She glanced over her shoulder. He sat back on the flowery pillowcases her mother had bought her, looking all rumpled and sexy with his hair sticking up and those amber eyes sparkling.

"Only you would think of something like that." He stroked her hair. "First I'm gay and now I'm a pimp?"

Bingo.

His dimples deepened. "Well, you're wrong."

Her eyes narrowed. Did pimps lie?

"I don't now—nor have I ever—owned an escort service." His gaze was direct and honest. When she continued to stare at him, he added, "You can call up Elite Escorts and ask them, if you want."

"Then why do you have all that office equipment?"

"Because I run a business."

"But not an escort service?" she said.

James looked away for only a second before looking back at her. "No."

Everything inside of Cassie released, and she sagged

against his chest. "I guess my imagination got the better of me. So what kind of business do you run?"

He smoothed back a strand of her hair. "Construction."

The information brought a huge smile to her face as everything slipped into place. No wonder he knew so much about architecture and building; it was what he wanted to do for a living. And no wonder she felt so drawn to the man. It all made perfect sense. He wasn't going to be an escort for the rest of his life. He was going to be a businessman, a businessman she could date. A man who got along with her brothers and who would have no problem getting along with her parents.

In fact, her father would love him.

It suddenly seemed as if she had received the best Christmas present ever.

Cassie lifted her head and looked up at him. He had bad bed head and there was a sleep crease on one cheek. Still, to her he looked as perfect as he had the first time she'd seen him standing in front of the glittering lights of the office Christmas tree. Suddenly she realized she wanted to see him like that again.

Right here in her home.

"Do you know what I want to do?" she murmured.

He arched a brow. "Hopefully, the same thing that I want to."

"Do you want to go get a Christmas tree?"

His other eyebrow joined the first one. "On the day before Christmas? I think most of the lots will be closed by now. Besides, I didn't think you wanted one."

She hadn't. Christmas trees were for families. Not a single girl who spent most of her time at work. But suddenly she didn't feel like a single girl. She felt like a couple. And she wanted a tree to share with the man who had changed a lonely one into a happy two.

"A person can change their mind, can't they?" she said before she leaned up and brushed a kiss over his lips.

A look passed over his hooded, whiskey-colored eyes that melted her like an acetylene torch to metal. "We'll go get a tree," he whispered, "but first we're going to do what I was thinking about."

"And that was?" She barely got the words out before he rolled her over and followed with his hard body.

"Well, I've been thinking about this headboard." James took each one of her hands in his and drew them up over her head. Her knuckles rapped against the brass. "You are way too controlling in bed, Cassandra." He opened her fingers, then closed them around a rung. "So I think I'm going to have to take drastic measures."

Cassie's eyes narrowed. "How drastic?"

"Pretty drastic." He gave her a lecherous grin, followed by a long, leisurely kiss that made her body puddle into the sheets. When she was good and limp, he released her hands. "Don't move." He bent over the bed to retrieve something from the floor. He returned with a skinny knit scarf, which he proceeded to entwine around her wrists and the headboard.

"What do you think you're doing?" She released the rungs and tried to sit up, but it was too late. The scarf tightened, and her wrists were caught against the cold brass. "This isn't funny, James."

"It's not supposed to be funny." His gaze dropped down

to her breasts as he finished tying the scarf. A tremor ran through her, and her nipples beaded into hard points under the warmth of his gaze.

"Let me go." She tugged.

"Now, don't be scared," he whispered. With his fingers resting on her wrists, he bent to place a feathery kiss at the base of her throat. "Anytime you don't like what I'm doing, all you have to do is say so and we'll stop."

"I don't like what you're doing."

Cassie had an aversion to being tied up after Rory had tied her to a chair for one of his magic acts, then left her there for over an hour while he checked out the tent Jake had made in the backyard with Mom's good sheets. Of course, Cassie was only seven at the time and completely convinced that her brothers wanted to permanently get rid of her every time their parents left.

James wasn't trying to get rid of her. And if the way he settled against her side was any indication, he wasn't going anywhere.

His lips traced a fiery path up to her ear. "Are you sure you don't like it? I feel like you haven't given it much of a chance." He flicked his tongue over her earlobe, then softly nibbled while his fingers brushed up and down the sensitive skin on the inside of her arm. "You need to learn to relax, Cassandra. Let someone else be in control for a change."

"For a change? You've been in charge ever since I met you."

"And has anything bad happened?"

"No, but—"

"Shhhh," he breathed against her ear, sending shivers

down her spine. "The only butt I'm willing to talk about is the one attached to your sweet body." Hot fingertips slid down her arm and skated over her breast.

Cassie's eyes closed.

Maybe she'd let him play his little game for a while. Just to see what happened. There was something rather thrilling about being completely at the mercy of a tall, dark, and very hot man. Something she'd missed in her other relationships. The men she had dated preferred taking orders rather than issuing them. So if any tying had taken place, Cassie would've been the one doing it. But she'd never tied them up. She didn't have to. They usually let her do what she wanted without rope.

Not that James was forcing her to do things she didn't want to do. Besides lying there with her hands wrapped around the brass rungs, she didn't have to do anything. Except enjoy the feel of his mouth and the glide of his fingers. Maybe being at the mercy of a controlling, wicked man was okay after all.

Maybe it was better than okay.

His lips opened and closed around the muscle that ran behind her ear to her collarbone. James sucked the firm flesh between his lips, not hard enough for a hickey, but just hard enough to send an explosion of tingling sensations coursing through her body. He gently bit down, and Cassie saw stars. She had erogenous zones, but not one guy had hit this one. Without conscious thought, her hips lifted and her toes curled around the sheets.

With his erection pressing into her thigh, he trailed moist kisses over her collarbone and down toward her breasts. When he reached her erect nipple, he slowly circled it with his tongue, grazing the center but never fully touching it.

"James," she groaned.

"Hmmm? Did you want me to stop, wildcat?" He leaned back and blew on the wet spot he'd made.

The cool puff of air made her nipple even tighter, and she groaned and shoved her head back into the pillow. "No, not yet."

His lips returned to their torture. After what seemed like hours, he took her stiff nipple into the heat of his mouth. A scorching shaft of desire shot through her, and she gripped the scarf and tried to wrap a leg around his waist and pull him on top of her.

"Now. Get in me now."

He stilled and lifted his head. "I'm afraid that's not how this game works, sweetheart. If you want me to stop, I will. Otherwise, I'm the one in charge."

Cassie wished her hands were free so she could smack the jerk. Instead, she glared at him before closing her eyes.

He chuckled. "One more word from those pretty lips of yours and the game's over. Got it?" When she nodded, he leaned back over her. "Now, where was I?"

This time the heat and suction of his mouth on her breast nearly did her in. He wasn't exactly gentle, but completely thorough. His tongue licked and his lips pulled, while his fingers ran over her skin. He treated her like an experienced carpenter with a fine piece of wood—his hands callused and rough, yet gentle and reverent. They slipped into places and massaged muscles that she didn't even know she had.

With her bottom lip tucked between her teeth, Cassie moaned, groaned, and squeaked her satisfaction. Funny, but she had never realized before how words could screw up great sex. All this time, she had followed the advice of the sex experts who believed in the importance of telling your partner exactly what you wanted. Now she realized that sometimes it was best to keep your mouth shut and just enjoy.

While she was enjoying, James eased her legs apart and slid between them. His lips feathered kisses along her rib cage, then slowly sipped his way to her navel. He circled it once with his tongue, dipping inside before he moved down. She knew where he was headed and part of her couldn't wait for him to get there. The other part was a little scared. Not that she hadn't experienced oral sex before, but there was something different about this time. For some reason, what he was about to do felt more invasive.

More intimate.

Cassie lifted her head up off the pillows to stop him, but before she could utter a peep, his hot lips covered her wet heat, and her words got lost in a tidal wave of sexual desire. She watched his mouth work its magic until the muscles in her neck turned to jelly and she fell back to the pillows.

After a few gentle sips, he settled into rhythmic flicks that took complete control over her mind and body. She felt consumed and devoured, and there wasn't a thing she could do about it except sit back and enjoy.

Her orgasm was explosive. Her thighs tightened around his head as the intense sensations washed over her. Once the last spark fizzled, her body relaxed. She puddled there for a few seconds before opening her eyes and looking down.

James lifted his head and everything inside of Cassie stilled except for the clamoring of her heart. His amber eyes were hot and glassy and filled with need, but they also sent a message that no man had ever sent. They asked the silent question—are you all right? But more than that, they revealed a man who cared. A man who cared not only about this moment, but about the moments to come.

"I..." she got out before words escaped her.

Easing her legs from his shoulders, he slid up her body, cradling her head with his forearms as he untied her hands. "I know, baby." He kissed her deeply, his mouth wet and salty. "It's okay." He took the time to massage her wrists, unconcerned with the erection that pressed against the damp spot between her legs.

With emotion clogging her throat, she nodded and ducked her head into his neck like a shy, sixteen-year-old virgin. She didn't know where Cast-iron Cassie had gone, but it didn't look like she was coming back anytime soon. And, surprisingly, she was okay with that. As long as this man stayed right where he was.

"Make love to me," she whispered against his hot skin.

James chuckled. "So I guess you're back to giving orders." He leaned over and got a condom from the nightstand. "I think I can live with that."

He wasted no time at all in slipping deep inside her. He stretched the still quivery muscles, causing her desire to build again as he cradled her head between his arms and touched his forehead to hers.

"God, Cassandra." He moaned. "I don't think I can wait."

"Then don't." She slid her arms around his neck.

James was right. Within seconds, his body convulsed. A second later, Cassie joined him.

Chapter Fourteen

So I'll see you in a couple hours?" Cassie had her hand on the Land Rover's door handle, but her lips were inches from those of a most delectable man.

"Only long enough so I can shower and shave." He brushed his lips back and forth across hers.

"You already showered."

"I wouldn't call that a shower."

She smiled against his lips. "Really? What would you call it?"

"A wet dream." The kiss deepened.

Her head dropped back as he nibbled on her neck. "Mmmm, it was pretty close to heaven."

"You're pretty close to heaven." He moved back up to her lips and kissed her long and deep before lifting his head. "You better go before I forget all about letting you out of this car."

There was a moment when Cassie actually thought about taking him up on the offer. But since it had been her idea for him to drop her off at the office, she couldn't exactly change her mind without looking like a ditzy female. Although, when he kissed her, she certainly felt like one.

She opened the door and got out, but before she could slam it, he stopped her.

"I'm dropping you off to get your truck, not to let you get so wrapped up in work you forget to meet me back at your place." When she didn't say anything, he added, "Right, Cassandra?"

She rolled her eyes. The man was completely insufferable—domineering—arrogant, and, as her Aunt Wheezie would say, as cute as a bug's ear. "I'll see you in exactly two hours at my place," she conceded; then she slammed the door and turned to walk to the front door of her office building.

The day was cloudy and cold with a hint of forecasted snow in the air. She pulled the ends of her down jacket together and zipped it up against the biting wind. Besides fighting against the wind, she also fought against the strong desire to turn back around.

Other men had dropped her off before. Not many, but a few, including Mike. But she never had the urge to turn back around to see if they were still there. Probably because most of them had let her out and driven off as if the hounds of hell were after them. But this time was different. This time she knew that if she turned around James would still be there. Watching and waiting until she was safely inside.

Another one of those damned baseball-sized lumps formed in the back of her throat, and she suddenly felt all happy, quivery, and girlie. Just another reason why she refused to turn around. No man had ever made Cassie McPherson feel all happy, quivery, and girlie. And no man would. It would pass. She just needed some time away from his gorgeous face and body.

Of course, she needed to be farther away from him than several yards, which was why she dropped her keys to the front door twice, missed the lock three times, and had the key upside down when she finally did hit the hole. By the time she opened the door, she was upset with herself and with the man who had turned her into this bizarre creature.

But that didn't stop her from looking when she relocked the front door and was hidden behind the tinted glass. He was there, his left hand rested on the steering wheel as he leaned down to see out of the passenger window. For a few seconds, she stood there watching him, feeling a weightlessness in the pit of her stomach. Then the beeping of the alarm caught her attention, and she rushed over to the security box to punch in the code. By the time she looked again, he was gone.

What did she expect? Did she think that he would sit outside the entire time like some lovesick fool? She moved to the elevators and punched the button. Her hand shook, and she jerked it beneath her arm and held it tightly against her body. The man wasn't the lovesick-fool type.

She stepped into the elevators, punched the fourteenth floor, and then slumped back against the wall as the doors closed. The elevator had started its ascent when Cassie glanced over at the mirrored wall across from her. A woman looked back, a woman with finger-tousled hair, sparkling green eyes, and well-kissed lips. A woman who looked as if she'd been thoroughly loved. A woman who looked in—

Cassie's eyes widened. She pushed away from the elevator wall and took a closer look. She didn't study the tousled hair, flushed face, or kiss-swollen lips; instead she studied the look in her eyes. She'd seen the look before. Not on herself, but on others. On Jake when he brought home Melanie for the first time and thousands of times on her father's face when he looked at her mother.

Oh, shit. James might not be a lovesick fool, but she was.

"No," she whispered. "I can't be. Not after only two days." Hadn't it taken God six days to create the Earth? Certainly it would take at least that long to fall in love.

The elevator doors opened with a *ping*, but Cassie didn't notice. Her mind was too consumed with this startling revelation. So the doors closed again while she stood there and stared…and stared…and stared. The look didn't change. She tried to harden her features and scowl, but her eyes remained soft. Wistful. Happy. Obviously, something inside had changed, and the windows of her soul were spreading the news.

Cassie McPherson was in love.

A grin slipped over her face, then widened into a full-out smile. So this was what it felt like. After twenty-eight years, she finally knew. She turned away from her reflection and pushed the button for the doors to open. In a trancelike state, she stepped from the elevator and walked toward her office. It was Sunday and the day before Christmas, so not a soul was there to witness their boss wandering through the lobby like a happy zombie. She left her coat on, zipped all the way to the neck, as she slipped into the chair behind her desk and leaned back against the leather.

Nothing in this part of her world had changed. Everything was just as she had left it. Her desk was cluttered with stacks of memos and invoices, groups of rolled-up blueprints, her open day planner, and a half-filled coffee mug. The clock she'd received as an office-warming present still hung on the wall over the couch, counting off the time with soft little clicks. Even the view of the city from her window looked just the same as it had on Friday. A steel-gray sky threatening snow.

Yet as she looked around the room, everything seemed different. Completely foreign. It was as if she had taken a long hiatus and returned to a place that no longer mattered to her. She was in no hurry to call Steve Mitchell about the Slumber Suites contract, go over her calendar for the next week, or even check her messages on the cell phone that blinked on its charger. Instead, she just wanted to sit and enjoy the feeling that coursed through her body. For once in a very long time, she felt as if everything was right in the world.

Friday seemed like a lifetime away instead of just two days. She hugged herself and laughed, twirling her chair around with her feet. Suddenly, she felt like Scrooge after finding out he hadn't missed Christmas after all. The ghosts had accomplished all their lessons in one night and given him a new lease on life, which was exactly what had happened to her. She felt as if she'd learned an entire lifetime of lessons in just two days.

Not just about a man with whiskey-colored eyes and sexy dimples, but about herself. About her feelings. About what she wanted. More than that, she had learned what she needed. And all it had taken was eight glasses of champagne and one pain-in-the-butt man to teach her.

In forty-eight hours, Cassie had laughed harder and cried more than she had her entire life. To say nothing of the intense passion she'd experienced. All her emotions had been bottled up, just waiting for someone to uncork them.

James had sure popped her cork.

She giggled just like all the other lovesick women she had made fun of in her life.

Her cell phone rang, and she swiveled her chair back around to her desk and answered it.

"Where have you been?" Amy's voice came through the receiver.

Grinning like an idiot, Cassie leaned back in her chair and plopped her boots on the desk. "I was home."

"So you don't pick up? I left you at least six messages. If I hadn't talked to Mattie, I would've thought you'd fallen off the face of the earth."

She sort of had. "I'm sorry. You know I'm not good about getting my messages at home, and I spent the day shopping."

"So what about your cell? I left messages on it too."

"I didn't get a chance to stop by and get it until now."

"So you're at the office?" Amy sounded thoroughly disappointed. "I was hoping that you and James were still hanging out. Mattie said that you guys looked pretty intense while you were playing pool."

"Leave it to Mattie to stick his nose where it doesn't belong."

"He didn't say all that much," Amy said. "Which is why I've been dying to talk to you." Cassie could almost see Amy leaning in to the phone. "So did you?"

"Did I what?"

"Did you heat up the sheets with James?" Amy asked.

"No."

"Liar."

Cassie laughed. "Okay, so I had sex. But I refuse to give you details over the phone."

"So stop by my house when you leave the office."

She glanced at the clock. "I can't. But maybe I could stop by this evening before I go over to my parents' house— Oh wait, I forgot. You're spending Christmas Eve with Derek's family."

There was a long pause. "Actually...I broke up with Derek."

Cassie dropped her feet to the floor and sat up. "You're kidding. Because of our conversation on Friday?"

"Partly," Amy said. "I guess it made me realize that I wanted the dream after all."

Knowing how much Amy wanted a real family for Gabby, she tried to cheer her friend up. "It will happen, Amy. I know there's someone out there for you. Look, why don't you and Gabby come over to my parents' tonight? It will give me a chance to give you all the dirty details, and my nieces and nephews will love seeing Gabby."

"I don't think so—".

"I won't take no for an answer. Christmas Eve is for family. And you and Gabby are family."

"But wouldn't you rather invite James?"

"Are you kidding?" Cassie picked up a pen and doodled on her day planner. "Having James meet the boys was bad enough. I won't subject him to Dad until I get to know him better."

"But you are planning on getting to know him better?"

Cassie stared down at the heart she had just drawn with the J + C written inside. There was no doubt about it. She had become one of those quivery, boy-crazed girls. "Yeah, I'm going to get a tree with him today."

"A tree? Like as in Christmas tree?" Amy sounded shocked. "Man, Cassie, you have fallen."

She wanted to deny it, but she couldn't with the lopsided ink heart glaring up at her and with her own heart thumping against her chest just talking about him. She laughed because she couldn't stop herself. "Oh, Amy, I have and I'm scared to death."

"Because he's an escort?"

"No. I mean I was worried about that at first, but now..." She took a deep breath. "Now I'm just scared that he doesn't feel the same way about me."

"What makes you think he doesn't?"

Cassie's mind ran over the last couple days, but she couldn't come up with one time that James had made her feel as if he didn't want to be right where he was. She glanced up at the clock again.

"Listen, Amy, I need to go. I'll expect to see you at the house tonight."

"I'll think about it," Amy said. "Oh, and, Cassie, while you're at the office, would you stop by my fax machine? I had the *Las Vegas Review-Journal* fax over the article they did on Sutton for the business section last year. It should be there by now, and your father wanted to see it."

After Cassie hung up the phone, she punched in the numbers to retrieve her messages. She needed to hurry if she wanted to call her parents, collect all her stuff, and get back to her apartment in time to meet James.

She had around twenty messages. The first few were from her mother, who had been looking for her while she'd been primping in the executive bathroom; one from Amy apologizing for taking her maroon dress and laughing about the condoms; and one from an electrical contractor who wanted to meet with her after the new year. Cassie listened to all of these with half an ear, her mind going back to how cute James had looked sitting in his Land Rover watching her.

Oh, brother. She needed to get a life.

While she listened to the next message, she got up and headed to Amy's office. The recorded voice wasn't one she recognized.

"This is Maggie Jane Robbins calling from Elite Escorts. I'm terribly sorry, but your escort for the evening just called to say he has a hundred and two fever. Unfortunately, we don't have any other escorts available this evening. But you will receive a full refund along with one complimentary night. I apologize for any inconvenience this may have caused you. Merry Christmas."

Cassie came to a halt by Amy's desk.

Huh?

She stared at her phone. What did the woman mean her escort had a hundred and two temperature? James was hot. But healthy. There had to be a mistake.

Maybe he'd started feeling better and decided to show up after all.

She punched a button and listened to the message again, then checked the time she received it. That was weird. She'd received the call *after* she'd left with James. But who else would come to an office dressed to kill, escort her to a Christmas party, and then...

Cassie's eyes slid closed in ecstasy. And then give her the best two days of her life.

No, the woman with the annoyingly snobby voice had made a mistake. Some other desperate female had missed out on an escort, but, luckily, Cassie hadn't. James had been all hers. Her brow crinkled. At least, he'd been all hers for two days. But what would happen now? Would he continue to be an escort even if he was starting a construction company? Starting a business took capital. Maybe he couldn't afford to quit. Especially with the biggest date night of the year only a week away. The thought of James escorting another woman to some New Year's Eve party took all the happiness right out of Cassie.

She sat down in Amy's chair. What had she been thinking? Did she think that suddenly James would stop being an escort? Even if it turned out he loved her, that didn't mean he would quit his job. Maybe he was like her little brother, Mattie, and loved women. All women.

Good God. She rested her head in her hands. Could she ever choose a guy that didn't have a bunch of weird excess baggage? At least Mike was only addicted to lacy underwear, not the women who wore them. Cassie might be able to overlook the occasional panty raiding, but could she overlook a guy who had sexual relations with half of

Denver? And even if he did quit, could she forget about all the women he'd been with before her? Every time James said hi to a woman, she would wonder if he'd taken her to bed. If she couldn't forget the women, then she couldn't be with James. The thought crushed her.

As her mind feverishly looked for an answer to her dilemma, Cassie glanced down at the stack of paper on the fax machine. A face smiled back at her from the top page, a face she had come to know very well. A frown marred her forehead as she reached for the picture. It was blurred. But not so blurred that she couldn't read the words beneath the smiling image. *James Sutton, owner of Sutton Construction, cuts the ribbon on the new Sunset Housing development.*

James Sutton?

Her insides tightened as her mind frantically tried to fit all the pieces together. It didn't take long. Now that she had the full picture, everything slipped into place. The confused look on his face when she ordered him into the elevator. His age. His nice SUV and house. All the computers and office supplies. His refusal to tell her his last name and his face whenever she mentioned his profession.

James wasn't an escort.

He was her number-one competitor.

And a big, fat liar.

Chapter Fifteen

For Christmas Eve morning and a Sunday, traffic was brutal. It took James forever to get to his house. Or maybe it just seemed like forever because he happened to be in a hurry. A hurry to get back to Cassandra. And why was that? Hell, she hadn't even turned around once on the way into the M & M building. He didn't know why something that stupid would bother him. It just did. His annoyance grew when he pulled into his driveway and saw half the neighborhood in his front yard setting up brown paper sacks.

For a moment, James thought about pulling into the garage and ignoring his neighbors, but then the guy who lived next door waved, and James figured that he didn't have much of a choice. Still, he couldn't help glancing at his watch before he stepped from the Land Rover. An hour twenty-two minutes and counting.

The guy next door stuck out the hand that didn't hold three lunch-sized bags. "Les Finley."

"James Sutton." He shook the guy's hand and then watched as a couple teenage boys in the back of a pickup handed off the bags to a group of women who then placed them on the front lawn. James didn't know a lot about luminaria placement, but it sure looked like a jumbled mess to him. While the other houses had them neatly lined along the driveways and sidewalks, the neighbors had placed James's in nine crooked lines they'd shoveled through the snow. Sensing James's confusion, Les clarified.

"Betty thought you might like to have them in the shape of a menorah like the Greenburgs."

Now would've been the time to mention that he wasn't Jewish, but James refused to add fuel to the conversation when he was in a hurry.

"I figure you and the Greenburgs would just as soon do without them altogether," Les continued. "But once Betty gets something in her head, it's best to just go along with it. She means well."

James's eyes narrowed on the older woman, who was issuing orders like Patton on D-Day. *Means well, my ass.* The woman just liked to issue orders. Speaking of people who liked to issue orders, he glanced at his watch and tried to bring the conversation to an end.

"I'd love to help out, but I have an appointment I need to get ready for."

Les glanced over at him and grinned. "Yeah, I saw you driving off with her yesterday morning." His eyes turned wistful. "I remember what it was like to have those appointments. Now I'm lucky if I have one every other week. Not that I don't love the kids, but once in a while..." His voice trailed off before he snapped out of his daydream and cleared his throat. "Don't worry about helping. We've got it covered. And my son and his friends will come back tonight and light them. That's if it doesn't snow." He grinned. "Of course, I don't know what I'm talking about. A little thing like a blizzard won't stop Betty from seeing her plan to fruition."

"Yeah, well, thanks again." James edged back toward the open garage, almost tripping over the gray, one-eyed cat. He sidestepped the cat and wasn't even aware that it had followed him until Les spoke.

"Oh no, you don't."

James turned to find Les scooping up the cat and walking out of the garage so James could close the door.

It took James just over twenty minutes to shower, shave, and get dressed. Which left him with an hour before he had to be back at Cassie's.

Standing at his kitchen counter waiting for the coffee to brew, he glanced at his watch for the umpteenth time. Was it his imagination or was the second hand slower than normal? He tapped the crystal face. Maybe it was broken. Maybe a lot more than forty minutes had gone by. Maybe he should grab his cup of coffee and head on over to Cassie's. Or maybe he should go to her office.

Or maybe he should pull his head out and quit acting like an idiot.

Just as the coffee machine hissed out its final drop, the lock on his front door rattled. A moment later, Sierra bounced into the kitchen wearing a pair of Tweety Bird slippers, pink heart pajama bottoms, a zippered hoodie, and a striped scarf wrapped around her neck.

"Where have you been?" She unwound the mile-long striped scarf. "Do you realize you were moments away from getting listed as MIA and your picture on a carton of milk? The last I saw of you, you were all dressed for prom and on your way to some party. Then I show up here yesterday to drop off your Christmas present— Oh, crap, I left it back at my apartment." She waved the hand that wasn't holding the Starbucks cup around in the air, fluttering the bangs of her short magenta hair. "Anyway, I stopped by and you weren't here, and you're never not here. Unless you're on site, but with all the sites shut down for the holidays, you should be here. So I tried calling and I kept getting your voice mail—"

James reached over and covered her mouth, something he did on a regular basis. She stopped talking, and her big brown eyes blinked at him.

"As you can see, I'm fine." He dropped his hand and smiled to reassure her. Sierra might be young, dramatic, and easily excitable, but she was also loyal, dependable, and hardworking. In the last year, he'd grown attached to her odd-colored hair, multiple ear piercings, and weird fish tattoo. Well, maybe not the weird fish tattoo.

"So why didn't you answer your phone?" she demanded.

"I was busy." Thinking about what he had been busy with had him blushing like a schoolboy, and he turned around and poured a cup of coffee to hide his reaction. "It happens."

"Not to workaholics who shiver with delight when their cell phones go off."

"I don't shiver with delight," he said, even though she was right. Since starting Sutton Construction, he'd always made a point of answering his phone. His phone was a direct line to his business. And business was his life. It was what made him get out of bed in the morning and what put him to sleep at night. It gave him a feeling of accomplishment and self-worth with only a few minor migraines.

His placed the carafe back in the coffee machine. But it wasn't as big of a deal as Sierra was making it out to be. Even workaholics needed a vacation. And it was Christmas. Or close enough to use it as an excuse. By the time he turned back around, Sierra had leaned back on the opposite counter with her arms crossed and her eyes narrowed.

"So where were you?"

He cocked an eyebrow. "Are we going to start asking personal questions? Because if we are, I'd love to know where you go on your hour and a half lunch breaks."

She blinked. "Well, I—I..." A smile tickled the corners of her wide mouth. "Fine. No personal questions. But that doesn't mean you don't need to check in every now and again. Especially when you deviate from your normal routine."

"You're right." He cradled his cup and blew a little before he took a sip. "I should've checked in. I'm sorry."

"You're forgiven." Sierra grinned the adorable grin that made him want to reach out and ruffle her hair. He didn't. Mostly because the one time he'd given in to the urge, she'd lectured him for a good hour on how degrading it was to work for people who treated you like a ten-year-old. She was right, but it still didn't stop him from wanting to do it. Probably because he'd always wanted a cute baby sister—minus the fish tattoo and magenta hair. Instead, he had a belligerent stepbrother who grunted one-word replies whenever James phoned home.

Sierra took a slurp from the straw that stuck out of the Starbucks cup. "I bet the reason you forgot your cell phone had to do with a woman."

"I thought we decided no questions."

"That wasn't a question. It was a statement."

"A statement I'm not going to acknowledge," he said.

"Whatever." She studied him over the straw. "But a woman would explain that confused lost-puppy-dog look you have. The one that men get right before they fall hard."

James choked and jerked the cup away from his mouth, splashing coffee on his boots. Wiping his mouth with the back of his hand, he glared at her.

She shrugged. "It's nothing to get all choked up about. So you finally found someone you like well enough to act stupid over. I'd say, it's about time."

"Stupid?" His eyes narrowed as he watched her grab a paper towel from the roll on the counter and bend down to wipe off his boots. "Being too busy to answer my phone is not stupid."

"No." She tossed the towel at the garbage can in the corner. It bounced off the wall and landed inside for a good three-pointer. "But your shirt's buttoned wrong and you missed a patch of whiskers on your chin." She pointed at him. "And is that toothpaste under your nose or something more disgusting?"

"Damn it." Setting his mug down, he grabbed a paper towel and wiped at his nose before turning his attention to the three buttons at the top of his sweater. Annoyed with himself as much as with her, he lashed out. "Aren't you late for the tattoo parlor?"

"I thought you said you'd fire me if I got even one more scale."

"As if that threat ever worked." He tossed the crumpled towel at the trash can, but it ricocheted off the edge of the counter and landed a good three feet away.

She walked over, picked up the paper wad and scored a two-pointer. "Don't get defensive. The stupidity will leave. Eventually. For now, I'd suggest staying away from sharp objects and moving vehicles." When he continued to glare at her, she held up a hand. "Fine. I'm going. But at a time like this, you probably shouldn't be alone."

James didn't know what he was angry at. He was talking with a twenty-year-old who still wrote her boyfriend's name in hearts all over his phone messages. But she was right. He did have a bad case of stupidity. Except it had nothing to do with falling and everything to do with getting back to a warm, delectable body.

"I thought you said you were going," he said.

She tipped her head. "Ya know, I think I like the new you. Usually when I stop by I'm forced to make phone calls, do copying and filing, and answer a hundred and one questions like 'Did you e-mail so-and-so,' 'Did you get the expense reports finished,' and 'Were there any important messages after I left on Friday?' "

"Were there any important messages after I left on Friday?"

"Hey, don't turn all businesslike now." When he just looked at her, she added, "No. There were no important messages. I already told you the *Denver Post* wants to do a story on you. Which is pretty exciting. Do you think they'll want a picture of me? After all, I'm your right-hand woman." She struck a pose, all wide eyes and pouting lips. "My mom would implode if I got my picture in the paper."

He placed a hand on the back of her neck and guided her toward the door. "I'll make you a deal. If they do an article on me, I'll be sure to get you in the picture."

"If? That Amy Walker sounded like it was a done deal. You should've heard all the questions she asked. Even personal things like where you lived and who was your girlfriend. Of course, I told her you didn't have one." When they got to the door, she turned to him with a knowing smirk on her pixie face. "I guess I was wrong."

James pulled open the door. "No. You weren't wrong." He stepped out on the porch with her, relieved to see that his neighbors were gone. "Don't party too much on Christmas. I expect to see you bright and early on Tuesday morning."

She shot him a pout. "Scrooge."

"That's not fair." He grabbed an end of the scarf, then proceeded to wind the stretchy wool around her neck and up over her mouth. "I always give you extra lumps of coal for your fire." He grinned down at the picture she presented with the striped knit wrapped around her lower face and her brown eyes snapping.

"Bahhh-hhhmmbug," she mumbled through the scarf.

"Bah humbug yourself, brat." He pulled her into his arms and gave her a tight hug followed by a quick kiss right on the top of her head. "I guess Wednesday morning will be soon enough to see your homely face. With pay, of course. I realize ugly tattoos are expensive."

Before he could pull back, she flung her arms around his neck and bumped her wool-covered mouth against his. "Thhanks, Bosh."

"Get going." He turned her around, then watched as her Tweety slippers thumped down the steps, walked between his menorah luminarias, and disappeared around the bright yellow Volkswagen Beetle. As he turned to go back inside, he noticed a half-ton truck parked down the street. Just the sight of it reminded him of Cassandra, and he smiled.

Okay, so maybe he did have a girlfriend. It wasn't like it was the end of the world. At least, it wouldn't be if he could slow things down a little and not let her control his mind so much that he forgot everything else.

Like business.

James ran a hand over his chin. Or grooming. God, he had lost a few brain cells over the last two days. But starting now, he intended to keep things in perspective. Which meant he didn't need to race over to Cassandra's condo and wait there like a little lost puppy.

After days of ignoring his business, there were a million things he could do. He glanced back at the truck.

Unfortunately, there was only one thing he was going to do.

Chapter Sixteen

Tweety slippers?

What kind of a woman wears Tweety slippers?

Cassie glared through the windshield at the woman who had just stepped off the curb on her way to her car. Suddenly, Cassie had the strong desire to pop her truck into drive and run right over those cutesy-wootsy slippers. Of course, it wasn't the young woman's fault. She probably had no idea what kind of lowdown, two-timing, lying bastard her boyfriend was.

Boyfriend.

The word sent a shaft of pain through Cassie's heart, and her gaze snapped back over to the porch where James still stood. He had changed and now wore a rust-colored sweater that brought out the highlights in his brown hair. His hands were stuffed in the front pockets of his jeans, one shoulder hitched higher than the other. He watched the woman get into her car and smiled a smile that not less than two hours ago had melted Cassie like a plastic bread bag on a hot toaster.

Her hands tightened on the steering wheel.

On second thought, why waste her time on Tweety when it was a peacock who deserved to be turned into roadkill? Unfortunately, before she could do more than gun the engine and calculate what path she wanted to take through his front lawn, someone tapped on the passenger-side window. She jumped and turned to find a woman in a down jacket and earmuffs standing on the sidewalk, motioning for her to roll down the window.

Cassie's first thought was to make a run for it. She had come here looking for answers, and she had gotten them in spades. But before she could even move her hand to the gearshift, a herd of cats slowly meandered across the street in front of her truck.

She wouldn't mind killing a Tweety bird, but cats were a different story.

The woman tapped again, and Cassie pushed the automatic button to lower the window. It wasn't even halfway down when the woman started her interrogation.

"Do you have business in this neighborhood?"

Cassie wondered if murder would be considered business. She glanced back at the porch, but it was empty. And the Volkswagen was already at the corner.

"The neighborhood watch doesn't put up with loitering," the woman continued. "And you've been sitting here for more than thirty minutes. I clocked you."

Funny, but it seemed like much longer to Cassie. She released the tight grip she still had on the steering wheel and tried to smile. It wasn't easy, especially when anger encased her body like the scarf James had lovingly wrapped around Tweety Bird's neck.

She scrambled through her mind for a good excuse for sitting there with the engine running. She had almost given up when she glanced down at her cell phone. "I was making a phone call. I've taken that oath—the one Oprah started—no talking or texting while driving."

The woman's eyes narrowed. "I didn't see you talking on any phone."

Cassie cleared her throat. "Speaker."

The woman looked like she was about to challenge that answer when a noise had them both glancing over at James's house. The garage door rolled up, and the Land Rover slowly backed out. An hour ago Cassie wanted nothing more than to confront James. A few moments ago she'd wanted to kill him. Now all she wanted to do was hide from him.

She couldn't explain her wacked-out emotions. All she could do was humor them. Without a second thought, she ducked down in the seat and pressed her cheek against the console. She didn't even consider the nosy neighbor until she glanced up and saw the woman peering in at her like she had a few screws loose.

Cassie's screws only got looser.

"Amy!" she yelled at the phone that sat on the console inches from her mouth. "Are you still there?" Her ploy might've worked if her phone hadn't started to ring. She smiled weakly at the woman, but still waited until the roof of the black Land Rover had passed before she sat up and answered the phone.

"Cassie?" Rory's voice came through the receiver. "Where are you? I just stopped by your apartment."

She tipped the phone at the neighbor. "Better get this." The woman sent her another one of those you-are-crazy-as-a-loon looks but stepped away from the truck. She didn't go far. Even after Cassie rolled up the window, she stood in the closest driveway with the herd of cats circling her snow boots.

Cassie tried to ignore her. "I had a few errands to run," she said to Rory. "What's up?"

"Dad told me about Slumber Suites, and I wanted to get your take on it."

Slumber Suites? She'd forgotten all about Slumber Suites. The realization made her twice as angry at James Sutton. The man had screwed her up so badly, she couldn't even function properly. She had no business sitting there worrying about her personal life when M & M had lost Slumber Suites to Sutton—

She straightened so quickly, she accidentally honked the horn, scattering cats like a hyper Doberman.

M & M had lost Slumber Suites to James Sutton.

The truth hit her right between the eyes like a fast-pitched softball. All this time she'd been worried about James lying to her, and she hadn't even thought about why. Even when the answer was right in front of her face. All the lies. Manipulation. And sex. Had been for one reason and one reason only.

To get Slumber Suites.

"That no-good, dirty bastard," she breathed.

Rory laughed. "I assume you're talking about James Sutton. I got to hear the same thing from Dad."

"I'm going to kill him," she hissed between her teeth.

"Get a grip, Cassie. Like I told Dad, we don't even know for sure that Sutton Construction is who Steve Mitchell is going with. There were a lot of companies in on the bid. I guess we'll have to wait until after the holidays to find out."

"Like hell we will." Cassie popped the truck into drive, completely ignoring the annoyed look of James's neighbor when she pulled away with cell phone to ear.

"Oh, no, Cass," Rory said. "Don't even think about going over to Steve Mitchell. Not on the friggin' day before Christmas."

"I don't know why not," she fumed. She took the corner a little too fast and hit a slick spot that had the truck's back end fishtailing. "He has interrupted more than one of our holidays complaining about one thing or another. Now, after we've put up with his anal nitpicking, he wants to drop us like a dirty shirt. I don't think so."

There was a long pause before Rory's voice came back on. "Fine, but for God's sake, call him before you show up at his door. And if he's busy, let it go until after the holidays. Dad's going to be pissed enough as it is that you're taking care of it without talking to him first."

"He won't be pissed if he doesn't find out," she said.

"So you want me to lie?"

"No, I just want you to keep the truth to yourself until I've talked with Steve. I certainly don't need Big Al busting in on the meeting."

"And what do you want me to tell Mom when you're late for Christmas Eve dinner?" he asked.

The last thing Cassie felt like doing was attending her

huge family's Christmas Eve dinner. But there was no hope for it. She could be late, but if she didn't show up, the entire clan would come looking for her.

"Just tell her I'm working. No one will question that. And tell her to set two more places for dinner. I invited Amy and Gabby over."

"What in the hell for?"

No matter how much Rory didn't get along with Amy, Cassie was surprised by the outburst. "What's the matter with you? Ever since you got back, you've been a real asshole to Amy. I understand you're upset about Tess leaving, Rory. But you need to pull your head out. Amy's not only a trusted employee, she's a friend. A friend who needs our support now that she's broken things off with Derek."

"So she's not marrying him?" Rory sounded more shocked than Cassie had been. "But why?"

"I don't know for sure. She said something about wanting the dream."

There was a long pause before Rory spoke in a dazed-sounding voice. "Yeah. The dream."

"Welcome, Ms. McPherson." Steve Mitchell's smile had always reminded Cassie of a used car salesman, insincere and kind of oily. "So nice to see you." He held open a door that would've been better suited for a storybook giant's house. Not that a giant wouldn't have fit very comfortably in the Mitchells' mansion.

"I'm sorry to bother you today of all days," Cassie said as she stepped into the foyer with its impressive high-domed ceilings and Italian marble floor.

"Like I told you on the phone, it's no bother at all," Steve said. His smile got wider as he closed the door with an echoing click. "In fact, I appreciate the company. The help has flown the coop for the holidays, leaving me all by my little lonesome until I leave for Vegas."

If it had been someone else, Cassie might've felt sorry for him, but Steve Mitchell was about as pitiful as a tarantula. A tarantula that owned Slumber Suites.

"Well, I certainly appreciate the time," Cassie said as she looked around. "And you have a lovely home."

"It's more my father's taste than mine." Steve held out his hand for her to precede him down a long hallway. "Which is why I plan on putting it on the market after the holidays. New year, new house."

And new construction company, Cassie thought as she stepped into the room he indicated. The decor of the room was much more contemporary than the rest of the house. Weird chrome and wood end tables bookended a funky black leather sectional that looked uncomfortable as hell.

Taking her silence as approval, Steve glanced around. "This is the only room I've really had the chance to redecorate after my father passed away." He moved over to the bar. "Could I get you something to drink? Some wine, perhaps?"

"No, thank you," Cassie said. After her run-in with champagne, just the thought of drinking wine gagged her. Or maybe what gagged her was the person she drank the champagne with. She pushed down the thought and moved over to the couch. "Your father was a good man. We were all saddened by his death." She sat down, and Steve joined her. The couch was huge, but he sat only inches away. Cassie had socialized with Steve on a few occasions, and every time, he seemed to have a problem with personal space.

"Let's be honest." He handed her a glass of wine as if she hadn't just refused it. "My father was a tyrant who wanted things done his way or no way. Very similar to your father."

Al McPherson *was* loud and controlling, but Cassie didn't talk about family with acquaintances. Or business associates.

"So is that why you decided not to renew your contract with M & M? You don't care for my father?" she asked.

He laughed. "That's what I like about the McPhersons. They always cut to the chase." He leaned back and swirled the wine around in his glass. "My father and I were never on the best of terms. And Big Al *does* remind me of him." He took a sip. "But like my dear old dad used to say, never let emotions get involved with business. The main reason I'm leaving M & M is that I've found a company that will fit Slumber Suites' needs better. The owner is young and hungry, which usually makes for meticulous work and excellent prices."

Cassie's hand tightened on the stem of the glass. "James Sutton."

Steve's eyes didn't register an ounce of surprise. "Now, what makes you think that?"

"So you're not going with James?" The name slipped out almost too easily, and Cassie wished she could take it back when Steve's smile got even oilier.

"No, you're right," he said. "I *have* decided to go with

Sutton Construction. I just wonder how you found that out when I haven't even mentioned it to James yet."

It took a real effort to keep herself from snapping the stem in two. She'd wanted answers, and now she had them. But Cassie would be damned if she'd go down without a fight.

"So the rumor is true? Sutton has been wining and dining you," she said as she set the glass of wine down on the end table.

Steve laughed. "I wouldn't say wining and dining, but James and I have struck up a friendship."

A few days ago, the news might've surprised her. Now Cassie realized that the two men were peas in a pod. Two arrogant, sly peas in a pod who, if the smirk on Steve's face was any indication, had already shared the sordid details of Cassie and James's relationship.

Just the thought of James confiding to his "new buddy" had her face heating and her temper rising. But she held it together. Steve's father was right. There was no place for emotion in business.

"Sutton might be young and hungry," she said, "but M & M is experienced and dedicated. For the last ten years, we've given you meticulous work and fair prices, and we don't intend to stop now." She paused. "If we need to lower our bid, we can do that. In fact, I'm willing to do whatever it takes to keep your business."

Steve studied her for only a second before he downed the rest of his wine and turned to set the glass down. "I wondered why you wanted to stop by this close to Christmas Eve. Now I have my answer." When he glanced back, his eyes glistened with a look that Cassie recognized instantly. Unfortunately, before she could clear up Steve's obvious confusion, he pulled her into his arms and onto his lap. A lap with a prominent hard-on that had Cassie's muscles tightening in anger.

"And I must say that I'm thrilled by the prospect," Steve said. "There's just something about you that's always turned me on. I think it's that tough exterior coupled with those sultry green eyes." He dipped his head and pressed a wet kiss to her neck. "I should've realized sooner that all it would take to get your attention was a little healthy competition."

"You're making a mistake," Cassie warned.

"No mistake." He kissed her chin, or more like licked it. "I might not mix emotions with business, but I have no problem mixing pleasure with it."

When he kissed her mouth, his lips were as slick and oily as his smile. But it wasn't his lips that had chills of disgust racing down Cassie's spine. It was the thick tongue Steve slipped into her mouth. The only thing that kept her from clocking him like she'd done to Foster was the fact that he had once been a client. However, that didn't stop her from biting down on his tongue.

"Oww." He pulled back and held a hand to his mouth. But it didn't take long for the hand to drop and the smile to reappear. "So you like to play rough, do you?"

"I guess you could say that." Before he could dip his head for another kiss, she threw the glass of wine in his face and slid off his lap.

The smile completely dropped and a look entered his eyes that was, no doubt, much closer to his actual personality.

"Why, you bitch!" He wiped off his chin with the back of his hand. "I thought the McPherson ice princess had thawed out. I see now that I was mistaken." He cocked his head, and his eyes narrowed. "Or is it just working-class men like James Sutton who make you melt?"

Cassie tossed the glass at him, enjoying his flinch when it hit the fly of his corduroys. "I melt for no man."

Chapter Seventeen

James pressed the buzzer next to Cassandra's garage door again before he stepped back and looked up at the window. There was nothing to get worried about. So she hadn't answered his first ten buzzes? He *was* a good twenty minutes early. No doubt she had gotten caught up in business and forgotten all about meeting him back at her condo.

He didn't know why the thought pissed him off. Maybe because he hadn't gotten all caught up in business. Maybe because he stood there staring up at her window like some goddamned rejected Romeo. With a grunt of disgust, he turned and headed back to his Land Rover. He would give her twenty more minutes. Just twenty more minutes before he brought an end to the craziness.

He gave her forty.

When she still hadn't shown up, he drove all the way

back to her office building. But the building was locked up tight for the holidays. Which didn't stop him from driving through both levels of the underground parking garage looking for her truck. He found the McPhersons' parking spaces right next to the elevators. But not one of them had a vehicle in it. Including "C. McPherson's." Which meant he had either passed her on the way or she'd ditched him altogether.

The whole ditching thing seemed more likely an hour later as he stood outside her home freezing to death like a damned idiot. It had started to snow, and huge flakes clung to his hair and the shoulders of his sheepskin jacket.

Still he waited.

He was a tenacious businessman, but he never realized that he could be that way about a woman. He loved women, but he never spent much energy on them. Money, yes. Energy, no. They were always just there. If one wasn't interested in hanging around, another one would come along sooner or later. Usually sooner.

Now all it had taken was one controlling wildcat to turn him into a pathetic stalker.

James's cell phone rang, and he quickly pulled it out of his pocket and answered, hoping that Cassandra was calling to explain why she wasn't where she was supposed to be. Unfortunately, that wasn't the case.

"James. It's Steve Mitchell."

James tried to keep the disappointment out of his voice. "Hey, Steve. What's going on?"

"Nothing much, which is exactly why I'm calling you. I'm fuckin' bored stiff. You want to get a drink with me? There's something I wanted to give you. An early Christmas present, so to speak."

It didn't take a rocket scientist to figure out what the early Christmas present was. But no matter how hard James had worked to get the contract, he was no longer excited about the news. In fact, just the opposite was true. He was depressed as hell. Which was crazy. What person in their right mind would want another company to get a multimillion-dollar contract? Sierra was right. Stupidity was a disease. And he had it bad. But not bad enough to screw up a deal he'd worked his ass off for.

"Sure, I'll meet you," he said. He looked back up at Cassandra's dark window. "Just give me about an hour."

After he hung up, James pressed the buzzer one more time before he jogged next door to Matthew's condo. He could've gone to Patrick's, but Matthew was the lesser of two evils and the one who would probably volunteer information more readily. He pressed on the buzzer and then shoved his hands in his coat pockets to wait.

When Matthew didn't answer, James looked back at her condo.

Give it up, Sutton, and accept it. She's just not that into you.

But he couldn't give it up because it didn't make any sense. Cassandra wasn't the type of woman who led a man on. If she hadn't liked him, she would've told him straight to his face instead of stringing him along with sultry kisses and mind-blowing sex. So there had to be another reason she wasn't there. A reason that had nothing to do with him.

The thought made him even colder than he was.

What if she'd gotten in an accident? The roads weren't that slick yet, but it was possible. Just the thought of Cassandra being hurt—or worse—had him pressing the buzzer even harder. It was a relief when Matthew's voice came through the speaker. At least he'd found someone who might be able to alleviate his fears.

"Patrick, you dick," Matthew yelled. "I told you I'm not going to run in this kind of friggin' weather. So leave me the hell alone."

James leaned closer and pushed the button to the intercom. "Hey, Matthew, it's James Sutton."

There was a long pause before Matthew answered. "Real funny, Paddy."

"I'm not joking, Matthew. It's James. I played pool with you yesterday."

"No shit?"

James might've laughed if he hadn't been so worried. "No shit."

The garage door rumbled open. James stepped into the garage and brushed off his shoulders and hair. By the time he got the snow stomped off his boots, the door opened and a tousled Matthew stuck his head out.

"Come on up, man." He disappeared, forcing James to follow him.

Matthew's condo had the same floor plan as Cassandra's and Patrick's, but a completely different decor. While Cassandra's living room felt feminine and Patrick's like a bar with its pool table and dartboard, Matthew's was a bachelor pad with a huge leather couch that was more bed than sofa. Although he was as messy as his sister. Pizza boxes and empty beer bottles were everywhere.

"Listen, I don't want to keep you," James said, "but I was wondering if you knew where Cassie was. She was supposed to meet me here."

Matthew stumbled into the kitchen and waved James along. James walked over to the breakfast bar and watched as Matthew yawned and stretched before he opened the refrigerator. He stood there for a couple minutes, scratching his bare chest before deciding on a bottle of Sunny Delight. Screwing off the lid, he guzzled down what was left before turning to James. He wiped off his mouth with the back of one hand. "So your last name is Sutton, huh?"

James was so worried about Cassandra, he hadn't even realized he'd given Matthew his last name. Of course, it didn't matter. Matthew had never struck him as the type who paid much attention to business. His next words proved James wrong.

"James Sutton of Sutton Construction." Matthew tossed the empty bottle of juice at the overfilled trash can. It bounced off the empty twelve-pack carton and rolled across the floor.

James had wanted to tell Cassandra the truth first, but he figured it was too late for that. So he nodded. "The same."

A smile spread across Matthew's face, quickly followed by hysterical, side-clutching laughter.

"Look, Matt," James said, "do you know where Cassie is or not?"

Matthew held up a hand. "That's—" He tried to take a deep breath, but ended up wheezing and doubling over.

James had lived through college. He knew how alcohol,

women, and lack of sleep could leave you a little crazed, but he didn't have time for this. Not when something serious could've happened to Cassandra. He turned to leave, but Matthew finally sobered enough to speak.

"Hold on, man." He straightened and wiped at his eyes. "I'm sorry to laugh, but you have to admit that it's pretty funny."

"What is?"

"You being James Sutton, dude." He walked over to the leather couch and flopped down. "I can't believe that Cassie just waltzed enemy number uno in right under our noses. Damn." He laughed and shook his head. "I didn't think daddy's little girl had it in her." He paused, and his eyes narrowed in thought. "Wait a minute—she doesn't know, does she?"

"What do you mean enemy number one?" James moved around the couch.

"You screwed the pooch this time, Sutton," Matthew said. "If you think Patrick is scary when he loses his temper, it's nothing compared to Cassie when she loses hers. My dad even gets the hell out of the way."

James flipped some magazines off the couch and sat down on the edge. "Cassie thinks I'm her enemy?"

"Not just Cassie, but the entire McPherson family." He reached over and thumped James on the shoulder. "Except for me. I like you, dude. You're a big improvement over Mike. And I think it's pretty funny that you spent an entire night with us and nobody had a clue." He flopped his bare feet up on the coffee table, knocking over an empty beer bottle in the process. He stretched his arms over his head, hooking his hands behind his neck. "Which is too bad, because I think you're pretty much history. If there's one thing McPhersons hate more than some new construction company trying to put them out of business, it's a liar."

"Put them out of business?" James couldn't believe his ears. "Who's trying to put them out of business?"

Matthew released his hands and allowed his feet to fall to the floor. "The evil Sutton Construction Company that happens to be run by the evil James Sutton."

James jumped to his feet. "That's bullshit! I have no intention of putting M & M out of business even if I could. The only thing I'm guilty of is underbidding you."

"Hey"—Matthew held up his hands—"you're preachin' to the choir, man. I'm not the one who you need to explain things to."

Matthew was right. There was only one person he wanted to talk to.

"Where is she, Matt?" he asked.

The grin disappeared, and the determined McPherson look came over his boyish features. "Patrick thinks you care about her. Do you?"

There were so many emotions going through James at the moment, it was hard to wade through them. He was pissed and disappointed that Cassandra had judged him without even meeting him. Frustrated and anxious that she had stood him up. But mostly, he was terrified that Matthew was right and she would never forgive him.

James took a deep breath and released it. "Yes, I care about her."

Matthew rolled to his feet. "Okay then. Give me a minute, and you can follow me over to my parents' house."

James held up a hand. "That won't be necessary. All I need are directions."

On his way up the stairs, Matthew stopped and turned around with a wide grin. "And miss all the fireworks? Not on your life."

Chapter Eighteen

Delany said her mom thinks it's weird that you dust our Christmas tree."

Amy froze with Swiffer in hand and looked down at Gabby, who was sitting on the floor shaking a present she'd just pulled out from under the six-foot artificial tree. "You told Delany that I dust the Christmas tree?"

"Books," Gabby said before she placed the present back and lifted another one. "I didn't tell her. Her mom walked by and saw you."

Amy glanced out the big picture window. If her daughter hadn't been there, she might've gone over and closed the blinds before she continued dusting. "Well, I don't see anything wrong with it," she tried to defend herself. "Lights and ornaments get dusty too." She flicked the Swiffer over a Hallmark ornament of Snoopy and Woodstock.

"It's okay, Mom," Gabby said. "Everyone is different. You clean when you are PMSing and Delany's mom has a glass of wine."

Amy stopped dusting. "PMSing?"

"Yeah, that's what Delany's mom calls it when she's grumpy. Delany and I think it stands for Pretty Mom Stressing since both of our moms are pretty." She squeezed the package. "Socks. I figure you're upset because you broke up with Derek."

It would make sense. Most women would be devastated after ending a two-year relationship. But the truth was that Amy felt more relieved than upset after breaking it off with Derek. No, her "PMSing" had nothing to do with Derek and everything to do with a handsome redhead.

Gabby grabbed another package and shook it. "Game."

"Would you stop that?" Amy swatted at her with the Swiffer. "Don't you want to be surprised tomorrow morning?"

"I'm looking for the one I want to open tonight." Gabby set the package away from the others. "I choose this one. We can play it after we get back from the McPhersons."

Amy set the Swiffer down on the coffee table. "About that, Gabby. I was thinking that maybe we would stay home tonight. We could pop some popcorn and watch *How the Grinch Stole Christmas*." She smiled. "And even play your new game."

Gabby stared at her as if she'd just killed a puppy. "You don't want to go to the McPhersons'? But when Mrs. McPherson called to make sure we were coming, she said we were going to make sugar cookies and Patrick and

Mattie were going to help the kids make the biggest snow-man ever. Besides, don't you want to see Uncle Rory?"

Rory.

Just the name had Amy reaching for the Swiffer. No, she didn't want to see Rory. Not when her emotions were a jumbled mess. With just a few words, Rory had turned her nice, orderly life upside down. And she wasn't exactly happy about it. After all the snide comments and mean glares, where did he get off telling her that he cared about her? Where were his sweet words five years ago when she was drooling over him at the water cooler? Why hadn't he explained how he felt then, instead of running off to Chicago and marrying Tess? And why after his speech at the toy store had he walked off and not called her once?

Amy knew that the only way to still the cacophony of questions was to talk with Rory. She just couldn't do it in a house filled with loud, partying McPhersons. She looked at Gabby's disappointed face. Nor could she deny her daughter a family Christmas filled with sugar cookies and snowman-making.

"Okay." She leaned down and ruffled her daughter's hair. "Go get on your snow boots while I see what I can whip up in the kitchen to take."

"Yippee!" Gabby bounced up off the floor and headed for her bedroom while Amy headed to the kitchen.

Fortunately, she had the makings for a relish tray left-over from the one she'd made for the Christmas office luncheon. She had just pulled a jar of green olives out of the refrigerator when she heard a car door slam. Closing the refrigerator, she moved over to the window and looked out. Patrick's black truck was parked in the driveway, but it wasn't Patrick who was pulling down the tailgate. The jar of olives slipped from Amy's fingers and landed on the floor with a crash, showering shards of glass all over her knee-high boots.

But she wasn't as upset by Rory being at her house as much as she was by what he was pulling out of the back of the truck. The mess on the kitchen floor was forgotten as she headed for the front door.

By the time she got outside, Rory was already setting the small dirt bike down in the driveway.

"Just what do you think you're doing?" Amy said as she stomped across the snow-covered lawn.

Rory glanced up, and even with the frigid temperatures, she could feel the hot sizzle of his gaze as it swept over her. "I could ask you the same thing." He leaned the motorcycle on its kickstand and pulled off his down jacket. In no more than three strides, he had it wrapped around her shoulders. "Are you crazy, woman? It's freezing out here."

She tried to push the coat off, but he snapped it under her chin. Still, it didn't stop her from pointing a finger at the motorcycle. "Do not tell me that is for who I think it's for."

He flashed a grin. "Okay. I won't tell you."

"Oh, no." She shook her head. "That is much too dangerous a vehicle for a seven—"

"Holy smokes!"

Amy's words were cut off by her daughter, who came flying out of the house with jacket flapping. "Is that for me, Uncle Rory? Is that mine?" She raced over to the bike and had no trouble swinging a leg over it. "Can we start it up? Can I ride it over to Delany's and show her what I got? Man, she's not going to believe it. Her parents are getting her a dumb battery-operated one."

Amy shot Rory a look that she hoped was filled with as many shards of glass as her kitchen floor. "Could I speak to you for a second in private?" she ground out through her teeth. She looked over at Gabby and issued a stern warning. "You can sit on it, but that's it. Do not start it up or move it an inch out of this driveway, young lady."

Completely consumed with the motorcycle, Gabby nodded. "No duh, Mom. I don't even have the key."

With anger boiling, Amy swirled and headed back inside. Of course, she headed straight to the kitchen. She had always done her best yelling while cleaning. She jerked off Rory's coat and threw it at him before she took the trash can out from under the sink, then knelt down and started picking up the glass.

"She's not keeping it. And if you think I'm going to tell her and break her heart, you can think again. You're the one who was stupid enough to bring over the gift without asking me, so you're the one who will have to figure out how to break the news."

"So you're not marrying Derek?"

Amy's gaze snapped up, and her heart skipped a beat. Even as mad as she was, she couldn't help but notice how handsome Rory looked in jeans and a green sweater that matched his eyes. He had one shoulder propped against the doorjamb, his jacket tucked beneath his arm, and a look on his face that took her breath away. She returned her attention to the mess on the floor.

"No, but that's not what we're talking about. We're talking about a motorcycle that is much too dangerous for a seven-year-old."

Tossing his jacket to the kitchen table, Rory walked over and pulled the roll of paper towels off the dispenser. "Why?" he asked as he squatted down and tore off a couple sheets and handed them to her.

She took the towels and started cleaning up the vinegar. "Because she could seriously hurt herself. She's been riding a two-wheeled bike for only a couple years."

"No, I mean why did you break it off with Derek?"

It was a good question. One Amy had been asking herself since ending their engagement. Why would she break up with a man she'd dated for years? A man who for all practical purposes was a perfect match for her? The answer came when Rory reached out and covered her hand with his.

Derek might be her perfect match, but he didn't make her insides tremble at just one touch. And he didn't make her want to scrub one damned toilet. He filled all her requirements for a husband, just not the ones for *her* husband.

"Would you stop cleaning and talk to me?" Rory said.

His knee was no more than inches away from her, his breath warming the back of her neck. She ignored the feeling his closeness ignited and pulled her hand away so she could continue to scrub the floor. "We didn't suit."

"And it took you this long to figure that out?"

She glanced up. "You should talk. At least I didn't marry Derek before I figured it out."

Releasing his breath, Rory sat back on the floor and

leaned against the refrigerator. "I figured out I didn't love Tess long before I married her."

"So why did you marry her?"

"I tried to convince myself it was because she was pregnant. But the truth is that I moved to Chicago and married Tess because it was easier than staying at M & M and having you treat me as if I didn't exist."

Amy stopped scrubbing and turned to Rory. "Tess was pregnant?"

"No. She lied to me just like she lied to you." He looked at her. "Except I had reason to believe her lie. Why did you believe her when she told you that you weren't good enough for me?"

She sat back against the cupboard. "Maybe because I was only nineteen and I had already been rejected by my daughter's father. At that point, I didn't think very much of myself. I didn't believe I could get what I wanted."

"And what did you want?"

"I guess I wanted the dream." She picked at the paper towel. "I wanted a knight in shining armor to come and sweep me off my feet. Someone who would pay the bills and fix a flat tire and the leaky faucet in the bathroom. Someone to hold Gabby and change her diapers when I was too exhausted. Someone to hold me and tell me everything was going to be all right."

Rory rested his hands on his knees and stared down at the tile floor. "And what do you want now, Amy?"

It was a good question. One she had thought about all night. One she felt as if she'd figured out.

"I no longer want, or need, a knight in shining armor. I want a partner. A man who will stand beside me, not behind or in front of me. A man who accepts my weaknesses and rejoices in my strengths. A man who is strong enough to be a husband and a loving father."

She got up from the floor, threw away the paper towels, and put the trash can back beneath the sink. When she turned, Rory was on his feet. He seemed to fill the entire kitchen. Needing some space, she moved into the living room.

The town house Amy shared with Gabby wasn't big or fancy, but she had worked hard to turn it into a home. Which was probably why she felt so happy when Rory glanced around the room and sent her a look of approval.

"This is nice," he said. "How long have you lived here?"

"Almost three years."

She wandered over to the window to make sure Gabby wasn't riding the motorcycle down the street. She wasn't. She still sat on it in the driveway, but now she was surrounded by all the neighborhood kids and a couple fathers.

"I'm sorry." Rory moved up behind her. So close she could smell the clean, fresh scent of his cologne. So close she thought she could hear the beat of his heart. Or maybe it was hers that thumped wildly as he continued. "I should've gotten your permission before I bought the bike. I guess I just wanted to make this Christmas special for Gabby—and for you." His hands settled on her waist as he stepped closer, and his mouth brushed the top of her head. "I want to be that man, Amy. The one who stands beside you. But I also want to be your knight in shining armor. The one who fixes your leaky faucets, teaches

Gabby the safe way to ride a dirt bike, and the one who holds you when you need holding."

Rory turned her around. His green eyes were filled with something that had Amy's stomach taking a nose-dive.

"I know I've botched things badly, Amy. I always thought I was the levelheaded one of the bunch, but it turns out that I have just as much stubborn pride as the rest of my family. Pride that kept me from claiming you the moment I first set eyes on you. Pride that kept me from telling you how much I love you." He touched her cheek with just the barest brush of his fingertips. "And I do love you, Amy Walker." He leaned down and kissed her.

Unlike the greenhouse kiss, it wasn't quick and desperate. This kiss was soft and sweet. He gently brushed her lips as if asking permission. She gave it by sliding her hands around his waist and pulling him closer. His fingers tunneled through her hair and cradled her head as he moved her away from the window and pressed her up against the wall. Desire flamed to life and sizzled through her veins, and she pressed closer as all the confusion of the last few days melted away. Suddenly everything became crystal clear.

Rory was right. No matter what had happened in the past, she belonged right here. Right here in his arms.

He pulled back from the kiss and rested his forehead on hers. "So I think this is the point where you tell me that you love me too. You do love me, don't you, Amy?"

"Yes," she said as she smoothed out the shoulders of his sweater. "And I have since you walked up to my desk and said, 'Welcome to M & M Construction.' It took me five seconds to figure out you were the man I wanted. But it took me five years to figure out that I'm the woman for you."

Rory kissed her again, this time with a lot more heat. When she was thoroughly dazed, he pulled back and held up a finger. "Don't go anywhere. I'll be right back. I forgot something in my jacket." He headed for the kitchen and, a second later, returned with a small box that had Amy's mouth dropping open.

While she stared in stunned disbelief, he got down on one knee and opened the box to reveal a beautiful square-cut diamond between two glittering emeralds the color of Rory's eyes.

"Amy," he said. "I've already wasted too much time, and I don't want to waste a second more. Especially since there will never be another woman I want to spend the rest of my life with. Marry me."

Amy placed a hand over her mouth as tears dripped down her cheeks. "Oh, Rory." Unfortunately, it only took a moment for reality to slip in. "I can't." When hurt entered his eyes, she tried to explain. "I love you. And if it was just up to me, I wouldn't think twice about marrying you today if you wanted me to. But I have a daughter to think about. An impressionable daughter whom I've already put through one relationship and breakup. I can't just jump into another one without consulting Gabby first." She reached down and cupped his chin in her hand. "So if it's okay with you, could we take things a little slow—"

"Hey, what's goin' on?"

Startled, Amy turned to see Gabby standing in the doorway of the living room with red cheeks and a baffled look. Amy's own cheeks flamed, and she tried to cover the ring with a hand while she stammered out an explanation.

Wouldn't you know that her headstrong daughter would figure it out all on her own?

With a loud whoop, Gabby jumped up and punched the air. "This is the best Christmas ever! A dirt bike and a McPherson!"

Chapter Nineteen

The kitchen was warm. Too warm. Both ovens worked overtime as the McPherson women fussed with the last-minute preparations for the night's big family potluck. The heated air carried with it the chaotic chatter of gossip along with a variety of scents—vanilla from the sugar cookies, spices from her mother's spaghetti sauce, evergreen from the huge Christmas tree, and cinnamon from the candles that flickered on the mantle.

It was enough to give Cassie a sick stomach to go along with her splitting headache. A headache that was the result of finding out she'd been played for a fool. How could she have willingly jumped into bed with the biggest, most deceitful man in Denver?

Cassie rammed the knife back into the bowl of red frosting and scooped up a glob, which she promptly smeared all over the top of a Santa-shaped sugar cookie. The thought of all the lies James had told her had her hand tightening on the knife.

Santa's head snapped clean off.

"Shit." She stared down at the decapitated Santa and the frosting that oozed between her fingers.

"Shit!" Chase, her eighteen-month-old nephew, yelled while beating a spoon on the top of his high chair. "Shit! Shi—"

Cassie quickly rammed Santa's head in between his rosy little lips. "Have a cookie, sport." She set the other half of the cookie down on the tray and licked her fingers.

"You shouldn't give him cookies, Aunt Cassie." Megan Anne sent her a reproachful look as she removed the cookie from her brother's reach. Megan was the oldest of Jake's brood and took her position quite seriously. "Mother doesn't want us acquiring a taste for sugar."

"Which is why you've eaten the last four I've broken," Cassie said.

Megan glanced over at the women in the kitchen, then replaced the cookie on the tray. "I guess one won't hurt."

"That's what I figured." Cassie jerked up another cookie, but before she could behead it, one of the twins stood up in her chair and started yelling.

"Mommy!" Her three-year-old niece, Kelsey, waved a frosting-covered plastic knife dangerously close to Cassie's left ear. "Aunt Cassie just broke-did another cookie! That makes eight cookies she broked!"

"Traitor," Cassie whispered as she looked up at the horde of McPherson women who had stopped what they were doing to stare at her as if she'd grown horns. "So I broke a few cookies." She waved her hand over the cookie-filled table. "I don't think they'll be missed."

"Cassandra," her mother moved forward with a look of concern, "are you feeling okay?"

She wasn't. She felt like hell, but she was bound and determined to work through it. "Of course I feel okay." She brushed back a piece of hair. "Why?"

Her mother shrugged. "Nothing. It's just that you don't usually like to be in the kitchen. Especially if you have to help with cooking."

"This isn't exactly cooking, Mom."

Her mother walked over and took off the oven mitt, then placed her hand on Cassie's forehead. "Still, you feel hot to me. Mary Louise," she called back over her shoulder, "go get Lisa."

Her cousin Lisa was getting her pharmaceutical degree and had somehow become the resident doctor for all family gatherings. She might not know what was wrong with you, but she could tell you what to take to get rid of it.

"Don't bother Lisa." Cassie removed her mother's hand and stood. "I'm fine, really. Just because I want to help out in the kitchen doesn't mean I'm sick."

"Yeah, it does," one of her cousins piped up. "You'd rather be burned at the stake than cook one."

"Boiled in oil rather than boil an egg," another cousin chimed in.

"Roasted—"

"I get it!" Cassie yelled.

Everyone laughed as they went back to their jobs. Everyone except her mom.

Her mother could work for the CIA, interrogating spies. Those deep brown eyes had a way of staring right through a person, which was worse than any water torture. "So tell me about this new man you've been seeing."

The last thing that Cassie wanted to do was tell her mother about James. It was one thing for Steve Mitchell to find out about your idiocy and another for your mother to find out.

"There's nothing to tell," she said. "He was just a guy I dated a few times."

"Your brothers really like him."

It figured. The guy they should hate the most, they liked. "Yeah, well, since I'm the person dating him, I'm the only one that counts. And I won't be seeing him again."

Those eyes turned soft and knowing right before she pulled Cassie into her arms. "When it's right, baby girl, everything will just fall into place."

Cassie believed her, which meant nothing was right because everything was out of place. Right now, all she wanted to do was tuck her nose against her mother's neck and sob out her anger like she had when she didn't make the varsity soccer team. Instead, she just rested there and breathed in the smell of vanilla and Joy perfume.

"I'm okay, Mom."

"No, you're not." Her mother kissed the side of her head. "But, unfortunately, heartbreaks are something mothers can't fix."

"I'm not heartbroken," she grumbled. How could a person be heartbroken over someone she'd known for only two days?

Her mother gave Cassie an extra squeeze before she

pulled back and smiled at her. "Why don't you go into the game room and beat some of your uncles at pool? If you continue to frost sugar cookies, the kids are all going to have stomachaches." When Cassie nodded, her mother gave her one last worried look before she went back to the kitchen.

"Does your heart hurted, Aunt Cassie?" Kyle, the other twin, asked.

Fortunately, Megan answered for her. "No, Ky. Aunt Cassie doesn't have a real broken heart. Brokenhearted is just another way to say her boyfriend broke up with her, and she's very sad. Isn't that right, Aunt Cassie?"

Cassie rolled her eyes as she jerked up a dish towel and wiped off her hands. "Something like that."

"So you're sad." Kelsey looked on the verge of tears.

"How can I be sad when Santa comes tonight?" Cassie leaned over and tickled her ribs. "And it's a good thing we've got plenty of cookies to give that jolly old elf."

"Santa! Santa!" Chase screamed from his high chair, which in turn set the three-year-old twins to shrieking.

It was more than Cassie's head could take, so after tickling each belly, she left the room.

But she didn't go downstairs to the game room to play pool. Instead, she slipped inside her father's study and closed the door behind her. She had always loved the room. It smelled of leather and lemon furniture polish and was dark, quiet, and soothing. Which was probably why it didn't have a pack of McPhersons in it. Her family loved to be together. Loved the mass confusion and excitement that went along with every family gathering.

Usually, she did, too.

Not today. Today she just wanted to be home in her little condo with her throbbing headache and her anger and, yes, even her broken heart. Because as much as she hated to admit it, her heart did hurt.

Why did James have to be so much fun to talk with? And why did he have to have soft, wavy hair and deep, golden eyes? And why did his body have to be so perfectly fitted to hers? But most of all, why did he have to be James Sutton? Lying, cheating, job-stealing James Sutton.

She released a long sigh and pushed away from the door. Even though she probably should lie down for a few minutes, she bypassed the cozy sitting area with its throw-covered couches and crackling fireplace and walked to the window by her father's desk.

The skies were dark and growing darker but had yet to produce heavy snow that would make traveling difficult. Not that anything short of a major blizzard would keep her mother and her aunts away from midnight mass on Christmas Eve. It was sacrilegious to even think about it.

Every year for as long as Cassie could remember, after they filled their stomachs and played games, the entire McPherson clan would load up and head to Saint Paul's.

Last year, Mike had already been history so Cassie had sat between Mattie and Patrick. In the flickering candlelight, she'd watched her nieces and nephews snuggle into their parents' shoulders and laps to sleep. While they dreamed about Santa and sugarplums, Cassie had dreamed about the strong shoulder she would someday rest her head on while her children slept.

Of course, tonight she wouldn't have such thoughts. Tonight she would be trying to forget about a certain man with a set of shoulders that looked strong enough to hold up a woman who sometimes felt weak.

Her eyes burned, and she swallowed down the lump that had risen to her throat. Okay, so she had gone and fallen for the wrong guy. It wasn't the first time, and it wouldn't be the last. She was a big girl; she could take it. Tears trickled down her cheeks. She just needed some time. Like a good twenty years.

The door to the study opened, and Cassie quickly brushed at her eyes before turning around.

"Hey." Amy hesitated just inside the door.

"Where have you been?" Cassie studied her friend, who looked all sparkly eyed and giddy. "I was beginning to think that you weren't coming."

A smile spread across her face as she held up her hand. A hand with a huge diamond on the ring finger. "I'm getting married!" Before Cassie could even register the words, Amy came flying across the room and threw her arms around Cassie.

"Wait a minute." Cassie pulled back. "I thought you'd decided not to marry Derek."

"I did." Amy giggled. "I'm marrying your brother."

"Rory?"

A guilty look took the sparkle out of Amy's eyes. "I know I should've told you that I loved him, Cassie. After all, you're my best friend. But I just didn't want you telling Rory. Not when he was already married to Tess. Can you forgive me?"

It was hard to smile when your world was crumbling, but Cassie tried her best. "There's nothing to forgive." She hugged Amy close. "I'm thrilled that you're going to be my sister-in-law." She pulled back. "So fill me in on all the juicy details."

Amy shook her head. "Oh, no. Not until you tell me all about what happened with your hunka-hunka-burnin'-love. Was he as good in bed as he looked?"

The wall of depression settled back over Cassie, and she couldn't keep the smile in place or the tears from her eyes. Amy was instantly concerned.

"What happened, Cass?" Her eyes turned mean. "Did the jerk love you and leave you? What an asshole."

Cassie swallowed. "You can say that again."

"Oh, Cass, I'm so sorry," Amy said. "I feel responsible. I mean, if I hadn't bought the dress and all those condoms—"

Cassie held up a hand. "Stop right there. I'm a big girl. Everything that happened, happened because I wanted it to. Not because of some stupid dress or a purse full of condoms. I was the one who hired him—at least, I thought I had hired him."

"What do you mean?"

Needing some space, Cassie moved over to her father's desk and sat down. The cushions of the leather chair had molded to Big Al's large frame and were comfortable and soothing. She leaned back and released her breath. "James isn't an escort. He's James Sutton."

"The James Sutton?" Amy asked as she moved over and sat down in one of the chairs across from the desk. "Why would he be parading around as an escort?"

Cassie flipped forward in the chair. "Exactly! Not unless the jerk wanted to make a fool of Big Al McPherson's daughter and steal Slumber Suites out from under our noses."

Amy rolled her eyes. "God, Cassie, you sound just like your dad. I'm sure there is some explanation that is far less dramatic."

"Really? I'd like to know what would make a guy continue to lie for two days straight right before we lost Steve Mitchell's account."

Amy's brow knotted. "That doesn't make sense. What excuse did James give?"

Cassie flopped back in the chair. "Who cares what he says? He's nothing but a big, fat liar."

"So you didn't even give him a chance to defend himself?"

"I tried to give him a chance," Cassie said. "Unfortunately, he was making love to another woman when I arrived at his house."

"He was having sex with another woman?"

"Not exactly." She nibbled on her thumbnail and refused to meet Amy's narrowed gaze. "But close."

"Close how?"

"They were making out on his porch." Not really making out. More like one quick kiss. But one kiss was enough. "Anyway, it doesn't matter. I don't care about the other woman as much as I care that the guy is James Sutton. The same James Sutton who's trying to put us out of business."

Amy sat back and crossed her legs. "I don't think he's trying to put us out of business. And if I remember correctly, neither did you. Maybe he has a very good reason for posing as an escort." Her eyes twinkled. "Maybe he really is an escort and he uses the extra money to underbid M & M Construction."

For just a second, the thought had some merit, the second right before Amy tipped back her head and laughed.

"Geez, Cass," she said. "You *have* really lost it. I mean, what's so bad about the guy turning out to be an independently wealthy builder who looks good enough to be hired as an escort? Most women would consider themselves lucky."

"Well, I don't consider lying a quality I want in a husband."

"Husband?" Amy stared back at her. "So you really have fallen for this guy?"

"No." She tried to backpedal, then realized it was too late. She ran a hand over her face and sighed. "Maybe I considered it, but not now."

Amy placed her hands on the desk. "But what if he's it, Cass? What if he's the one?"

It seemed that Amy had stumbled on what had been bothering Cassie for some time now. What if James was the one? The one and only man who could make her laugh and keep up with her verbal barbs. The man who gave her control when she needed it, but took control when she needed someone to lean on. The perfect man for her.

Except he wasn't the perfect man. He was the most imperfect.

He was James Sutton. A liar and the enemy.

"Well, he's not the one." Cassie pushed up out of the chair and walked back over to the window. "I just let my emotions get away from me, is all. I mean, I've just gotten over Mike." Eighteen months wasn't exactly "just," but beggars couldn't be choosers. "This was just a rebound thing. A sexual thing."

Suddenly, she wondered if she was trying to convince Amy or herself. But it really didn't matter. For some reason, voicing her thoughts seemed to relieve some of the pressure in her head. Unfortunately, her heart still hurt.

"I mean, look at the man. Who wouldn't think they were in love with someone who looks as great as he does? The man looks like a friggin' model. And when a person hasn't had sex for eighteen months, it's easy to see how they could let bodily urges get tangled up with emotions. I didn't love the guy as much as I lusted after him."

There was a soft click before Amy spoke.

"Uh, Cass—"

Cassie didn't turn around, not when she had finally gained some kind of perspective on her screwed-up emotions. "It's the truth. James Sutton was nothing more than a hot one-night stand."

"But, Cass—"

"Okay, maybe he was a hot two-night stand, but it doesn't make any difference. It was nothing but sex—"

"Cassie McPherson!"

"What!" She whirled around. Amy stared at her with a look of horror. After looking behind her, Cassie understood why.

James stood in the doorway, his arms crossed and his eyes as chilly as the ice that frosted the window.

Chapter Twenty

Hey, sis," Mattie said with a bright smile. "You remember James Sutton, don't you?"

The air left Cassie's lungs, and all she could manage was a strained groan. James didn't seem to have the same problem.

"Hello, Cassandra," he said as he moved into the room.

"And this is Amy Walker," Mattie continued as if he were introducing his best buddy. "Or did you meet her the other night at the party?"

James's eyes narrowed on Amy. "The same Amy Walker who called my office?" When she didn't say anything, he made the correct assumption. "How's the news room at the *Post*?"

Amy sent Cassie a sympathetic look before clearing her throat. "Well, I better help your mom in the kitchen." She glanced at Mattie. "Come on, Mattie."

"Not on your life." Mattie went for a chair, but before he could take two steps, James stopped him.

"I need to speak to your sister alone."

The grin slipped from Mattie's face, and he glanced over at Cassie. "You want me to leave, Cass?"

She didn't really want him to leave. If anyone was going to leave, she wanted it to be her. But it didn't look like that was going to happen, so she nodded.

Mattie shrugged and followed Amy out the door. James closed it behind them. This time the click was deafening. He turned and looked at her. No, more like glared at her.

After spending countless hours going over all the things she wanted to say to him since finding the fax, suddenly her mind was a confused jumble. Needing something to do, she returned to the comfort of her father's chair. If nothing else, the thick wood desk would serve as a barrier between them. Because as much as her mind might hate him, her body didn't seem to feel the same way. Just being in the same room with him set her pulse to throbbing. She tucked her trembling hands beneath her legs and spoke.

"So? What brings you here?"

"A one-night stand?" His voice was as chilled as his eyes. "Is that what you think of me?"

Cassie tried not to cringe at the fact that he had overheard her. "You lied to me."

He strode across the room and placed his clenched fists on the desk. "Answer me, Cassandra. Was that what we had, a one-night stand?"

She looked up at him towering over her in the rust

sweater with a collar that framed his smooth, clenched jaw. Snowflakes still clung to his hair, slowly melting into the mussed chocolate brown. Just the sight of him caused something to melt inside of her. It was that melting feeling that drove her to ask, "Wasn't it?"

He raised a fist and slammed it down. "Not to me! But if that's what it was to you then there's no need to stay here a minute longer." He turned and started for the door.

His condescending attitude cleared her mind, and she jumped up, sending the chair back against the wall. The loud whack had him turning around. "That is such bullshit, Sutton!" She rounded the desk and pointed a finger at him. "You lied to get laid. Don't try to pretend that emotion was involved."

He moved toward her, his eyes sharp, his voice low. "Oh, we had sex, all right. No doubt about it. A real hot two-night stand. But the question is, Cassandra, who was the one who initiated it? Because if my memory serves me—"

"Shut up!" The pressure in her head grew. "You manipulated me."

Those whiskey eyes widened. "I manipulated you? Really? Just where did this manipulation take place? When I forced you to drink too much champagne? Or maybe when you ordered me to get you to a bathroom, then stripped off your clothes and got in my shower? Or, possibly, it was when I woke up and you had your mouth on my—"

Her head felt as if it might explode. "You've had your fun, so you can just leave!"

But he didn't leave. Instead, he took two steps closer. "Have I hit a sore spot, Cassandra? Worried that word might get out that Cassie McPherson is a controlling sex fiend who pays for escorts?"

He was close enough that she didn't have to reach far to hit him. Except he didn't wait like Foster for the punch to land. He caught her fist in one hand and jerked her close to him with the other. "Ah, I have hit a sore spot. Well, join the club. You have been hitting sore spots with me ever since you weren't waiting for me at your condo."

She struggled to get out of his arms. "I don't date liars."

"I never lied."

She stilled and glared up at him. "Really? What would you call masquerading as an escort? Halloween?"

He ground his teeth. "I wasn't masquerading. You were the one who jumped to the wrong conclusion."

"And you didn't correct me."

"When a beautiful woman throws herself at a man, what do you expect him to do? Say no?"

"Obviously not! You didn't stop the woman who threw herself at you this morning."

"This morning? Are you nuts—" He paused. "Are you talking about Sierra, my twenty-year-old assistant?"

"Which is even more disgusting." Her eyes felt as if they would pop right out of her head. "And I never threw myself at you."

"Really?" He backed her up against the desk. "And what would you call wanting to pay me for sex?"

"Stupidity!"

He snorted. "That doesn't change the fact that you threw yourself at me."

"Nor does it change the fact that you lied."

His nostrils flared as he took a deep breath. "I tried to tell you the truth and, obviously, you didn't believe me."

"When was that? Before or after you made a fool of me?" She leaned back and crossed her arms to show her anger—and to keep her breasts from touching his chest.

His eyes narrowed. "I never made a fool of you, Cassandra. You seem to be able to do that all by yourself."

"Really? Then what would you call it when someone conceals their identity in order to play with another person's emotions?" She lifted a finger and poked him in the chest. "Is that what James Sutton calls fun?"

He grabbed her finger and refused to let go. "So now you're saying that I played with your emotions. I thought I was just a hot one-night stand."

She lowered her gaze. "You were."

There was a long moment of silence in which the space between them seemed to shrink, taking all the air with it. She swallowed and watched as the hand that still held her finger moved to her chin and tipped it up. His eyes were no longer cold as he searched for the truth she struggled to hide. He found it much quicker than she'd hoped.

"Now who's the liar," he whispered before he lowered his head.

His lips were scorching, rivaling the fire that blazed behind him. He didn't punish her with a hard, devouring kiss. Instead, his warm, moist mouth gently slid over hers. Cassie tried to collect herself enough to give him the hell he so richly deserved, but her body wouldn't cooperate. Her eyes closed right before he slipped his hands to her waist. The edge of her sweater was lifted and cold hands tingled over her bare skin as he easily lifted her to the top of the desk.

She trembled and placed her hands on his chest. The fact that she was kissing James Sutton—a lying, conniving jerk—didn't seem to matter to her treacherous body. The hormones that had been so easily controlled with a simple shower nozzle were now raging out of control. And all it had taken was one little kiss.

Or one big heart-stopping, soul-touching kiss.

A kiss too good to let her mind take control. So she released her brain and let her body do what it would. Of course, she hadn't expected her body to be so ravenous it forgot where it was and proceeded to cling to James like spray-on insulation.

Which was exactly how her father found them.

"What the hell is going on in here?" Big Al McPherson's voice resounded through the room like a sonic boom, causing James to pull away from the kiss.

Of course, he couldn't get very far away with Cassandra's legs wrapped around his waist. It took only a second to figure out she wasn't going to move. She had frozen in place with her nose pressed into his sweater and her eyes squeezed shut. When James lifted his gaze to the man who stood by the open door, he understood why.

Big Al McPherson deserved his nickname, not only because he was a large man, but because he filled the room with a powerful presence. It radiated off him like heat off hot pavement. His thick red hair was faded with age and peppered with gray, but the large muscles in his arms and chest were those of a thirty-year-old.

He walked farther into the room while James tried to untangle himself. It didn't take him long, not once Cassandra cooperated by dropping her hands and legs and jumping down from the desk.

"Hi, Dad. Is dinner ready?"

James had to give it to her. She tried her best to look as if nothing had happened, which wasn't easy when her lips were swollen, her hair was mussed, and her eyes still held the glaze of desire. James probably didn't look much better. Fortunately, the appearance of her father had caused his erection to quickly deflate.

Big Al snorted and turned to him. "Matt informed me we had company. I assume you're James Sutton."

James cleared his throat. "Yes, sir." He stretched out a hand.

Big Al gave him a handshake that almost sent him to his knees. "I'm sorry I missed our meeting the other night. I left a message on your cell phone."

"Yes, sir." James nodded, then shot a glance over at Cassandra. "But I'm afraid I didn't get it in time."

Her eyes darkened to a deep emerald filled with fire. No doubt he would catch some hell for not mentioning the meeting with her father.

Big Al nodded. "So I assume that's how you met my daughter." He walked around his desk and sat down. "Since I couldn't meet with you on Friday, we can do it now. Have a seat, Sutton."

James remained standing. "Actually, sir, I need to talk with your daughter."

His bushy red eyebrows lifted. "Really? Because it

didn't look like you two were doing much talking when I came in."

There really wasn't much to say to that, so James pulled out a chair and sat down.

"You staying or leaving, Cassie?" Big Al asked.

For a moment, James thought she would bolt for the door. Then the cool businesswoman he had come to admire took control. "Staying." She took the other chair, trying her best not to look at James.

Her father smiled. "I figured as much." He opened the humidor that sat on the top of his desk and pulled out a cigar. He didn't smoke it, just held it in his hand and rolled it between his fingers. He leaned back in the chair. "So let's cut to the chase. How much will you take for your company?"

His words completely broadsided James. "Excuse me, sir?"

"Your company. How much do you want for it?"

Up until this point, James had been more interested in getting Cassie alone than anything her father might have to say. Now his mind struggled to catch up. The man wanted his company?

"My company's not for sale," he stated.

"Come now, Sutton. Almost everything's for sale. Especially to a young, single man like yourself." Big Al stuck the cigar in his mouth and chewed on the end. His green eyes, so much like his daughter's, piercing. "Name your price."

The room seemed to shrink around James as he worked to comprehend the drama that was playing out before him. "So let me get this straight: You wanted to meet with me last Friday night to make me an offer for my company?"

"Exactly." Big Al smiled.

It was the smile that finally had the truth slamming into James. He'd been a fool. While he had been excited about getting to meet the man and talk construction, Big Al had only wanted to get his hands on his company. A company he had built from the ground up with a lot of sweat and blood. What an idiot he was.

"Dad—" Cassandra interrupted.

"Not now, Cassie," he ordered as he continued to watch James. "Do you realize how many companies smaller than yours have gone out of business in the last year?"

"Is that a threat?"

"Just a fact."

James wondered how the arrogant man had lived so long without getting his ass whipped. "So you're making the offer out of the goodness of your heart? Do you try to help out all small companies, or just mine?"

"Just yours."

So Matthew was right. His family saw him as a threat and wanted him out of the picture. Completely. But what James didn't know was if the man was working alone or if the woman who had come very close to stealing his heart knew about it and wanted the same thing.

He swiveled around in his chair and stared at her. "Did you know about this?"

Cassandra's face was white, her eyes wide. She looked innocent and surprised, but James wasn't about to fall for that charade. She was a smart businesswoman, a real work-aholic. Something as big as acquiring another company wouldn't get past her. That was why her good friend Amy Walker had called Sierra claiming to be a reporter for the

Post. Cassandra was getting information for her father. Information that would help them decide if he would be open to selling his company. He thought that after spending two days with him, she would've known better.

Unless she really did just think of him as a one-night stand.

When Cassandra didn't answer, James swallowed down the lump that had formed in his throat. He was surprised at how much the realization hurt. But he had always been able to turn his hurt to anger.

"It must've been quite a shock to learn that the man you were screwing was also the man you planned to screw," he said.

Big Al slammed his fist on the desk. "Watch the way you speak to my daughter, Sutton!"

James stood and glared back at the man. "No. The answer is 'no.' I don't care how much you offer me. Sutton Construction isn't for sale." He glanced down into the green pools of Cassandra's eyes and felt his chest begin to cave. With the pain came anger, steel-cold, punch-a-friggin'-wall anger. He knew if he didn't get out of there soon that was exactly what he would do.

He turned and walked to the door. But before he reached it, he couldn't help glancing over his shoulder at the man who casually leaned back in the chair studying him as if he were some damned science project. "And if you think I took some of your business this year, just wait for the next."

James jerked open the door just as Big Al's laughter echoed off the high ceilings. The laughter took him by surprise. What didn't was finding all of Cassandra's brothers standing in the hallway. He'd had little doubt that Matthew would spread the word about who he was. And the brothers didn't look very happy with the news. All except for Matthew, who stood there, grinning.

"I'd ask you to stay for dinner," he said, "but I think that might be pushing it."

Ignoring the comment, James strode past them. Matthew had taken his jacket when he first arrived, but damned if he would stick around to find it. To hell with the jacket. To hell with the McPhersons. And to hell with Cassandra. Her complete silence let him know exactly who she sided with. Who she would always side with. And he sure as hell didn't want some daddy's girl as a wife.

A wife?

Where in the hell had that come from? After two days of knowing the woman, only an imbecile would be thinking of marriage.

He jerked open the front door, then slammed it behind him. Snow gathered on his head and the shoulders of his sweater as he walked to his SUV and tried to come to grips with the fact that he very well could be an imbecile. Or at least had been one until a green-eyed vixen and her father brought him back to his senses. Now there wasn't a snowball's chance in hell he would even consider marrying a McPherson.

No matter how much she had made him laugh.

Or how much she had made him feel.

Chapter Twenty-one

The slamming door snapped Cassie out of her daze, and she turned to her father. "What do you think you're doing? Why would you decide to buy Sutton out and not tell me?"

"Watch your tone, young lady." Her father sent her a warning look. "I still run this business, and I don't need your okay on my decisions. Although you need to explain what you're doing cavorting with our main competitor."

"I'm not cavorting," she said, and heat infused her cheeks at the bold-faced lie. "Besides, I didn't know he was our main competitor."

"You didn't know? What do you mean you didn't know? Who do you think we've been discussing for the last few months? Some other James Sutton?"

"No. I just thought—" She cut off when she realized who she was talking to. The last person she wanted to know about her escorts was Big Al.

When she didn't continue, her father looked out the door. "Matthew, get in here. Since you showed up with the man, maybe you can explain what's going on."

Mattie strolled into the room, followed by the rest of her brothers. "Sorry, Pops. I don't know much more than what I told you."

Her father's gaze touched on each brother, and when no one spoke up, he looked back at Cassie. "Fine, I'll drop it. But I expect you to find another boyfriend. Sutton is too cocky for his own good." A smile played with the corners of his mouth. "Although he does remind me a little of myself when I was his age. It will be a challenge to go up against him." The smile got even bigger. "But there's little doubt who will come out on top. In another six months, Sutton will be begging us to buy him out." He glanced over at Rory. "Rory, I hope you set up a meeting with Steve Mitchell this week. Whatever it takes to keep Slumber Suites, I expect you to do it."

"Slumber Suites?" Her mother walked into the room with a scowl on her face and a dish towel in her hands. "You're not talking business, are you, Albert? Because if you are, I'm calling the doctor—"

"Calm down, Mary Katherine." Her father got up from the chair and came around the desk. He hooked his arm around his wife and gave her a loud, smacking kiss on the cheek. "But you're right. Christmas Eve is no time for business. It's a time for family and celebration. And a big plate of meatballs and spaghetti."

"Oh, no." Cassie's mother shook her head. "You're getting salmon."

Her father groaned as they walked out of the room.

Once they were gone, Jake closed the door behind them. Always the lawyer, he immediately started the interrogation. "What's going on, Cass? What were you thinking, dating James Sutton? Especially when you know how Dad feels about the man. And what did you mean when you said that you didn't know who he was? Did he lie to you?"

"I'm kicking his ass," Patrick stated.

"Lay off," Mattie said. "It's Cassie's business who she dates and who she doesn't. Besides, I like James."

Patrick snorted. "That's because you've never had a problem lying to women to get them into bed."

Mattie clenched his fists. "I've never lied to a woman in my life! Unlike you, I don't have to."

Rory jumped in. "Calm down. Mattie's right. Unless it affects business, we have no right to meddle in Cassie's personal life. We've got other things to worry about. Like Slumber Suites." He looked at Cassie. "Please tell me your meeting went well."

She had spent her entire life trying to prove to her father and brothers that she was tough. That she wasn't some prissy female that let emotions get in the way of business or life. Yet here she sat, an emotional wreck over their main competitor. And now she had to break the news about Steve Mitchell. Could things get any worse?

She sat up in the chair and took a deep breath. "Steve Mitchell is going with Sutton Construction."

"And you couldn't talk him out of it?" Jake asked. "There has to be something we could do to change his mind."

"Oh, there was something I could've done," Cassie said,

"if I was willing to prostitute myself for the company." Before she could explain exactly what had happened, Patrick growled and charged out the door. Rory and Jake hurried after him while Mattie took his good, sweet time.

"I gotta hand it to you, sis," he said as he walked out the door. "You sure know how to liven up a holiday."

All Cassie could do was stare at the empty doorway.

"He's got a point, you know?"

The softly spoken words had Cassie looking over her shoulder in time to see a mussed white-haired head peek up over the back of the leather couch.

"Aunt Louise?"

Her aunt's green eyes twinkled. "I was trying to take my afternoon nap, which wasn't easy in a room filled with yammering fools." She yawned and sat up, tossing the colorful afghan over the back of the couch. "You'd think a person could find one empty room in a house this big."

Funny, but Cassie wasn't even shocked to see her aunt. In a day filled with surprises, what was one more? She walked over to the sitting area and flopped down in a chair across from her aunt. She put her feet up on the ottoman and tipped her head back on the soft leather.

"So I guess you pretty much heard the entire story."

"Pretty much."

Cassie stared up at the ceiling. "And?"

"And what?"

She looked over at her aunt. "What do you think about the entire fiasco I've gotten myself into?"

Her aunt stared back at her. "If you're talking about Steve Mitchell, I'm with Patrick. It sounds like the man needs a good ass-kicking—never did like the son as much as I liked the father. If you're talking about being in love with Jimmy Sutton, then I guess I'd say it's about damned time."

Cassie lifted her head. "Are you serious? Obviously, you missed some of the conversation. I couldn't possibly be in love with him."

"Of course you can. And you are. You just won't let yourself admit it. It's all that McPherson pride, you know. Damned nuisance, if you ask me." Her aunt shook her head. "It took your father a good six months to cut through all that crap and get to proposing to your mother. Unfortunately, after what happened today, I don't think you've got six months. Or even six hours, for that matter."

Now Cassie knew for a fact that her entire family had gone off the deep end. "Six hours for what, Wheezie?"

"Six hours to get back the love of your life."

"James is not the love of my life. He's the man who's trying to put us out of business."

"Pssht." Aunt Wheezie flapped a hand. "It sounds to me like the man had no desire to put anyone out of business until your father opened his big trap. James was doing what any good businessman would do; he was being successful. You're just hurt that he lied to you."

Wheezie's words were like a hard slap of reality. And it took only a second for the truth to sink in. Cassie *was* hurt that James had lied to her. So hurt that she'd been blinded to the facts. James hadn't been trying to put them out of business. He'd been trying to succeed. And he hadn't shown up at M & M's offices with the intent of collecting damaging information on his competitors. He'd shown up at the request of her father.

"So why did he lie to me, Wheezie?" Cassie said. "Why didn't he tell me who he was from the beginning?"

Her aunt got up and came over to sit down on the arm of Cassie's chair. "All men will lie to get a beautiful woman in bed. But you can't throw out the baby with the bathwater. Besides being a great kisser, Jimmy was resourceful enough to pose as an escort so he could get to be with you. You aren't gonna get any better than that, young lady."

A good kisser? Obviously her aunt hadn't slept a wink.

"You watched?" Cassie gasped.

"At my age, I get my thrills where I can. So you never answered Amy's question. Is he as good in bed as he looks?"

Cassie rolled her eyes. "For God's sake."

"Don't for God's sake me, young lady. I was having hot sex long before you were even a twinkle in your daddy's eye." Her eyes narrowed. "I used to own this red negligee that drove your Uncle Neill wild. When words don't work, naked flesh always does." She looked away in thought. "Where did I put that?"

Wheezie got up and slipped on her black velvet flats with the huge poinsettias stitched on the toes. "Well, it doesn't matter anyway. We don't have time to get it. You need to leave now if you want to catch Jimmy before he does something stupid like get back with his tart of an assistant. I can't tell you how many men I watched sob in their beer and then end up leaving the bar with some slut."

The thought of James with any slut made Cassie see red. Still, she couldn't bring herself to chase after him. "I'm not going to go running after him. Not when he never once apologized for lying to me."

"You didn't really give him a chance. First you insulted

his feelings by calling him a one-night stand and then you insulted his intelligence by wanting to buy his company. If someone treated you like that, you wouldn't apologize, Cassie McPherson. You'd punch them in the face."

She had a point. Cassie hadn't given James much of a chance to do anything other than get angry. And kiss her. She couldn't forget the kiss. Her lips still tingled.

"So what do you want me to do?" she asked. "Besides go to his house in a red nightie?"

"You have a red nightie?" When Cassie shot her an annoyed look, she held up her hand. "Never mind the nightie. All you need to do is show up at his house."

Cassie got to her feet. "And say what?"

"I'm sure it will come to you." Wheezie's eyes lit up. "And if it doesn't, get naked. Men will forgive a naked woman much faster than a clothed one." She took Cassie's arm and walked her to the door, but Cassie stopped a few feet away.

"What am I going to tell Mom and Dad? They aren't going to just let me walk out the door on Christmas Eve without an explanation."

Aunt Wheezie released her arm and gave her a shove. "You let me handle your mother and father. You just worry about Jimmy."

Wheezie waited until Cassie was safely out the front door before she walked back to the study and sat down in Alby's big leather chair. Things were working out better than she'd expected. Rory and Amy were engaged. And it looked as if Cassie and Jimmy wouldn't be too far behind. To celebrate, she leaned over and opened the lid of the humidor. But before she could pull out a cigar, Gabby came skipping into the room.

"Grandma Mary told me to tell you and Aunt Cassie that it's time for dinner." She glanced around the room. "Where is Aunt Cassie?"

"I sent her on an errand." Wheezie grinned at the young girl. "So I hear our plan worked."

Gabby glanced behind her before she moved closer to the desk. "Like a charm. You were right. All I had to do was get Uncle Rory some alone time with my mom. Which wasn't easy since I had to spend a good twenty minutes with Dodo Derek, looking at stupid dollhouses." She flashed a grin. "Did you get Uncle Rory to buy the dirt bike?"

"I might've mentioned it. But it didn't take much convincing."

"Thanks, Aunt Wheezie. You're the best." She held out her fist.

Wheezie bumped knuckles with her. "And don't you ever forget it, sister. Now, run along and tell Mary Katherine that I'll be there in a minute."

Once Gabby had left the room, Wheezie selected a cigar and lit it. As the smoke curled around her head, she eased back in the chair and sighed.

Soul-mating was fun, but exhausting, work.

Chapter Twenty-two

James drove home with anger boiling in his gut, and he couldn't even take his frustrations out on the road. The storm hadn't been as bad as expected, but the streets still had slick spots and traffic moved at a snail's pace. Looking for some kind of distraction, he turned on the radio. But the only things on were traffic reports and Christmas music. Annoyingly cheery Christmas music sung by every singer who ever lived. After trying several stations, he clicked on the CD player. The Black Eyed Peas blasted from the Bose speakers, conjuring up a memory of him sitting in his Land Rover in the cold-assed weather, waiting for Cassandra. He thumped the steering wheel with his fist, but it wasn't enough. Not nearly enough. He should have punched Big Al. The man needed to be brought down a peg or two.

He turned the corner and barely missed the bumper

of a Cadillac that had stopped for no apparent reason. He swerved and fishtailed before he gained control. As he drove around the car, he yelled out a few choice cusswords. An elderly man glanced over at him, his aged face tense and fearful. James snapped his mouth shut.

Get a grip, James. It's not his fault you fell head over heels for an arrogant, stubborn woman.

His cell phone rang. Thankful for any distraction, he quickly answered.

"Hey, buddy." Steve Mitchell's voice came through the receiver. "I'm running a little late, but I should be there in a few."

James had forgotten all about meeting Steve. He started to make an excuse—he wasn't fit company for anyone, let alone a wealthy prospective client—but then Al McPherson's laughter echoed through his head and he changed his mind.

Buy my business?

When hell freezes over.

"Yeah, I'll see you in a few," he said.

It took him only fifteen minutes to get to the sports bar Steve had chosen. But instead of hurrying inside, he stood out in the cold for a few moments in a last-ditch effort to cool off his temper. Unfortunately, it succeeded only in making him more pissed off at the McPhersons for having his jacket.

"We close in an hour," the bartender yelled as he stepped in the door. The bar was warm and dark and, fortunately, had no Christmas music playing. There was just the noise from the multiple football games on the flat-screen televisions.

"That's fine." James stomped his feet and brushed the snow off the shoulders of his sweater, then took a seat at the bar. "Can I get a beer?" He actually needed something a lot stronger, but that would have to wait until after he met with Steve.

"What kind?" the bartender asked.

"Anything but Coors," he said. Cassandra drank Coors.

"What? Are you a Communist?" a man who sat two stools over asked with a smile. He was seated a couple stools from the only woman in the bar. A redhead with well-displayed cleavage.

"That's bullshit," a man at the end of the bar chimed in. "Just because we live in Colorado, home to the famous beer made from Rocky Mountain spring water, doesn't mean everyone has to drink it. Personally, I think it's shit." He burped loudly before he continued. "I mean, who wants to drink beer made from water that a bear probably pissed in?"

The smiling man looked down at his glass. "Could you bring me something else, Joe?"

Joe the bartender laughed as he set a dark beer down in front of James. "That's four fifty. Unless you want something else. The kitchen's closed, but we have cold sandwiches."

"I'm good," James said as he pulled out his wallet to pay. Joe took the money and was handing him back his change when Steve came in the door. Spying James, he walked over and sat down, uncaring that he tracked snow across the wood floor.

"Man, it's a bitch out there." He took off his ski coat and flipped it over the stool next to him before he thumped

James on the back. "Glad you could make it. I was worried you'd have other plans."

"No," James said, ignoring the sinking feeling in the pit of his stomach. He'd had plans. Plans to spend the day, and hopefully the night, with a woman whose kisses he couldn't seem to wipe out of his brain. Now he had no plans. No plans at all.

"Chivas on the rocks," Steve said to the bartender, then leaned in closer to James. "This is a dump, isn't it? The app on my phone was way off on their four-star rating." He shrugged. "But what can you expect on Christmas Eve? I hate the friggin' holiday. There's never a good bar or restaurant open and my chef always expects the day off."

He went to pay for his drink, but James beat him to it. Without even a nod of thank-you, he continued. "I swear its entire purpose is to get single men married off. It seems every event is wrapped around couples and family. Which is why I used you as an excuse not to go to my aunt's. She always tries to fix me up with her friend's divorced daughters. Thanks, but no thanks. I've seen too many of my buddies hung out to dry after getting divorced. Even with a prenup."

Damn straight, James thought. Here was a man after his own heart. He was successful and intelligent enough to stay away from the marriage trap and all it brought with it. Like conniving females and overbearing fathers.

Steve took a deep drink of his whiskey. "Now, New Year's Eve, that's a holiday. A night where most women are just looking to get laid."

As if on cue, the redhead leaned over the bar, displaying her cleavage to James and Steve. "Excuse me, Joe, but could I get another cherry?" She flashed a smile over at them. "I seem to have misplaced mine."

"Maybe this bar wasn't such a bad idea after all," Steve said. He waited for the bartender to toss a couple more cherries in the woman's drink before he motioned him over. "Give her another one of whatever she's drinking on me." He winked at James. "Who knows, she might have a friend she could call." He took a sip of his drink. "Speaking of that, me and a couple of my buddies are headed to Vegas to celebrate New Year's. Why don't you come with us? Since you used to live there, you'll know all the great places to party."

James did know all the great places to party. But partying had gotten old, which was one of the reasons he'd moved to Denver. If tonight was any indication, he was partied out. All he wanted to do was go home and crawl into bed.

"I'm afraid I'll have to pass," he said. "I'm pretty swamped with work."

Steve pulled his gaze away from the woman and smiled. Until that moment, James had never realized how sly Steve's smile was. "And you're about to get more swamped." He toasted him with his glass. "Congratulations, you're the new contractor for Slumber Suites."

James had known it was coming. What he couldn't figure out was his reaction to the news. Instead of being thrilled, he just felt numb. And he knew exactly who to blame for his lack of enthusiasm.

"Hey, how many of those have you had?" Steve asked as he pointed at James's beer. "I'm giving you a multimillion-dollar contract and all you can do is sit there and look at me?"

James pulled his head out of his ass and plastered on a smile. "Sorry, Steve. I guess I'm a little stunned. You told me you were happy with M & M, so I didn't see this coming."

He shrugged. "I was happy with M & M, but it was time for a change." He slapped James on the back. "And you were the man who showed the most interest."

The bartender handed the redhead her drink and nodded at Steve. The woman flashed a smile and waggled her fingers. "Thanks a bunch."

"My pleasure," Steve said before turning back to James. "Besides, I don't exactly care for Big Al McPherson. The man is too full of himself."

James nodded. "I know what you mean. He had the gall to try and buy me out."

"No shit?" Steve said. "Well, I can't say as I blame him. I've bought out my fair share of smaller hotel chains. But only the ones I take as a threat. And I would say that the McPhersons consider you a big threat. Your name was the first name that popped out of Cassie's mouth when she stopped by today."

James choked on the swallow of beer he'd just taken. It took a couple hard whacks on the back from Steve before he could catch his breath. "Cassandra stopped by today?"

One of Steve's eyebrows lifted. "Cassandra? Is there something you're not telling me, buddy? She seemed to be pretty familiar with you as well."

James ignored the question. "What was she doing at your house?"

"I had assumed she'd come by to sweeten the deal."

Steve's gaze followed the redhead as she got up from the bar and walked to the bathroom. "And I must say I was looking forward to getting into those snug jeans of hers. Unfortunately, it turns out she's an ice bitch just like I'd heard. A little slap and tickle was all I got."

There was a moment when everything seemed to freeze. The bartender cleaning off the bar. The woman smiling at Steve on her way to the bathroom. Steve lifting his glass for another drink. The football games on the televisions. Everything froze except the wall of rage that welled up inside of James.

One minute he was sitting there enjoying a drink, and the next his fist was connecting with Steve's face. The punch sent Steve reeling off the barstool and landing hard on the floor. James got up and stood over him.

"If you ever touch Cassandra again, I'll take your fuckin' head off. Do you understand me?"

"Hey." Joe the bartender came over. "Take it outside."

Steve held a hand over his eye and glared at James. "I hope you know that you just fucked yourself, Sutton. All over a frigid tomboy who wouldn't give you the time of day."

Since it was pretty much the truth, all James could do was toss down money for the tip and walk out the door.

The snow had stopped falling by the time James got home. He pulled into his garage, barely glancing at the menorah-shaped luminarias that flickered on his front lawn. Obviously, his next-door neighbor had been right. A little snow wouldn't stop the crazy cat woman's plans to make the block festive. Of course, he had no business calling other people crazy. Crazy was a man who had just lost a multimillion-dollar contract over a woman who thought he was nothing more than a one-night stand.

He shoved open the door of the Land Rover so hard it hit the wall of the garage and ricocheted back. One-night stand. The woman didn't know crap. He'd had plenty of one-night stands and not one of them was anything like what he'd experienced with Cassandra. One-night stands didn't last for two of the best days of your life. They didn't make you feel like you were the luckiest man on earth. And they sure as hell didn't make you this pissed off when they were over.

James got out and slammed the door. A *meow* had him glancing down. The mangy gray cat sat at his feet, looking up at him with his one green eye. James pretty much hated green at the moment.

"What do you want?"

The cat meowed and rubbed up against James's legs.

"Oh, no," he said. "I don't do cats." He picked up the matted ball of fur and carried him to the open door of the garage. "Go hang out with your crazy owner." He set the cat down in a tire track of his Land Rover and turned to go inside.

The damned cat followed him.

James tried it two more times—putting the cat farther and farther down the driveway—but before he could run back and close down the garage, the stubborn cat would end up right behind him. He finally had to push the button for the garage door, then wait for it to almost close before he shoved the cat underneath it.

He had second thoughts about getting rid of the cat

the moment he stepped into his dark, silent house. A house that suddenly felt cold and empty. He tried to shake the feeling off by making himself something to eat. But his cupboards were almost as bare as his soul, and he ended up grabbing a vitamin water and heading to his desk in the dining room to see if he could get some work done.

It proved to be impossible. Cassandra appeared in every account he looked over, her green eyes mocking, her smile devastatingly beautiful. Unable to take a moment more of his solitude, he reached for his cell phone and scrolled through the numbers until he found his dad's. He punched the button, probably harder than he should have, but better a button than a wall. His stepbrother answered.

James cleared his throat. "Hey, Robby. It's James."

There was a moment of uncomfortable silence. The poor kid probably didn't remember who he was. He really needed to take a trip home.

"Hey, James. How's it goin'?" he said.

James smiled. "Pretty good. How's school?"

"Boring."

"Not all, I hope. I'm sure there are a few girls that aren't too boring."

Robby laughed. "A few."

"Good, always keep a spare. That's my motto." He frowned. At least, it had been his motto until a few days ago. "So, is Dad around?"

"Yeah, he's right here." There were muted noises; then his father spoke.

"James?"

"Hi, Dad." Weird, but just hearing his father's voice gave him the sudden urge to start sobbing like he had when they sent him to camp.

"You usually call tomorrow," his dad said. "Is everything okay, son?"

James swallowed and reminded himself that he wasn't eleven and covered with mosquito bites. Although his heart felt as if someone had taken a bite out of it. "Sure, I'm fine. I just wanted to see how you were doing."

"We're all fine here. Marge has the entire house looking like the Walmart Christmas section exploded in it. The only space without some Santa or baby Jesus is my garage and Robby's room. And both of us had to fight for that much space."

James tried to laugh, but it came out just forced enough to alert his father.

"Jimmy? You sure there's nothing wrong?"

James pressed on the bridge of his nose. "No, there's nothing wrong. I was just thinking that maybe next year I'd come up for the holidays."

"Really, son?"

"Yeah. I mean, I'm my own boss. So why not?"

His father pulled the phone away from his mouth. "Hey, Margie! James thinks he might come up for Christmas next year!" There was some excited, muffled talking; then his stepmom got on the phone.

"Oh, James, that would be just wonderful. I know how busy you've been, but your father has missed you so much." His father grumbled something in the background, but Marge ignored him. "And I think you should take some time off in the summer as well. Your father told me how much you loved fishing together. You could come in June for Robby's graduation and then head up to the lake. You might even want to stop by and see some of your old friends." She rambled on. "Of course, if there is someone you'd like to bring with you, she's more than welcome."

"No one," he snapped; then softened his voice. "I'll probably just come by myself, Marge. But thanks for the offer."

"Of course, James. This is your home too. By the by, did you get your Christmas box?"

James glanced guiltily over at the big box that sat in the corner of the room still unopened and kicked himself for not mentioning it sooner. "Yeah, I got it. The baked goods were delicious." God, he hoped she had sent baked goods.

"I'm glad you liked the peanut brittle. It was the only thing I thought would ship well." She paused, then yelled, "Robby, don't you dare touch that package. Listen, I better go before your brother breaks something. Merry Christmas, sweetheart." Then the phone was handed back to his father.

"Now, son, you don't need to worry about coming here this summer and fishing with your old man if you're too busy. That's just Margie gabbing. I understand how hard it must be to run your own business. And, well...I've always been real proud of you."

James squeezed his eyes shut and leaned his head back. "Look, Dad, I'm sorry about not coming back to see you more often. It's just..." He struggled to find the words that would explain how hard it was for him to be in the same house where his mother had lived and laughed and loved. Luckily, his father didn't make him find the words.

"I know, Jimmy." He paused. "Sometimes I think it's been harder for you. I mean, I had Margie and Robby to help me through. You didn't have anyone."

"I didn't want anyone, Dad."

"That might have been your mistake, son."

James sat there for a moment, too stunned to reply.

"I love you, Jimmy," his father said.

It took a second for James to find his voice. "I love you too, Dad. Merry Christmas."

"Merry Christmas." The connection was broken.

James remained there with the phone pressed to his ear for a few moments before he finally put it down. His father's words had nailed the coffin of his depression shut with a final bang. His father was right. He had chosen loneliness over companionship. A loveless life over a love-filled life. Work over pleasure. All because he had tried to run from the pain he'd felt after his mother died.

Somewhere along the way, he had convinced himself that if he worked hard enough and long enough he would never again have to deal with the loss of a loved one. All he would have to deal with were business transactions and money. Except business and money didn't keep you warm on a cold winter night. In fact, it couldn't even hold off the pain of losing someone, because eventually it catches up to you.

He got up, walked into the den, and sat down on the couch. His mind wandered back to the bar and Steve Mitchell, and he couldn't help but wonder if that would be him in twenty years. A middle-aged, single guy stuck in a bar on Christmas Eve, trying to get in some lonely woman's pants. A guy who had nothing to look forward to over the holidays except a raunchy weekend in Vegas.

It was a pathetic thought.

The doorbell chimed, pulling him from his depressed musings. He stared in the direction of the front door for a few seconds, his mind tired and sluggish. On the second chime, he finally got up. He flipped on the entryway and porch lights, wondering who would be ringing his doorbell—he glanced at his watch—at ten thirty on Christmas Eve.

James threw open the door, expecting to find his nosy neighbor and her cats. Instead the sight that greeted him made his heart jump up to his throat.

Chapter Twenty-three

Cassie stared into James's surprised eyes and felt like throwing up. This was a very bad idea. Especially when the warm surprise melted from his eyes and was replaced with hard, cold anger.

"Hi," she said, and was really annoyed by how wimpy her voice sounded, especially when he continued to look at her as if she were a glob of dog poop on the bottom of his shoe.

She cleared her throat and tried to think of a good conversation opener. "Your luminarias look pretty. Mom and Dad usually just put up lights." Figuring it probably wasn't such a smart thing to bring up her father, she moved to another topic.

"I'm sorry I stopped by so late. It took me a while to find it." She looked down at the Christmas tree she'd dragged up onto his porch and then back at James. His dark expression hadn't changed one iota, which caused her to ramble even more. "I know it's not much, but it was the only one I could find. You were right." She adjusted her grip around the trunk of the tree. "All the lots *were* closed down. Luckily, this one was left behind."

He finally spoke. "What's your point, Cassandra?"

Point? Darn, she had hoped she wouldn't have to make a point. She'd hoped he would take one look at the tree and get what she was trying to say. It was a ridiculous fantasy. Why would James remember something she had said about a Christmas tree? A tree was a tree to him, certainly not a symbol of wanting to share your life with someone.

Which meant she would have to just come out and say it. Except Cassie had never been good at expressing her emotions. She could give orders and articulate her physical needs, but emotions were something else entirely.

She took a deep breath and released a fog of moisture into the frigid air. "So that thing I said about the one-night stand." She swallowed hard. "I didn't really mean it."

He cocked an eyebrow and crossed his arms over his chest. "So what did you mean?"

The tree might have been half-dead, but it was really heavy. She dropped the trunk and then set down the bag of decorations she'd gotten at the twenty-four-hour Walgreens. A gray cat lay in one corner of the porch with a leg hiked over its head, grooming a part of its anatomy that had Cassie taking a second look. She glanced back at James, who didn't look the least bit more welcoming than he had a few seconds ago.

"What I'm trying to say is that I enjoyed the time I spent with you," she blurted out. "I mean, it was fun."

"Fun?" His arms dropped to his sides, which she took as a good sign.

"Actually"—she smiled—"it was more than just fun. It was…uh…well, it was…" She struggled to find the right words, but they just weren't there. Instead of bringing a stupid tree, she should've brought an interpreter who understood incoherent idiots.

"Sorry," James said. "But I don't have time for this." He nodded at the sheepskin jacket she wore. "So if you'll just give me my coat."

Cassie hadn't planned on taking off the jacket until she'd had a chance to clear things up. But she couldn't seem to get her feelings out verbally, so taking it off seemed like the next best thing. She glanced around, hoping no little children were peeking out their windows in hopes of seeing Santa before she flicked open the two buttons on the jacket. She pushed it off her shoulders and let it drop to the porch.

If she'd thought it was drafty before, it was nothing compared to how she felt when wearing nothing but her UGGS. The frigid air felt like a thousand tiny needles. Fortunately, it got the reaction she had wanted.

"Jesus!" James reached out and jerked her inside, slamming the door behind them. "Have you lost your mind? This is a family neighborhood."

"I'm sorry. I just thought…" Her voice trailed off. "Oh, to hell with it!" She launched herself at him, pushing him back against the door.

James opened his mouth to protest, and she took the

opportunity to kiss him for all she was worth. She thought he was going to continue to fight her, but instead his hands closed around her waist and he jerked her closer as his lips molded to hers.

It seemed like a lifetime since she'd kissed him instead of only hours. But even hours was too long to wait for something as wonderful as kissing James. He kissed like it wasn't a prelude to sex. He kissed like kissing was the beginning and the end. Then, as if realizing what he was doing, he pulled back. But she didn't give him time to change his mind. She grabbed his sweater and pulled it over his head.

James had the nicest chest. Not too muscular and not too skinny. She ran her hands over his rib cage and up to his pecs. They flexed against her palms, and she squeezed them as she pushed him more firmly against the door. She kissed him again, but this time he allowed it more than participated. Thinking he was ready to move on to other things, she undid the top button of his jeans and slid down his zipper, then reached under the band of his boxer briefs and encased him in her tight fist.

"Shit," he breathed against her lips. "Your hand is cold."

"Maybe I can warm it up," she said as she stroked up and down his shaft.

He groaned and switched positions, pushing her up against the door. He didn't waste any time getting to the heart of the matter. His hand moved down between her legs, and he stroked her a few times before slipping a finger deep inside. Then he jerked down his jeans and briefs and hiked one of her legs around his hips. In one smooth thrust, he was deep inside her.

"Is this what you were after?" he panted against her ear as he pumped out his desire. "Is this the fun you were talking about?"

"Yes," she breathed and tipped her head back. "Yes."

It must've been the wrong answer. Because suddenly he wasn't inside her anymore. Suddenly he was standing a few feet away, looking at her as if she were something that had just crawled out from under a rock.

"Get out."

She blinked. "What? But I thought—"

"You thought you could come here and show a little skin and all would be forgiven." He pulled up his jeans and struggled to zip them over his erect penis. "Well, you thought wrong, Ms. McPherson. But you seem to be doing that a lot lately. Like thinking that I'd be willing to sell a business I built from the ground up. And standing me up so you could run over to Steve Mitchell's and take care of a little business. I think that pretty much defines our relationship. Business before pleasure."

"But I—"

He tugged her away from the door and jerked it open. "Save it for someone who cares." None too gently, he shoved her outside and slammed the door in her face.

Cassie stood there staring at it for a moment, trying to figure out what had just happened. The lock on the door clicked and so did Cassie's mind.

He'd thrown her out? After she had spent the last three hours running all over town looking for a tree lot that was open and had to Dumpster dive to get the tree she'd gotten, he'd thrown her out?

Ughhh!

She leaned down, jerked up the coat and put it on. Try naked! Aunt Wheezie should be shot. And so should she for listening to a ninety-year-old woman who probably hadn't had sex since Reagan was in office. All naked had gotten Cassie was frostbite on some very private areas, splinters in her butt, and humiliation at the hands of an arrogant asshole.

She glared at the door and thought about beating on it until the asshole opened up so she could scream out her frustrations. How dare he reject her apology? Just who did he think he was? She turned and headed down the steps. Up and down the street, luminarias flickered. Normally, she would've enjoyed the beautiful sight. But now she wasn't so sure that she didn't hate Christmas.

All the mistletoe and eggnog and flickering lights could turn a perfectly normal woman into a crazy lovesick idiot. And she refused to suffer through a second more of it. She didn't care if her father got angry with her; she didn't want to go to midnight mass tonight or her parents' house tomorrow. She was going home. Home to her lonely little condo with no Christmas tree. Hopefully, in another week, all this craziness would be behind her and her life would get back to normal.

She headed down the sidewalk to the spot where she'd parked her truck. She had just stepped off the curb when a deep voice had her almost jumping out of her UGGs.

"You know he's Jewish, right?"

Cassie turned to the man who stood on the sidewalk in

flannel pajamas and a huge parka. A little white poodle sniffed around the man's boots, almost disappearing in the snow.

"You scared me." Cassie held a hand to her chest and, when she felt nothing but bare skin, jerked the lapels of the jacket closer together.

"Sorry," the man said. "Just walking the dog." He glanced down at the poodle. "I wanted a Rottweiler, but the wife was worried about it eating the kids." He shrugged. "Anyway, I just didn't want you to be too mad at the guy." He glanced at James's house. "He's probably pretty sick of us trying to shove our holiday down his throat. Ms. Ellis insisted on the luminarias, and now you brought a tree."

"James is Jewish?" What kind of person didn't mention something like that? Especially when she'd gone on and on about getting a tree? Obviously, she didn't know James Sutton at all.

The poodle lifted its leg on a luminaria, dousing the candle inside. The man tugged him away in midstream. "Maybe if you tried again without the tree, he wouldn't slam—" He stopped and looked up, and even in the darkness, Cassie knew he blushed.

Great. If she wasn't humiliated enough, she had now stripped for the neighbor. A neighbor who was stupid if he thought Cassie was going to try again. James had made it perfectly clear how he felt. She had apologized for the entire one-night-stand thing—or close enough—and if James wanted to hold a grudge for something her father did then she didn't want him anyway.

"I like trees, though," the man said. When Cassie's gaze narrowed on him, he stammered. "I—I mean, if I wasn't...married with a family, I'd like trees. Because I used to like them...a lot."

Somehow Cassie didn't think they were talking about Christmas trees.

"Les?" A woman appeared around the hedge of tall juniper bushes. She wore flannel pajamas that matched her husband's and a pink down jacket. "What's an Allen wrench?" She waved a piece of paper. "And I think we're missing some instructions—" She stopped and her gaze drifted over to Cassie, then down to her bare knees. Which set Les to jabbering and supported Cassie's theory that he'd been thinking about something other than trees.

"This is a friend of Mr. Sutton's, honey. She just stopped by to bring him a tree. But I guess he wasn't at home." Obviously, Les wasn't willing to go into details about what he'd seen. "Well, it was nice talking with you." He steered his wife down the sidewalk.

"But I thought Mr. Sutton was Jewish," his wife said.

"Merry Christmas," Les said as he tugged the poodle behind him.

"Merry Christmas," Cassie called back, even though she wasn't going to have one.

She reached for the handle of the truck and then stopped. Wait a minute. Why shouldn't she have a Merry Christmas? Why should she let the actions of one jerk ruin her holiday? And why did she think that only couples and families could have a tree?

She had a tree. A little Charlie Brown tree that deserved a home.

Cassie whirled around and stomped back to the porch.

The gray cat was still sitting there grooming, this time its front paw. When she reached for the bag of decorations, it stopped and stared at her with one very spooky green eye. *Poor animal. What kind of a pet owner leaves their cat out in the bitter cold?*

Tucking the bag under her arm, she picked up the trunk of the tree. It seemed to have gotten even heavier, which was strange considering she'd left behind half the needles when she dragged it down the steps. Taking a shortcut across the lawn, she headed for her truck.

She didn't know what alerted her. The crinkle of a paper luminaria bag. Or the hiss of a flame as it caught fire. All she knew was that when she turned around, it was too late. No wonder Christmas trees were fire hazards. The little six-foot Scotch pine went up like a torch.

With a good foot of snow on the ground, everything might've been okay if not for the low-hanging branch of the maple tree. Did green wood burn? Her question was answered only seconds later when the branch caught fire. She watched a trail of flames zip up one branch to another.

Jesus, Mary, and Joseph.

For a second, Cassie was mesmerized by the tall, glowing flames. Then sanity returned, and she raced to her truck. As she grabbed her phone and dialed 911, James came running out the front door in his stocking feet with his phone to his ear. He glanced her way as he hurried down the pathway. Even from that distance, she could read the hatred on his face. Still, she might've tried to explain if his neighbors hadn't converged. People came out from almost every house in bathrobes and slippers.

Les raced over to James while the nosy woman with the cats tried to pull her garden hose across the street. The rest of the people just circled around and stared at the towering blaze.

At the arrival of three fire trucks and an ambulance, Cassie fled the scene of the crime.

Chapter Twenty-four

The reality of what she'd done didn't fully hit Cassie until she was sandwiched between her two little brothers in the eleventh row of Saint Paul's a few minutes before midnight mass. She stared at the flickering candles at the altar and wondered when she'd lost her mind. The night of the party? The day after? Today? Or maybe it had been a slow process that started with finding Mike in her closet in thigh highs and heels and ended with arson.

Not that she had purposely set fire to the tree, but it had been her fault. And instead of taking responsibility, she'd slunk away like the coward she was. A coward who had no business sitting in God's house.

As if to verify this, Aunt Wheezie, who sat in the pew in front of Cassie, craned her little white head around and whispered loud enough for the entire congregation to hear, "So did you try naked?"

"Someone's getting naked?" Mattie asked. His gaze was caught by a pretty young woman across the aisle, and he flashed his trademark smile. The girl blushed and smiled back.

"Mattie, don't even think about it," Rory warned, repositioning a sleeping Gabby on his lap.

"Think about what?" Amy lifted her head off Rory's shoulder, looking all lovesick and annoyingly content.

"Getting naked," Patrick said.

"Mattie's getting naked?" Jake leaned around Patrick.

"I'm not getting naked," Mattie said. "Cassie is."

"Shhhh!" Her mother turned around from her spot next to Wheezie and glared at Mattie.

"Don't look at me." He held up his hands. "Cassie started it."

"Matthew, don't argue with your mother," Big Al warned from his place right next to his wife.

"I wasn't arguing. I was just stating a fact. Although I guess it wasn't Cassie who started it. It was Wheeze."

"I wasn't talking to anyone but your sister," her aunt said. "And if the rest of you would shut your traps, I could get an answer."

It was too much. The emotional stress from the last few days caught up with Cassie, and she giggled. Since she never giggled, her entire family stared at her. She tried to get a grip on her hysteria. It wasn't easy, not when images of the last few hours kept popping into her head. Standing outside James's door naked as the day she was born. Sex against the wall of his foyer. A towering inferno.

Good Lord.

Fortunately, before she dissolved into a fit of laughter, the procession started down the aisle with Father Thomas, the deacon, and the altar servers. Everyone rose to their feet, and Patrick leaned over and whispered in her ear, "Are you okay?"

Just like that, all the laughter drained right out of her and was replaced with the hard press of tears. After days of trying to hide her true feelings from her family, Cassie gave up and told the truth. "No."

"Sutton?"

All she could do was nod.

"You want me to take care of him for you?" Patrick asked.

She shook her head. Almost setting the man's house on fire was revenge enough. Since she was being honest with Patrick, she might as well be honest with herself. She couldn't stand the thought of James being hurt. No matter how many lies he told or how many jobs he took from M & M.

"Good," Patrick whispered. "I like the guy. Especially after he kicked Steve Mitchell's ass."

Cassie turned to him. "He kicked Steve's ass?"

She spoke loud enough that her family weren't the only ones who turned to look at her. She tried to bluff her way through it by glancing back over her shoulder and then shrugging. It seemed to work, and as soon as everyone looked away, she leaned closer to Patrick.

"When did this happen? And how did you find out about it?"

Her mother turned back around and shot Cassie a look

that promised severe retribution if she didn't shut up. Cassie snapped her mouth closed.

Enduring the rest of the service without answers was the worst form of hell. She tried getting a pen from Amy so Patrick could write out the information. But before she could do more than lean over Matthew and Rory and tap her on the leg, her mother reached her hand back and pinched her arm.

The priest had barely concluded the service when Cassie forced the rest of her siblings out of the pew.

"Get a grip, Cassie," Jake said. "Where's the fire?"

His choice of words had her shoving Mattie even harder.

"Okay. Okay," her littlest brother said. "Geez, Cass, I want to get home too, but Mom is going to make sure none of us sees another Christmas if you don't cool it."

Except Cassie couldn't cool it. When she got to the end of the pew, she genuflected and did the quickest sign of the cross she'd ever done before grabbing Patrick's hand and pulling him through the crowd. Her intention was to get him in her truck, away from the rest of the family so she could interrogate him. But before they got even halfway down the aisle, she was accosted by the women of the church and pulled into a sea of ugly Christmas sweaters.

"Cassie." Tara Miller gave her the kind of hug you give an influenza victim. "I'm glad I caught you, sweetheart." Tara was only two years older than Cassie, but she looked and acted at least twenty years older. She would never stand naked on a front porch or almost set fire to someone's house. Although she had gotten smashed at

St. Paul's Annual Harvest Festival and thrown up on the hayride.

"Doesn't she look great?" she gushed to the other women. "Just look at all that hair. I used to have hair that thick, but that's what four kids and a demanding husband will do for you." She laughed and placed her hand on her Christmas tree sweater. "And speaking of husbands, my little brother is home for the holidays and would love to meet you."

"I thought Alex just got divorced, Tara." The woman in the snowman triplets sweater butted in. "Cassie doesn't want someone on the rebound. Now, my nephew, on the other hand, has never been married and likes masculine women."

"You mean rich women," said the bleach blonde in a sweater that had Rudolph's red nose strategically placed on the tip of one large breast. "I hear he's looking for someone to support his gambling habit. My cousin Brian has his own money. He wrestled professionally until he dislocated his shoulder fighting Mad Dog Dan."

"As if Cassie would want a pumped-up wrestler," Tara said before her eyes lit up like a flaming tree. "There's Alex now. Alex!" She waved her hand and moved farther up the aisle.

Cassie seized her opportunity and pulled a grinning Patrick down an empty pew to the other side of the church. But the move didn't stop Tara's matchmaking efforts. She latched on to a skinny man in glasses and started after them, forcing Cassie to duck behind a group of people and hide in the first room she came to.

"Cass," Patrick said when she pulled the door closed

behind them, "I've never been overly religious, but even I think this might be pushing it."

She glanced around the tiny confessional and figured he had a point. Still, she had too many questions to let a little thing like God's wrath deter her.

"So how did you find out James beat up Steve?"

Patrick sat down and peered through the latticed window before he started talking. "After you told me about what Mitchell had done, I drove to his house. He wasn't home, so I waited. It didn't take long. He arrived with some redhead who started this high-pitched screaming when I jerked Mitchell out of his Mercedes. But before I clocked the bastard, I noticed his swollen eye. From what I could get out of his whining plea for mercy, Sutton didn't care for him mauling you any more than I did."

Cassie's heart started to thump wildly. "He punched him because of me?"

"Good enough that I figured Mitchell had paid his dues and let him go with only a few words of warning about touching my sister."

Cassie shook her head in disbelief. "But Steve was giving him the contract for his hotels."

"Not anymore." Patrick laughed. "I believe Mitchell's exact words were 'I'm getting an out-of-state contractor. Colorado is filled with nothing but barbaric mountain men.'" He got up, towering over her in the cramped space. "Look, Cass, I need to get out of here. Not only am I getting claustrophobic, but I'm starting to want to confess all my sins. And believe me, you don't want to go there." He reached for the door handle. "Come on; let's go home."

Home.

It was funny. Instead of picturing her condo, she pictured a man with dark brown hair and rich whiskey eyes.

"Just give me a couple minutes, okay?" she said.

Patrick studied her face for only a second before he nodded and slipped out the door.

When he was gone, Cassie sat down and tried to collect her thoughts. It was hard to do when the giddy, girlie feeling was back and worse than ever.

James had punched Steve Mitchell. For her. And a multimillion-dollar contract hadn't even made one speck of difference. Wheezie had been right. James hadn't lied to her just to dig up dirt so he'd get the Slumber Suites contract. He lied to get her in bed. And while most women might be offended, it made Cassie extremely happy. Probably because she didn't believe for a second that the time he spent with her had been only about sex. James cared for her. He had proved that by showing up at her parents' house.

She froze and started nibbling on her thumbnail. At least, he had cared for her until her father had gotten involved. Until she had botched her apology and almost set fire to his house. Now he hated her. She slumped back against the wall just as the door opened on the other side of the partition.

"Is someone in here?" Father Thomas asked.

Cassie really wanted to keep her mouth shut and hope that he went away, but she figured she was in enough trouble with God without ignoring a priest. "Yes, Father."

"I'm sorry," he said. "But I'm afraid that confession

isn't being held tonight or tomorrow. But if you come back on—"

She cut him off. "That's all right. I was just…taking a moment."

Father Thomas chuckled and closed the door behind him. "I need to take those every now and again myself. Any particular reason for needing one on Christmas Eve?" He paused. "Or should I say, Christmas morning? It's well past midnight."

She thought about making up some excuse and bidding the priest goodbye. But since she was there, it seemed a shame to waste a good confessor.

She leaned closer. "There's this man, Father. This man I've been dating—well, sort of. And I did something really stupid, Father. Actually, I did a lot of stupid things. The main one being not giving him a chance to explain why he lied—oh, and calling what we had a one-night stand." She froze. Who did she think she was talking with? This was a priest, not a talk-radio host. "I mean, I shouldn't have made him think that what we had together wasn't special."

"It's always important to make people feel special," Father Thomas said.

"I know, and it's really my weakness. People in my family have trouble letting their true emotions show." She slumped back against the wall. "I can't even tell my father that I don't want to be a paper pusher for the rest of my life. People think I'm so tough, but I'm just a wimp."

"The meek shall inherit the earth."

"I don't want to inherit the earth, Father. I just want

James to forgive me. I just want to get back what we had before."

"And what makes you think that this James won't forgive you? Sometimes all people need is a little time to find forgiveness."

"That might've been true to begin with, but after I almost burned down his house, I'm thinking it will take more than time."

Father Thomas cleared his throat. "Perhaps I could make an exception, and we could do a confession after all."

"No, Father, I don't need a confession—well, maybe I do, but it will have to wait. What I really need is for you to tell me what to do to fix it. How can I get James back?"

There was a long pause before Father Thomas spoke. "I'm sorry, my child. I can't tell you what you need to do to get your young man back. All I can tell you is that God has a plan, and if you will release yourself to his loving care, he will guide you to your destiny. No matter what has happened in the past. No matter what obstacles lie ahead in the future."

"But how will I know if I'm going in the right direction?"

"Prayer and meditation have always worked for me. If you're patient, your heart will lead you in the right direction."

The only thing Cassie felt in her heart was a whole lot of love for James. But somehow she didn't think that was going to be enough. And maybe she needed to listen to Father Thomas and give James some time. She'd rushed over to his house earlier and look what had happened.

"Thank you, Father," she said as she got to her feet.

"You're most welcome," Father Thomas said. "Perhaps

you should bring in this young man so I can talk with him."

She paused with her hand on the door handle. "I don't think that's going to work, Father."

"Why not, my child?"

"He's Jewish."

Chapter Twenty-five

"Well, Mr. Sutton," the short fireman with the abnormally large upper body said, "you're a lucky man. A minute or two more and your entire roof would've gone up in flames."

Sitting on the front steps of his porch wrapped in a blanket because he couldn't find his ski jacket and his sheepskin had been taken by a lunatic pyro, James didn't feel very lucky. Just exhausted. And stunned. What kind of a woman brings you a tree, gets naked, has sex with you, then almost torches your house? She was nuts. Completely nuts. And he was nuts for not keeping a closer eye on her.

"Even your tree looks like it will survive." The fireman leaned back and stared up at the charred branches of the maple tree. "So I guess you learned your lesson about waiting until Christmas Eve to pick up a tree. By this time, they're nothing but fire starters. One tiny spark and whoosh."

Oh, James had learned his lesson, all right. About Christmas trees and hot-tempered women. At that moment, he wanted nothing to do with either one ever again.

"It's a good thing you hadn't taken it inside yet," the fireman continued. "I've seen dead trees burn entire homes straight down to the ground."

James nodded, wondering if that had been Cassie's plan to begin with. Snuff out the competition with a dead tree and a match. He rubbed his eyes. God, he needed to get some sleep.

"Well, it looks like the guys are all packed up and ready to go." The fireman held out his hand. "Hopefully, you won't need to call us again."

James stood to shake the man's hand, forcing the gray cat that sat on his feet to move. "Listen, I really appreciate how quickly you guys got here. You're right; a few minutes more and I'd be looking for another place to live."

"Not a problem. It was a slow night. Nothing to do but miss my family."

"I know what you mean," James said. What he wouldn't give to be in Pittsburgh with his family at that moment, as far as he could get from Cassandra McPherson.

"So you got kids?" the fireman asked.

"No."

The fireman pulled his wallet out of his back pocket and flipped it open. "I've got two. A girl and a boy." He pointed to the picture. "That's my wife, Haley."

James studied the picture in the light from the porch. The woman was dark-haired with pretty brown eyes. The kids were teenagers but still cute.

"Nice family."

"Yeah." He looked at the picture for a few seconds before he closed his wallet. "I got the bad rotation this year. But next year I'll be off." When James didn't say anything, he put the wallet back in his pocket and lifted a hand. "So take care, man."

James nodded. "Thanks again."

"All in a night's work," he said. Halfway down the path, he stopped and turned. "Merry Christmas."

"Merry Christmas," James mumbled. Suddenly too tired to make it the short distance to the door, he sat back down and watched as the firemen clambered up into the truck and pulled away. The other two fire trucks and the ambulance had left as soon as the blaze was under control. Along with all of his neighbors. It wasn't as exciting to watch the cleanup as it was to watch flames shoot up in the sky. Still, it was nice of them to come over and try to help him. The guy next door had invited him over for a drink, and it was the busybody's blanket that was wrapped around his shoulders. What were their names? Drew? Ms. Ellison? Hell, he'd just met them, and he couldn't even remember their names?

His father was right. He needed to start letting people in or he was going to end up a very lonely old man. But for now, he needed to get some sleep. He started to get up when Sierra's bright yellow Volkswagen pulled up to the curb. After the emotional roller coaster of the last few hours, a familiar face was a welcome sight.

"Hey." She scampered up the icy path in her knee-high boots and a pink coat. "Guess I missed all the excitement." She flopped down on the step next to him and stared at the large circle of charred remains in the center of the yard. "I heard it was a doozy."

"A doozy? And just how did you hear about the doozy of a fire?"

"Ms. Ellis."

"Ellis, that's it. The woman with the cat zoo."

She giggled. "The same."

"And how did Ms. Ellis get your number?"

"She takes in a lot of stray cats that would otherwise get gassed, and I help her find homes for them when I can." She reached out and scratched the cat that had plopped back down on James's feet. "Like One-eyed Willie here."

James hooked the edge of the blanket around her shoulders and hugged her close. "You're a nice person, Sierra. Even if you have ugly tattoos."

"Whatever." She ducked away. "So what happened?"

"I got a Christmas tree, and on the way inside, I let it get a little too close to the luminarias." It was the same lie he had told the firemen. He wasn't willing to mention Cassandra, not when it would involve talking about the events that took place before the tree burning. Unfortunately, Sierra had connections.

"Was this before or after the woman got naked on your porch?"

He turned to her. "Ms. Ellis?"

She nodded. "She likes to look out her window." She waved at the house across the street. It was dark, but James had little doubt that the woman was watching.

He lifted a hand in greeting before looking back at Sierra. "How much did she see?"

"You tell me." Sierra counted off on her bright, orange-gloved fingers. "Beautiful woman drags a tree up to your front porch; you reject tree; she gets naked; you pull her inside for an indecent amount of time before you toss her back out." She paused and glanced over at him. "She torches the tree." She grinned. "I like this girl."

"Figures." He stared out at the yard. Up until then, there was still hope that some wild neighborhood kids had gone on a tree-burning rampage. Now he was forced to accept the fact that the woman he couldn't get out of his mind really was a raving nut with pyro tendencies.

"So? I'll ask again." She leaned over and rested her chin on his shoulder. "What happened? And I'm not talking about the tree. What happened to turn the smiling, dopey guy who couldn't wait to get back to his new girlfriend to the sad, depressed guy who has nothing better to do on Christmas than sit on his front porch step with his cat and stare at a pile of tree ashes?"

He might've denied ownership of the cat if something else she'd said hadn't caught his attention. "Christmas?"

She grabbed his wrist and turned up the face of his watch.

"Crap," he said.

"You can say that again. Ms. Ellis pulled me away from a very in-depth discussion I was having with Slater on the pros and cons of getting married."

"Married? You're twenty, for Christ's sake."

"Not me, stupid. You."

"Me?" He shook his head. "Not likely. Not to some crazy woman who gives fire hazards as gifts."

"Whatever. Although bringing you a Christmas tree doesn't make her crazy. It makes her thoughtful."

"It barely had any needles on it."

She glanced back out at the yard. "It looks like it had enough."

"My point exactly." He jumped up, dislodging Willie from his feet again. "Hell, she could've burned down my entire house."

She stood. "If she'd wanted to burn down your house, she would've left the tree on the porch. She was just sending you a message."

"Burn in hell?"

She laughed. "Something along those lines."

"Great." He stomped the snow off his boots. "I got the message."

"I told you love makes you do stupid things."

"Believe me, this woman doesn't love me."

"If you say so. But take it from a woman who squirted Krazy Glue in her boyfriend's hard drive when he kept e-mailing an old girlfriend: Women who don't care don't waste their time on revenge. They just leave."

For being twenty, Sierra made a lot of sense. Or maybe it was the fact that he hadn't slept well in three nights. Two because of hot sex. And one because of hot sex followed by an even hotter fire. If he wanted to think clearly, he needed sleep. Minus the sex. And fires.

"I'm going to bed," he proclaimed.

"Not until you open my present." Sierra pulled a package out of her coat pocket that looked like it had been put through a paper shredder. "Sorry. The new puppy I got Slater for Christmas used it as a teething biscuit."

He smiled as he took it from her. "A new puppy, huh? Is that what you spent your bonus on?"

"No. You'll be happy to hear I saved my bonus. The puppy I got at the pound."

"Good girl." He ruffled her hair, too tired to worry about the consequences.

Excited about her present, she let it slide. "It's Christmas, so it's okay to open it."

The chewed-up paper fell away with little effort. *"A Christmas Story."* He flipped the DVD over and looked at the back. "Thank you. As a kid, I loved this movie."

"So did I." She grinned from ear to ear. "Which is why I think we should watch it." She pulled another package out of her other pocket. "I even brought some microwave popcorn."

"Listen, Sierra—"

She held up a hand. "Believe me; no matter how tired you are, you won't sleep a wink. You'll just lie there, thinking about naked women and flaming trees. What you need is a distraction." She jerked the DVD out of his hand and marched into the house.

Figuring she might have a point, James followed.

"How did you get so smart?" he asked. He waited for the cat to come in before he closed the door. He couldn't very well leave the animal out in the cold. "I thought Slater was your first true love."

"He is. But I have three older sisters who fall in love every other week."

"That would explain it." He flopped down on the couch and slipped off his boots, ignoring Willie when he jumped up next to him.

As she struggled with the shrink-wrap, she glanced over at him and smiled. "I think we're making progress."

"Huh?"

"That's the first time you didn't claim you weren't in love."

Somewhere before Ralphie got his Red Ryder BB gun but after he beat the shit out of the bully, James fell asleep. Not a deep sleep, but a troubled sleep, involving a really bizarre dream.

Or more like a nightmare.

He was back in his old Pittsburgh neighborhood, walking home from school with two of his best childhood friends, Kevin and David. The snow was piled high along the shoveled sidewalks, the air crisp and cold. They were doing what boys do on the way home from school, dawdling. Right before the alleyway, the neighborhood bullies jumped out in front of them. Kevin and David took off, but James was too scared to move.

"Look at the little wimp." Sierra marched up and shoved him in the chest with her orange-gloved hands. "He's shaking in his snow boots." She unwound the striped scarf from her neck and wound it around and around his body until his arms were pinned to his sides. "He's over thirty and doesn't know the first thing about love. So what do you want to do with him?" She stepped back to reveal the worst bully of all.

Cassie stood on the path in front of him, wearing the sexy red dress, spike heels, and a look that made his knees weak. Her dark hair fell around her shoulders, her green eyes sparkled, and her lips were a glossy red.

"So say it." She took a step closer. "I dare you." She slipped her arms around his neck and kissed him, a warm, wet, and delicious kiss that clouded his mind. "Say it. I double-dog dare you," she whispered right before her tongue slipped into his mouth.

He tried to shove her away, but he couldn't. His tongue was frozen to hers. He pulled and tugged, but it wouldn't come off. It was stuck.

"One spark and whoosh." The disproportionate fireman appeared next to him. "Just one spark."

Suddenly, his tongue was free. Except now he was tied to a dead, brittle Christmas tree with the entire McPherson clan standing around him dressed in pink bunny costumes like Ralphie's aunt had given him.

"Say it!" Cassie jerked the flaming torch away from Big Al Bunny.

James opened his mouth, but nothing came out. He watched in horror as Cassie set fire to the pile of condoms that surrounded his feet. He looked out in the crowd for help, but no one lifted a hand. Not the Bunny McPhersons. Not his business associates. Or his neighbors, including Ms. Ellis and her three thousand cats. Not even his own family—his father, Marge, and Robby.

Or his mother.

She stood closest to the fire, her golden eyes bright and loving, her smile soft and caring. She wore the same robe he remembered from his childhood. A tattered blue chenille with large pockets that held tissues, Band-Aids, and peppermints.

"Don't fight it, Jamie," she said. "It'll be all right. I promise."

But he had to fight. If he didn't, he'd die. He struggled against the knit scarf as Sierra raced around the tree, flashing her creepy fish tattoo and chanting, "You really love her! You really love her!"

Then everyone joined in.

"You really love her! You really love her!"

James woke up. Something *was* choking him. He pulled the cat off his neck before he looked around the sunlit room. His breath was ragged. His heart rate elevated. And his body sweat-drenched. But, fortunately, there were no pink bunnies or burning trees. No chanting Sierra. No sexy Cassie.

No smiling mother in a tattered robe.

Just James.

Alone.

Again.

Pushing the blanket off, he looked down at his watch.

Ten a.m.?

He felt as if he'd slept for only a few hours, all drained and sore. No doubt from sleeping on the couch. Or the weird night. Or the even weirder dream. Whatever it was, all he wanted to do was crawl back in bed and sleep for another eight hours. And why couldn't he? He had nowhere he needed to be. Nothing he needed to do. At least, nothing that couldn't wait until tomorrow.

Slowly, he rolled off the couch and headed to his room. Except once there, he stood in the doorway and stared at the rumpled bed that he hadn't made since a certain raven-haired beauty had bewitched him in it. The pillow still held the imprint of her head, and the robe she borrowed still lay on the floor by his chair.

James turned away. The guest room would be better. He wanted to try out the new bed anyway. He didn't want his dad and Marge to sleep on a crappy mattress when they came to visit. Not that he had ever invited them to visit. But he would. In fact, he would call them today. As soon as he had a few more hours' sleep.

On the way to the guest bathroom, he stripped down to his boxer briefs, unconcerned with the trail of clothing he left behind. As he stood in front of the toilet, he decided he would invite his entire family for New Year's. He'd even send them tickets. With all his frequent-flyer miles, he could send them tickets every couple months if he wanted to. And he wanted to. Family was important, and he needed to spend more time with his. He might not have a pretty wife and two cute kids like the fireman, but he had a great dad and a nice stepmom and a typical teenage stepbrother. It was more than a lot of people had.

He walked into the guest room and crawled into the queen-sized bed with its new scratchy sheets. Willie jumped up next to him, and James had to admit he was thankful for the company. He lay there with one arm tucked beneath his head and stared up at the sunlight that danced across the ceiling. He wasn't angry anymore. In fact, he didn't feel anything. Just kind of empty. It reminded him of the feelings he'd experienced right after his mother's death. The tired emptiness that came once all the anger drained away. And he *had* been angry when his mother died. Angry at his father for not taking better care of her. Angry at his mother for not fighting harder to live. Angry at God for taking her. But mostly, angry at himself for loving her so much that losing her made his life not worth living.

The room grew hotter and even kicking the covers down to his feet didn't stop the sweat from breaking out on his brow. How long had it been since he had thought about his mother? Not just in passing, but really thought about her?

Without much invitation, the memories swarmed around him, ghosts of Christmas past: His mother standing in her worn bathrobe in the doorway of their house as he rode by on his brand-new bike. The smell of her perfume when she hugged him for giving her the lopsided coffee mug he'd made in school. The sound of her laughter when his father had dressed up like Santa and pulled her down on his lap.

She had always laughed so easily. He couldn't remember the features of her face; they had blurred with time. But her laughter was there, would always be there—sealed inside the walls of his heart. It had been husky and unconfined, and just hearing it made his day.

Similar to Cassandra's.

Funny, but it didn't seem like such a stretch to go from thinking about his mother to thinking about Cassandra. Probably because their laughter wasn't the only thing they had in common. His mother had been just as strong-willed, stubborn, and hot-tempered. She was a loving mother and wife, but when she got mad, both he and his father had run for cover.

James grinned.

His mother probably would've set the tree on fire too. Especially if his father treated her like James had treated Cassandra. James had just been so angry. He had expected an apology. Instead, she'd acted as if the only thing she wanted from him was fun sex. But if that was the case, then why bring along a dead Christmas tree?

His mind wandered over the last few days. Bits and pieces of conversation drifted in and out until one came to the forefront. *A tree isn't a Christmas tree unless you have someone to share it with.*

Suddenly, all the pieces of the puzzle fell into place.

It wasn't just a lame gesture. She had been trying to tell him something without coming right out and saying it. If he hadn't been so angry, he would have read the message, not just in the tree, but in those beautiful green eyes.

Cassandra wanted to share a tree with him. To her, it was a symbol of more than just the season. It was a symbol of family and love. Which was why she didn't have one. She wasn't willing to share a tree with just anyone. She was willing to share it only with someone she cared about.

The revelation set James into action. He jumped up from the bed and hurried down the hall, grabbing up his clothes as he went and trying to figure out the fastest way to get to her. Was she at her condo? At church? More than likely with her parents, but he couldn't go racing over to her parents' house like a madman. He'd tried that once and look where it got him. This time he didn't want raving fathers and eavesdropping siblings interrupting them. He wanted to talk with Cassie alone. Which meant he needed to wait for her at her condo. He looked down at his wrinkled clothes. But first he needed a shower.

Then he needed to find a tree.

Chapter Twenty-six

Christmas at the McPherson house was mayhem at its finest. Cassie barely made it in the back door with her bags of gifts before she was greeted by screaming children.

"Aunt Cassie's here!" Kelsey came charging at her with a toy baby stroller, stopping inches before slamming into Cassie's legs. "Now we can open presents."

Kyle grabbed a package out of one of the bags. "Is this one mine? Is it that remote control truck I asked for?"

"Twuck! Twuck!" Little Chase toddled after his brother. Kyle turned and clipped him with the corner of the package, knocking him down. He started to cry, but stopped when a creature in a helmet and lime green and black motocross gear picked him up.

"You're late." Cassie's mother walked up and took Chase from the creature that was having trouble hanging on to the toddler while wearing bulky motorcycle gloves.

"Sorry," Cassie said. "I slept in." It surprised her mother as much as it had Cassie. She wasn't the type who slept in. She was the type who liked to get her day started early. But she had been exhausted. Not only from the late mass, but from a weekend of very little sleep. The restful night had left her more at peace than she'd been in a while.

Or maybe what had her feeling so peaceful was the acceptance of her love for James.

As if reading her mood, her mother smiled and kissed her cheek. "I'm glad you got things settled with James."

Things weren't even close to being settled with James. But Cassie had settled things with herself, and that was a step in the right direction.

"Well, let's get these presents under the tree," her mother said. "The kids have been chomping at the bit to start unwrapping. You would think that they hadn't just spent the morning unwrapping presents at their own houses." She took a bag from Cassie and headed for the twelve-foot Christmas tree that filled an entire corner of the family room.

Within thirty minutes, the room was piled high with crumpled wrapping paper, ribbons, tags, and enough toys to start their own store. Even her brothers had given one another toys and stood clustered around Mattie, waiting their turn, as he tried out his new remote control helicopter.

"They're really just big kids," Amy said as she flopped down on the couch next to Cassie. "You should've seen how excited Rory was to give Gabby her first lesson on that stupid dirt bike. He rode behind her with his knees practically touching his ears and a big grin on his face."

Cassie glanced over at Gabby, who still wore the moto-cross pants and jacket, but had taken off the helmet and gloves to play with the LEGOs Cassie's father had given her. "She reminds me of myself when I was her age. I loved boy's toys."

"And what about your new boy toy?" Amy asked.

Cassie looked back at her and grinned. "I'm working on it."

"Working on it?" Wheezie came over and sat down on her other side. "It doesn't look to me like you're working on it. If you were working on it, you wouldn't be sitting here."

"I'm not taking any more of your advice, Wheezie," Cassie said. "The last advice you gave me caused me nothing but trouble."

"Hmm?" Wheezie's eyes crinkled. "Naked always worked for me. Of course, there was that one time when Melanie tried to fix me up with her great-uncle. The old coot couldn't see a thing. Even with his glasses. So naked hadn't worked real well with him either." She tipped her head. "Does Jimmy need glasses?" Amy laughed and her aunt continued. "So you got naked before or after you told him you love him?"

"I didn't tell him that I love him." Wheezie started to open her mouth, but Cassie held up a hand. "But I plan to. Just fully clothed."

"So what are you doing sitting here?"

"Father Thomas said I need to be patient. Besides, it's Christmas day."

Wheezie's forehead knotted. "Father Thomas? What the heck does he know about relationships? Listen to a woman who's been around the block a few times. If you sit around too long being patient, that cute man of yours is going to get away. Just ask this one." She pointed her thumb at Amy.

"She's right," Amy said. She glanced over at Rory, who was maneuvering the remote and trying to keep the helicopter from crashing into the painting over the fireplace. "I almost lost your brother because I didn't stand up for what I wanted. And who cares if it's Christmas day. Isn't love what Christmas is all about?"

Cassie stared at the two women as the truth of Amy's words sank in. What *was* she doing sitting there? She loved James. And what better time to let him know that than on a holiday that was based on love?

Except suddenly she was scared to death.

"But what if he doesn't feel the same way?" she breathed.

"It's doubtful," her aunt said. "Especially with the way he was kissing you in the study."

Cassie cringed. "A few things have happened since then."

"It doesn't matter what happened." Amy took her hand and squeezed it. "If he really loves you, he'll forgive you. That's how it works." Her gaze locked with Rory's. Without saying another word, she got up and walked straight into his arms as the helicopter crashed into the wall.

"And what about Dad?" Cassie voiced another fear. "He's not going to take the news sitting down. Steve Mitchell was right about one thing: Big Al doesn't listen to anyone but himself."

"And whose fault is that?" Wheezie said. When Cassie

turned to her in surprise, she continued. "If you're planning on bringing home that man you love, you're going to
have to learn how to stand up to your father. Otherwise,
your life is going to be nothing but hell." She lifted one
penciled-in brow. "You might want to start with telling
Big Al how much you hate being an accountant."

"I'm not an accountant," Cassie stated. "I'm a vice
president."

"Phsssshh." Her aunt waved a hand in front of her face.
"Nothing more than a glorified title."

"It may be a glorified title, but it's where Dad needs
me. Especially since his heart attack."

Aunt Wheezie pointed a bony finger at her. "That's a
bunch of crap and you know it, Cassie McPherson. You
stay where you are because you're too afraid to go against
the Great Al McPherson."

The truth struck home with painful accuracy. Cassie
was afraid of going against her father. The fear wasn't
so much about him having another heart attack as it was
about wanting to please him. The thought of not pleasing
her father terrified her.

As if reading her thoughts, Wheezie patted her arm
and spoke in a voice that was soft and caring. "Cassie,
my sweet, you're a daddy's girl. You have been ever since
you were born. And that was just fine and dandy when
you were a child. But it doesn't work so well for adult
women who need to have lives of their own. Adult women
who need to fight for the jobs they want and the men they
love."

With her aunt's words, all the emotions Cassie had
experienced in the last few days came crashing in around

her. The weight in her chest dissolved into a heavy wall of tears that worked their way up to the back of her throat. Wheezie's red silk blouse and cardigan blurred before her eyes as she was enfolded against a tiny chest that smelled of roses.

"I know you love your family and would do anything for us," her aunt whispered against her head. "But I think it's time to do something for yourself."

Resting there against her aunt's fragile strength, Cassie silently released her tears and, with them, her stubborn refusal to accept the truth. Her aunt was right. Somewhere she had forgotten how to fight for herself. Or maybe she had never known how. Family and business had been her entire life. She had liked it that way. Hidden in her office and living between two of her brothers, she had felt safe from the world. Unfortunately, it had kept her from living a normal life. A life filled with laughter and passion— and, yes, even pain.

"What happened?" Melanie asked.

Cassie lifted her head to find her entire family clustered around the couch. Her brothers had stopped playing with the helicopter and the children their toys.

"Her heart's broken," Megan supplied.

"Who broke it?" Gabby said. "Because I bet Uncle Patrick will make them pay."

"No one is going to make anyone pay." Her mother sat down on her other side and handed her a tissue. "At least, not until I find out what's going on."

"What *is* going on?" Her father moved to the front of the group and waited for Cassie to finish blowing her nose. "I hope you're not upset over losing Slumber Suites to

Sutton. It ups the ante, but I think I've come up with a new offer that Sutton won't be able to refuse."

"I don't think she's crying about business, Albert," her mother said.

His brow furrowed. "Well, then, is she sick? Should we call Dr. Matheson?"

"Tassie's sick! Tassie's sick!" Chase yelled.

For a second Cassie almost latched on to the excuse. It would've been so easy to put off talking with her father and just say she was sick and needed to go home. But that would be the wimpy way out. And she was tired of being a wimp. Especially with her father.

"I don't need a doctor, Dad." She got to her feet. "I need you to listen to me."

Her father's face got that look it always got when he didn't like your tone of voice. But Cassie ignored it and forged on.

"James Sutton is not selling his business, and we're not making him another offer."

Anger turned her father's face a bright red. "I don't think that's your decision, young lady."

"And I think it is," she said, then wished she hadn't said it quite so sharply. A hush fell over the room. Everyone froze in shock. Even the children knew you didn't talk back to Papa Al. But it was too late now. Cassie swallowed hard and continued. "Since your heart attack, I've been working my butt off." She glanced around at her brothers. "We all have. And it was wrong to make an offer to James without consulting us."

"M & M is my company," he growled.

"No," she said. "M & M is our company. Every McPherson in this room has given up something to make the business successful, and every person in the room deserves to be heard. And I'm not blaming you for that, Dad. As Aunt Wheezie just pointed out, if people want to be heard, they need to speak up. So I'm speaking up. I don't want you making another offer to James Sutton."

Her father opened his mouth to speak, but before he could, Patrick beat him to it. "I agree with Cass."

Jake stepped up. "The offer's on the table. If he changes his mind, he'll contact us."

"I think that makes sense," Rory said.

Everyone looked at Mattie, who grinned from ear to ear. "Sorry, Pops, but it doesn't matter how I vote. Majority rules."

There was a moment when Cassie thought her father might explode. His face got even redder, and his chest puffed up. Then her mother stood and slipped an arm around his waist.

"She always was the outspoken one of the bunch, Albert." She kissed his cheek. "Reminds me of someone else I know."

"Outspoken and smart," Aunt Wheezie said.

Her father glared at Wheezie before returning his attention to Cassie. "This decision wouldn't have anything to do with you being in love with Sutton, would it?"

"No. Although, just so you know, I am in love with him."

"And he's in love with you?" her father asked.

"I'm not sure about that." She glanced at the clock on the wall. "Which reminds me, I need to be going."

"You're not going anywhere," her father said. "I'm

willing to concede the fact that you might be right about the offer I made Sutton, but this is Christmas. And the family's always together at Christmas."

"What about that Christmas when you were chasing after Mary Katherine?" Aunt Wheezie said. "I don't think you got home until well past midnight, Alby."

Her mother laughed. "She's right. Besides, as much as we'd like to keep Cassandra as our little girl, I think she's proven today that she's all grown up and needs a life of her own." She gave Cassie a hug. "If you don't have other plans, why don't you invite James back for Christmas dinner?" Her father started to speak, but she sent him a warning look.

"I'll try, Mom," Cassie said, "but I have a lot of apologizing to do."

"Then call me tomorrow, honey. Albert"—her mother spoke in a tone that few people messed with—"give your daughter a hug goodbye."

It took a moment for her father to comply. Even then, he didn't give her his usual bone-crushing hug. This one was softer, gentler. When she pulled back, he didn't look angry anymore. He wasn't smiling, but in those dear green eyes, she saw resignation and a lifetime of love.

"I love you, Daddy," she whispered.

He nodded, then cleared his throat. "Don't forget your coat."

"That's it?" Mattie asked in amazement. "She just gets to leave without any yelling or cussing? Man, I can't believe it. All I ask for is a tiny little sports car for Christmas, and I get the lecture of my life. But let the baby girl fall in love with our major competitor, and all she gets is

'Don't forget your coat.' ." He tossed his broken helicopter to the couch. "It's not fair, I tell ya. It's just not fair."

Cassie laughed. "Life isn't fair, baby brother. Remember that." She socked him on the arm on her way past him.

As she grabbed James's sheepskin jacket and headed for the door, the rest of the clan put in their two cents.

"Apologize, but don't show any weakness," Jake the lawyer directed.

"Best defense is a good offense," Rory agreed.

"Give him hell, Cass," Patrick ordered.

"Hell! Hell!" yelled Chase before Melanie picked him up and offered him a candy cane off the tree.

Her mother followed her to the door. "Show him what's in your heart, Cassandra. That will be enough."

Cassie was still smiling when she stepped outside. It wasn't snowing, though the afternoon sun was still well hidden behind thick clouds. The ground and trees were all blanketed in white, and the hushed stillness of the scene had her pausing and taking a deep breath of crisp air. A feeling seeped up from the region of her heart and spread through every part of her body. Even her gloved fingertips tingled with the sensation. The feeling was light and airy as a snowflake, but warming as hot cocoa.

She felt as if she'd emerged from a cocoon. For the first time in her life, Cassie McPherson was free. Free to work where she wanted to work, to live where she wanted to live, and to love who she wanted to love.

Cassie laughed, and the sound rang out like the clearest of church bells.

Chapter Twenty-seven

"Hey, mister, whatcha doin'?"

James straightened up so quickly, he banged his head on the bottom branch of the tree. He grabbed his head as he turned and looked into the wide eyes of the two boys who were scrunched down by the tree, peering under the low-hanging branch he'd just cracked his head on.

It was official. James had lost his mind. He just hadn't wanted anyone knowing it. Not even two adolescent boys. He went back to carving on the tree trunk and mentally kicking himself for not having a saw at home. He owned a construction company, for God's sake.

"Ya choppin' that tree down?" The littlest boy in the bright blue stocking cap fell down to his stomach in the snow and placed his mittened hands on either side of his face.

"He's not choppin', stupid," the other kid said as he

crawled on his elbows under the tree. "Can't you see he's using a knife? He's cuttin' the tree down."

James continued to whittle, hoping that if he didn't answer, the kids would get bored and leave. It didn't work. The sight of a grown man cutting down the large spruce tree in his front yard with a kitchen knife wasn't even close to boring.

"How come you're cuttin' the tree down?" The little boy scooted closer. "Did you get that knife for Christmas? I got a bike, but I can't use it yet 'cause of the streets being too slick. My dad moved the cars out of the garage and I rode it around in there until I ran into my dad's work-bench and knocked his table saw off and I had to stop 'cause Mom said I could've cut my leg off 'cause it's real sharp. A lot sharper than your new knife."

"Shut up, stupid. He doesn't want to hear about your dumb bike," the bigger kid said. He leaned closer. "What is that, a steak knife?"

James cleared his throat. "You boys better go on home. I don't want you to get hurt when this tree falls."

The older boy laughed. "I don't think that's happenin' anytime soon. Hell, you haven't even gone an inch."

"Aww." The little boy pointed a finger at his brother. "I'm tellin' Mom you said a bad word."

"Go ahead, you big tattletale." He reached out and cuffed him in the back of the head, almost dislodging the blue cap.

The little boy sent up a wail that made James's ears ring before the kid scrambled from beneath the tree and raced off through the snow.

"Baby," the bigger kid mumbled as he turned back to James. "Hey, can I help?"

He thought about declining, but his fingers had started to cramp up in his gloves. Besides, the kid was right. There was no danger of the tree falling. Not when he'd been at it for a good forty minutes and gone less than half an inch.

James turned the handle of the knife to the kid. "Don't cut yourself."

"Hey, Dylan, what's goin' on?" Another boy leaned under the tree, his chubby cheeks red with cold.

"I'm helpin' this old guy cut down his tree," Dylan said. *Old guy?* He found the groove and started to saw. "I guess he's tryin' to replace the one that burned down last night."

The other kid scooted under the tree. It was a tight fit. "Did you see the way that thing went up? Geez, it was so cool. Can I help?"

Dylan shook his head. "Not yet. I got a rhythm."

"Hey, my dad's got a chain saw. You want me to go get it?"

James opened his mouth, but Dylan answered for him. "Nah, we want to do it this way."

"Oh." The chubby kid rested on his elbows and continued to watch in silence.

As great as a chain saw sounded, the kid was right. After the commotion of the night before, James's neighbors might string him up in the charred maple if he ruined their Christmas celebrations with the loud revving of a chain saw.

"Dylan?" Footsteps crunched through the snow. White snow boots appeared right before a pretty blonde poked her head under the tree. "You get out·from under there this minute, young man." Little brother dropped to his knees next to the woman with a triumphant look.

Dylan tossed the knife at the chubby kid, but didn't seem to be in any hurry to climb out.

"I mean it, Dylan," his mother said. "I'm giving you to the count of three."

"You better go," James said. "But I appreciate the help."

"What's going on?" Black men's boots joined the white ones.

"Les, Dylan won't come out," the woman whined.

"He's under there?" His neighbor's face appeared a second later. Les glanced at Dylan, then at the chubby kid who was madly sawing, and finally at James. He stood back up. "Go on back home, Kelly. I'll take care of this."

The boots hesitated for only a second before they walked away, hauling a wailing little brother behind them.

James wondered if he was in for a ball busting for letting the man's kid play with knives when Les dropped down and scooted under. Instead, he nodded at the tree trunk. "You cutting it down?"

"Yeah, Dad," Dylan piped up. "He wants to replace the one that burned down last night."

Les glanced at him. "I thought you were Jewish."

James rolled his eyes. "No."

"Hmm?" Les watched the chubby kid for a few seconds. The kid didn't seem to be getting anywhere even though sweat dripped like a leaky faucet from his forehead to the needles that encircled the trunk. "You need a saw?"

"As a matter a fact," James said, "that would be—"

"No, we're good." Dylan reached for the knife. "I think we almost have it. Want a turn?"

Les shrugged. "Sure." He took the knife from his son and moved up closer. "Maybe we should start on the other side." As he sawed, he cleared his throat and looked over at James. "Sorry about your tree. Women can get pretty upset over things."

"Women?"

Les shot a quick glance at the kids before he looked back at James. "I was walking the dog. I would've said something to the firemen, but I figured if you wanted them to know about her, you would've told them." He stopped sawing, and his eyes glazed over. "You're one lucky sonofagun. I used to be that lucky. Not that Kelly ever did that, but she used to do some fun things. One time, she—" He stopped and looked at his son. "I'll have to tell you later." He went back to sawing.

James wondered how his solitary life had suddenly become so crowded. He had wanted to meet his neighbors, just not all at once. Willie joined the neighborhood party. The cat circled the tree three times before prancing through the middle of the group and swooshing his bushy tail in their faces.

"I'm sure there's nothing to worry about, Ms. Ellis." A pair of dark blue pants appeared, followed by the face of the fireman from the night before.

"Mr. Sutton?"

Yellow and green hiking boots tromped up. "That's Mr. Sutton under there? Well, I wouldn't have called you if I'd thought it was Mr. Sutton. I was worried someone was trying to set another tree on fire."

"We're not tryin' to set it on fire. We're tryin' to cut it down," Dylan offered as he took the knife from his father and went after the trunk with a vengeance.

"Cut it down?" The fireman looked puzzled. "Why do you want to cut it down?"

"To replace the burned one," Les said. "Of course, now that I think about it, I don't think this tree's going to fit in his house. It's a little big."

"Not if we cut off a few of the lower branches," the fireman said. "I've got an ax in the truck."

James groaned and rested his head on his forearms. Couldn't a man cut down his own tree without a bunch of interruptions? Not that he was ever going to succeed in cutting down the tree. The entire tree idea was just another example of Sierra's theory on lovesick stupidity. He should've skipped the tree altogether and just gone to Cassie's bright and early this morning. Now she was probably at her parents' and dragging a spruce up to their front door would be even more ridiculous than cutting one down from your front yard.

"Look." James lifted his head. "I really appreciate all the help, but I've changed my mind. I'm not going to cut down the tree after all."

"You can't change your mind," Dylan said. "We're almost there."

"Let it go, son." Les took the knife. "I'll let you cut down the pine in the back. Your mother has been after me for the last year to do it."

That seemed to pacify the kid, and he and his friend crawled out from beneath the tree. Les and James followed. James barely had time to brush the dead spruce needles off his coat when Ms. Ellis shoved a plastic-wrapped cake at him.

"I thought you might like some fruitcake. It's kosher."

"Thank you," he said as he took the heavy cake. "But I'm not Jewish."

"You're not?" She looked almost angry about the news. "Then why did you let us put a menorah in your front lawn? And why did that woman burn down your tree?"

"What woman?" The fireman came back up with the ax. "A woman started the fire?"

"That's exactly what I was trying to tell you last night," Ms. Ellis said, "but you were too busy to pay any attention. I hope you realize that it's my taxes that pay your salary."

"Who was this woman?" the fireman asked James. But before he could answer, Ms. Ellis jumped in.

"Why don't you ask her yourself? She's standing right over there."

James turned, and his breath lodged in his throat. Cassandra stood on the sidewalk, not more than ten feet away. She wore jeans tucked into the same boots she'd worn the night before, and her hair fell in dark waves over the sheepskin jacket.

His sheepskin jacket.

Without saying a word, he moved toward her. With every step, his heart pounded louder and louder in his ears. He stopped close enough to see the tiny flecks of brown in her green eyes, but not as close as he wanted to be.

"Hi," he said.

"Hi." She smiled and everything inside him jumped for joy.

"That's her." Ms. Ellis came up, pointing a finger. Her trail of cats followed. "That's the woman who burned down Mr. Sutton's tree. I would recognize that coat anywhere."

"Is that true, Mr. Sutton?" the fireman said. "Was arson involved?"

"No," James said as he continued to look into Cassandra's eyes. "Just a little misunderstanding."

"Well, it didn't look like a misunderstanding to me," Ms. Ellis said. "She was naked, and then she set the tree—"

"Ms. Ellis." Les rushed over and took the older woman's arm. "Did you know that Kelly makes the best eggnog? In fact, why don't you come over right now and have some? It's way too cold to be standing outside." He glanced back at the two boys. "Come on, Dylan. Tyler can come, too."

"Fine," Ms. Ellis said. "But if this tree catches on fire, we'll know who to blame." She glanced at the gray cat, who was now rubbing against Cassandra's boots. "Come on, Willie."

The thought of her taking the cat pulled James's attention away from Cassandra. "Ms. Ellis," he said. "I was wondering if I might be able to adopt Willie." He shrugged. "I mean, he seems to like my house."

Ms. Ellis looked at him for a few seconds before she smiled. The first smile the woman had ever given him. "Cats don't like houses, Mr. Sutton. They like people." She nodded her head. "I'll get together some care and feeding pamphlets and get them to you within the hour."

James glanced at Cassandra. "I think tomorrow will be soon enough."

Les tossed him a smile as he led Ms. Ellis and the boys next door.

"Dave!" one of the firemen, who were sitting in the truck, called out. "Everything okay?"

"Yeah!" Dave yelled before he looked back at James. "Since it's Christmas, I'll let it go. But do me a favor, would ya? No more fires. Planned or accidental."

James waited until he was out of hearing before he turned to Cassandra. "What do you say? You want to start a fire?"

Chapter Twenty-eight

Now that they were finally alone, Cassie didn't know what to say. She had gone over and over her speech on the way to his house, but now, looking into his golden eyes, all the words evaporated. Fortunately, James took matters into his own hands. Before she could start stammering, he kissed her. The heat of his mouth had barely melted into hers when he lifted her up in his arms. She snuggled against him and listened to the steady thump of his heart as he carried her up the steps, through the door, and into the den, where he deposited her on the soft cushions of the couch.

He turned to the fireplace, and she couldn't help but admire his butt in the Levi's when he leaned over to turn on the gas logs. Flames leapt to life. He adjusted them, then pulled off his gloves and coat and tossed them down on the hearth.

He turned around, his eyes bright but unreadable. She wanted his attention, and it looked as if she had it. So what was she waiting for?

"I owe you an apology," she said. "I tried to give you one last night, but I was too much of a wimp to get the words out. I'm sorry about how my father acted. I didn't know about the offer until after he'd made it. I'm sorry for referring to what we had as a one-night stand. I guess I was scared of letting you know how intense my feelings are."

James continued to stare right through her.

Suddenly, she felt extremely hot. She unbuttoned the coat and fidgeted with one of the buttons. "I should've just come out and told you instead of bringing a stupid tree and stripping down and..." She blushed. "And you know."

The silence was deafening. James just stood there with the matted gray cat sitting at his feet. After what seemed like hours, he chuckled. The chuckle quickly turned into a laugh. An out-and-out, belly-grabbing laugh that had Cassie glaring.

"What's so funny, Sutton?"

The question just made him laugh harder.

"Why, you jerk!" She jumped up. "That's the last time you'll get an apology from me." She turned and headed for the door, but he caught her before she had taken two steps and lifted her off her boots. His laughter had died, but his eyes still twinkled merrily.

"Thanks for the stupid tree." He kissed the tip of her nose. "And thanks for the...you know. I liked them both. A lot."

"Put me down," she ordered.

James shook his head. "Not in this lifetime."

She gritted her teeth. "Which could be all of two seconds more if you don't put me down."

The dopey smile deepened, showing off his dimples, as he let her slide down his body. "Two seconds, huh? Then I better not waste any time."

James lowered his head, and his lips found hers with gentle accuracy. It didn't take more than the first touch of his sweet lips to banish all anger and replace it with warm, deep desire. Besides, he liked her tree.

With his lips still attached to hers, he took off the sheepskin coat and tossed it to the floor. His hands slid down her back, over her waist to her hips, then cupped each cheek as he rubbed against her melting center.

"I want you," he muttered against her lips.

She tugged at his bottom lip with her teeth. "I think you have me."

"Thank God," he said as he fell back on the couch with her.

They landed with arms, legs, and tongues entangled—and her on top. But she had time only to wiggle against his rock-hard body once before he rolled her over. She didn't mind. He gave her one deep, heated kiss after the other as if she were the best thing he'd ever tasted. As if he had an eternity to do nothing more than kiss her.

"I've missed you," he breathed between kisses.

"It's only been a day."

"Too long." He slid his hand under her sweater and captured her breast nearest her pounding heart.

Too long. She ran her hands over his broad shoulders. *Way too long.*

Their kisses and caresses became more frenzied. Sweaters were jerked off and a bra removed. Naked flesh explored and tasted. Finally, when their breathing was hard and ragged and their bodies clamoring for release, James rolled off her so they could remove the rest of their clothing. Once they were naked, he didn't waste any time. He slid over her body and entered her. The sensation took her breath away, and she pressed up against him. He groaned and started to thrust, each deeper than the one before. The heat and friction consumed her. With each stroke, he touched something that wasn't just physical. It was emotional. Spiritual.

Suddenly, everything fell into place.

Cassie McPherson had finally found "the one."

A quicksilver orgasm rocked through her, and before she had completely floated back down to earth, James reached his own pinnacle. When the last tingle of sensation was over, James rested against her. At another time, with another man, she would've complained about the position. She would've felt suffocated and not in control. But not now. Not with this man. Tucked beneath his hard body, she felt safe. Protected. Loved. The feelings didn't make her feel weak.

They made her feel strong.

Unable to contain her happiness, Cassie smiled and dropped a kiss to his shoulder. "I love you."

His breath halted, and he pushed up to his forearms. It took a minute for his gaze to focus; then a smile tipped the corners of his mouth and his eyes turned a deep, watery gold. "I love you too, wildcat."

"Why?"

He chuckled and leaned on one elbow to smooth the hair away from her cheek. "I don't know, especially when you're so controlling—and so aggressive—and spoiled rotten."

Cassie scowled at him.

"And..." He kissed the tip of her nose. "I love all of it. The control freak. The wildcat. And the princess. But most of all, I love the woman who was strong enough to go after what she wanted. Even if she had to drag a tree to my doorstep and strip naked."

"Oh," she breathed, too overwhelmed to say more.

Tenderly, James rolled to the side and drew her into his embrace. He nestled his chin into her hair, and she buried her nose into his chest and clung to him as any needy woman would. They remained there for long moments, just holding each other, just feeling what they felt without egos involved.

"So how did you get away from your family?" he asked.

"It wasn't easy. I had to contend with Big Al."

"Hmm." He looked down at her through his dark lashes. "And how did that go?"

"Pretty well, actually."

"So are you saying your father doesn't plan on taking a claymore to my throat the next time we run into each other?"

"No."

"Great."

"Stop being such a wussy, Sutton. At least you don't have to worry about my brothers jumping into the fray. For whatever reason, they all seem to like you, even after finding out who you are." Her eyes narrowed. "Which reminds me, I think you owe me an apology."

"Really? For what?"

Cassie thought about sitting up in anger, but she was too comfortable where she was. "What do you mean, for what? How about for lying about who you are and what you do for a living?"

His gaze lingered on her lips for what seemed like an eternity before he finally brought his attention back to the discussion. "I didn't lie. I merely didn't correct you."

"Which is lying," she pointed out.

"True. But answer me this: Would you really have given me a chance at dating you if you had known who I was from the beginning?"

She thought about it and had to admit he was right. "Point taken, but the least you could've done was mention something before we had sex."

"You were drunk before we had sex."

"Okay, so what about after?"

"We were too busy after." He dipped his head and nuzzled her neck.

"You still owe me an apology." The warmth of his lips caused her eyes to slide closed. "After all, I stood naked before all your neighbors to say I was sorry. The least you could do—"

A loud crash halted her words and jerked them apart.

"What the—?" James slid out from under her and headed down the hallway with her following close on his heels.

They both stopped at the doorway of the spare bedroom and stared at the top of the blue spruce that stuck in through the broken glass of the window.

"Well, I'll be damned," James said with a smile on his

face. "The kid was right. We were only inches away from cutting it down."

"Cutting it down? Why were you cutting your tree down?"

He slipped an arm around her and tugged her close. "I was planning on giving it to a certain dark-haired beauty in the hopes she wouldn't burn it to the ground."

"You were going to give me a tree?" Her eyes got all watery as she looked up at him. "So you figured it out."

He nodded. "But only after a night of hell and large pink bunnies."

"Pink bunnies? What—?"

"Marry me."

She blinked. "Huh?"

There wasn't a hint of a smile on his firm, chiseled lips. "Marry me, Cassandra McPherson. I'm sorry for lying, but even then I was smart enough to know I didn't want to lose you. So say you'll marry me, and I'll share a Christmas tree with you every year for the rest of our lives."

After everything that had happened, her mind wandered around with no place to land and nothing to say. Thank God her heart knew.

"Yes."

"Yes?" His arms tightened.

She paused. "But we probably should talk about how we want to raise our children. I mean, what religion—"

"You're not Catholic?"

"Yes, but your neighbor said you were—"

James tipped back his head and laughed before hugging her close. "I was raised Catholic, Cassandra, so the only major obstacle we have is your father."

She smiled. "In that case, how would you like to have Christmas dinner with a family of loving, but sometimes annoying, Scots?"

A couple hours later, they stood outside Cassie's parents' home, staring at the huge holly wreaths on the double doors. The house was lit with a mass confusion of colored lights while the lawn boasted a nativity scene, Santa and his reindeer, and a blow-up Frosty. All of which had been placed there earlier in the month by her brothers after numerous bottles of Guinness.

"I guess he wouldn't kill me with so many witnesses," James said dryly.

"That wouldn't stop him." Cassie tucked her arm through his and tried to pull him toward the front steps. "But my mother doesn't allow fighting in her house. So you have nothing to worry about."

"Right." James didn't look convinced; nor did he budge.

She shivered in the cold. "Come on, you big chicken. Let's get this over with so we can get back to a warm bed. Although the plastic we taped over your window doesn't exactly keep out the cold."

"I'll keep you warm." He pulled her into his arms, seemingly unconcerned with the falling snow or the freezing temperatures. "So let's skip telling your family and go back to my house to enjoy our Christmas tree. Who knows, maybe Santa left you something."

"That trick's not going to work. Santa's already given me my present."

He arched his brow. "Really? And what would that be?"

Snow drifted down around his shoulders and head, glistening in the deep greens, blues, and reds of outdoor lights. It reminded her of the first time she had seen him, framed by the lights from the office Christmas tree.

She *had* been given a gift this holiday.

The best gift of all.

Love.

She smiled up at her best present ever. "He gave me you."

All teasing left his eyes, and his arms tightened around her with the strength she'd come to know and trust. "In that case, let's not keep your family waiting."

From inside the house, Wheezie watched out the frosted window as James led Cassie up the pathway. If the arthritis in her hips hadn't been acting up, Wheezie might've done a little jig. Instead she moved into the dining room, where the rest of the McPhersons had congregated for Christmas dinner.

"Set two more places, Mary Katherine," she said. "Cassie's here with Jimmy."

Albert sent her a sour look as Mary Katherine smiled and got up to head for the kitchen. "I don't know what you're so happy about."

"Give it up, Alby. Cassandra made a good choice." She moved over to her seat between Patrick and Matthew. They were a handsome couple of bookends, she'd give them that. She shouldn't have any trouble whatsoever finding them soul mates.

Albert released his breath in a weary sigh. "I guess I was just hoping to keep her with us for a while longer."

She nodded her thanks to Patrick when he poured her a glass of whiskey. "What are you talking about? Cassandra isn't going anywhere."

"I wouldn't be too sure about that," Jake said as he strapped Chase into his high chair. "Why would she work for us when she could work for her husband?"

Wheezie studied the amber liquid in her glass. "Well, I've been thinking about that. And it seems to me that M & S isn't such a bad name for a construction company."

Her words surprised the entire room, and every adult turned to Big Al to get his reaction. It didn't take long. "M & S, huh?" he said thoughtfully.

"Personally," Matthew said with a wicked sparkle in his eyes, "I think S & M has a better ring to it."

The entire room erupted in laughter. The only person who didn't laugh at the joke was Big Al. Although his eyes sparkled almost as mischievously as Matthew's.

"What's so funny?" Cassandra walked in with her arm hooked through Jimmy's. It was obvious by her stance that if anyone wanted to tangle with her man they would have to go through her first. She didn't have anything to worry about. McPhersons were stubborn, but loyal. If this was the man who made Cassie happy, they would welcome him with open arms. And there was little doubt that Cassie was happy. She looked as if she'd just found the rarest of treasures.

Wheezie figured she had.

"Matthew was just teasing your father," Mary Katherine said as she set a place for them. "Now, sit down before the prime rib gets cold."

"Prime rib?" Just the mention of beef had Albert smiling.

For the next few minutes, conversation remained at a minimum while Cassie and Jimmy took their seats and serving dishes were passed and glasses filled. Wheezie ignored her own plate in favor of watching her family. At the head of the table, Albert selected a huge slice of prime rib before flashing a loving look at Mary Katherine. Jake and Melanie hustled around, cutting up food for their brood of children, but still found time to share a quick kiss. Patrick and Matthew fought over why the Broncos hadn't won their last game. Rory leaned down to whisper something in Gabby's ear before shooting an innocent look at Amy. And Cassie and Jimmy just continued to stare at each other as if they were the only two people in the room.

Talk about treasures, Wheezie thought. God had certainly blessed her with a bountiful one. He hadn't seen fit to give her children, but he'd given her a beautiful niece and four handsome nephews. And that was enough to keep her busy until her time here on earth was up.

She waited until the children had been served and everyone's plate was filled to overflowing before she lifted her glass. "To the McPhersons! Merry Christmas and the happiest of New Years."

Glasses were raised and the clinking of crystal filled the room, followed by a joyous echo. "Merry Christmas and Happy New Year!"

Librarian Elizabeth Murphy lives
a quiet life in Bramble—until
she inherits the most infamous
house of ill repute in Texas...
and soon finds herself in
bed with an even more
infamous cowboy.

Please turn this page
for a preview of

Trouble in Texas.

Chapter Two

*Henhouse Rule #12: When unexpected
things arise . . . rejoice.*

The second hand of the wall clock ticked past the ten, then on to the eleven. Elizabeth Murphy waited until its slender arm was perfectly aligned with the black minute hand, between the one and the two of the twelve, before she got up from her chair.

"The library is now closed," she stated in the same no-nonsense voice she'd used since first accepting the job as librarian over fifteen years earlier. It was irrelevant that not a soul was in the library to hear her words. Her mother had taught her that rules and routine were what kept a person's life on the straight and narrow.

And no one's life was more straight and narrow than Elizabeth's.

Without the slightest hesitation, she pushed open the gate in the circular counter and proceeded to walk down each long aisle. As she went, she tucked in protruding spines and checked for any misplaced titles.

Books were her babies.

She loved their woody, earthy smell. Loved the smooth, crisp feel of their pages. Loved the colorful book jackets and their straight, even spines. To a shy, awkward girl, they had been her teachers, her storytellers, her friends. To a single woman, they were her life.

She read all types of books, from nonfiction to fiction, from *New York Times* bestsellers to the reliable classics. If she had one fault, it was that she lost herself in a good story, forgoing sleep and food until she'd finished the last page. That was why she never started a book during the workweek. But this was Saturday afternoon, the start of her weekend, so she took the time to pick out a number of books to take home. She had just selected a historical romance from the paperback rack when someone spoke from behind her.

"What kinda books are those, Ms. Murphy?"

The paperback slipped from Elizabeth's hand as she whirled around. Kenny Gene stood there in his tight Wranglers and pressed Western shirt, his eyes squinting at the cover of the book on the floor.

"That woman sorta looks like Shirlene Dalton," he said. "Although if Shirlene paraded around with her bosom showin' like that, not one man in Bramble would get any work done."

Elizabeth held a hand to her chest. "You scared the daylights out of me, Kenny Gene. The library is closed. Didn't you hear my announcement?"

His gaze flickered up from the book. "Uhh, I must've been in the men's room."

She released a long sigh at the obvious lie. "Kenny, I

thought we had this discussion before," she said as she picked up the book. "If you don't want to marry Twyla right now, you need to tell her—instead of avoiding her so you don't have to set a date. Sooner or later, she's going to figure out where you've been hiding."

Kenny shook his head. "That's doubtful, Ms. Murphy. The library is the last place on God's green earth anyone would come lookin' for me—although I gotta tell you that them Scooby-Doo books are downright entertainin'."

It was hard to keep a stern face. Of all the people in Bramble, Texas, Kenny was the most lovable.

"Well, I'm glad you're enjoying them. But that doesn't change the fact that you need to talk with Twyla. Just tell her what you told me—that you were thinking more a long engagement than a short one."

"That might work with someone like you, Ms. Murphy. Old maids are much more logical than ordinary women. Probably because their hopes for snaggin' a man are slim to none."

His words should've offended Elizabeth, especially since she was only thirty-seven, but she couldn't blame him. Or any of the people in Bramble. Not when she had worked so hard to achieve her old-maid anonymity.

"But Twyla don't think the same way as you do," Kenny continued. "That girl is hell bent for leather on being hitched, and after three times, I'd say she's pretty good at it."

Elizabeth bit back a smile. "I guess that depends on your point of view, Kenny."

"Well, her point of view is targeted on me, especially with Shirlene's weddin' tonight. If Twyla catches that bouquet, it's all over for me. The town will have us hitched by winter."

She couldn't argue the point. The folks of Bramble loved weddings as much as they loved football. And everyone knew how much Texans loved their football.

Kenny's eyes took on a speculative gleam. "'Course, I wouldn't have to worry so much if some other woman caught it."

"Excuse me?"

He did an excited little hop that looked like he needed to go to the men's room after all. "You could catch the bouquet, Ms. Murphy, and then Twyla might think it was fate and be willin' to give me a little more time."

"Oh, no." Elizabeth held up a hand. "It's bad enough that I'm forced to stand there with all the young girls. I'm certainly not going to make an effort to catch it. I have no desire to get married."

"Well, of course you don't," Kenny said. "And you won't have to. No one will expect you to find a man."

She ignored the insult and shook her head. "I'd love to help you out, Kenny, but I don't think that's a very good idea."

"Just think about it, won't you?" Kenny begged. "All I'm asking for is another year of freedom."

It was hard to ignore his plea, especially when she enjoyed her own single status so much. "I'll think about it." She waved a hand toward the glass doors. "But for now, you need to let me close up so we can get ready for the wedding."

Exactly fifteen minutes later, Elizabeth stood outside the double glass doors of the library. After checking them twice to be sure they were locked, she slipped the keys in the side pocket of her tote bag and headed home.

Her house was not more than a few blocks from the library, a pretty little yellow brick with a picket fence and a festoon of colorful mums growing in the flower beds. The front gate got stuck when she tried to open it, and she made a mental note to buy some WD-40 at the hardware store on Monday. Once inside the front door, she was greeted by a soft *meow* as a warm, furry body pressed against her legs.

"Hello, Atticus. Did you miss me?" she asked as she leaned down to stroke the cat's soft, orange fur.

Atticus allowed her fawning for only a few seconds before he headed for the kitchen cupboard where she kept the cat food. At a good six pounds overweight, he had always been more interested in Meow Mix than her affection.

After feeding the cat and refilling his water dish, Elizabeth walked back in to the living room to get her tote bag. The wedding was hours away. She'd have plenty of time to get in a little reading before she had to get ready. Unfortunately, after deciding on a book, she made the mistake of checking her cell phone messages. There was only one. One breathy message that completely obliterated her plans.

"Lizzie? You need to get out here. And quick."

The drive that normally took her close to an hour took only forty-five minutes, during which Elizabeth envisioned all kinds of catastrophes. Which explained why she was so surprised when she walked into the kitchen of Miss Hattie's Henhouse and found three women calmly going about their business. Minnie was sitting in her wheelchair playing solitaire at the table. Sunshine was sitting on the floor contorted in some kind of weird yoga pose. And Baby was standing at the stove, stirring something in a saucepan and staring up at the ceiling.

"What's the emergency?" Elizabeth asked as she looked around for signs of fire, flooding, or robbery.

"The Realtor came by on Tuesday," Minnie said nonchalantly.

Elizabeth released her breath and dropped her tote bag to the floor. "That's it? The reason you had me drive all the way out here was to tell me that the Realtor came by?" She glanced over at Baby, but Baby quickly looked back up at the ceiling.

"That is an emergency." Minnie took another drag of her cigarette, her eyes squinting through the smoke. "I told you we weren't leaving." She gave Elizabeth the once-over. "Where in the hell do you get those ugly suits?"

Elizabeth wasn't the kind of person who lost her patience, but the last six months of dealing with Minnie was more than anyone should have to endure. Still, she took a deep breath and tried to remain calm.

"We can't hold on to this house, Minnie. Your social security checks put together won't even cover the gas bills for the winter." She waved a hand around. "Just look at this place. It's falling down around your ears, and it would take more money than any of us have to fix it. So, yes, I'm selling it."

The wheelchair zipped away from the table and straight toward her. But Minnie had pulled the stunt before, and Elizabeth wasn't falling for it. She stood her ground, even when the wheels of the chair came within inches of the toes of her conservative brown lace-ups.

"Let me tell you something, girlie." Minnie shook a gnarled finger at her. "You might've inherited the house, but your ancestors would be rollin' over in their graves if they knew you were plannin' on throwin' out their sister hens!"

Hens. Elizabeth cringed. She had come to hate the word. So much so that she'd sworn off chicken, eggs, and feather pillows.

"So what do you expect me to do?" she said. "You want me to just let you live here until they turn off the utilities? Until you're forced to eat cat food—again?"

"That happened only once," Minnie said. "And only because Sunshine mistook it for a can of tuna."

Sunshine giggled. "Cathouse. Cat food."

"So are you telling me that you weren't almost starving by the time the lawyer finally located me?" Elizabeth asked.

"No." Minnie rolled back over to the table and snuffed out her cigarette. "I'll admit that we were pretty close to eating the mice that have taken over the attic. But the hens and I would've been just fine if you hadn't showed up. In fact, we just came up with a new plan."

"A plan?" Elizabeth rolled her eyes. "Is this plan similar to the one about starting your own line of lingerie?"

"That one would've worked," Minnie said, "if I hadn't let Baby come up with the slogan. 'Nighties that will entice your man to take his choo-choo on a ride in your tunnel.' What the hell does that mean?"

"Speaking of choo-choos…" Sunshine stretched a leg up over her head, something Elizabeth was quite certain she couldn't do now, let alone when she turned seventy. "Can I go upstairs now, Min? You said I could do it later. It's later. Right?"

Minnie shook her head. "In a little while, Sunshine. Right now we need to make sure Lizzie is in."

Elizabeth heaved a sigh and sat down in a chair. As much as she wanted to sell the house and completely forget her connection to Miss Hattie's, she also couldn't stand the thought of kicking the three women out of a home they loved.

"So what's this great plan, Minnie?"

Numerous cards were played and another cigarette lit before the ornery old woman finally spoke. "We're reopening the henhouse."

"Excuse me?" Elizabeth leaned closer, figuring she'd misunderstood. "Reopening as in selling sex?"

Minnie's eyes narrowed. "I don't know what that crazy mama of yours told you, but the hens never sold sex in their lives—that's what prostitutes and whores do. The henhouse was a place where men could come to be pampered and loved." She shrugged. "And if they wanted to show their appreciation with money and gifts, that was their decision. Miss Hattie never spoke of money. And neither did any of the hens."

"Which might explain why you don't have any now," Elizabeth couldn't help adding.

Taking another drag of her cigarette, Minnie flipped a queen of diamonds down on the king of spades. "Did you realize that, unlike the Chicken Ranch, the henhouse was never closed down? We remained open until the last rooster flew the coop. Age is what screwed us up. Nobody wants an old hen when they can have a spring chicken." She tapped a crooked nail on the table. "'Course, the spring chickens can't just be anyone. Hen blood is either in you, or it ain't." Her eyes narrowed on Elizabeth. "And I'm havin' my doubts about you, Lizzie."

Exasperated, Elizabeth got up from the chair. "I'm selling the house, Minnie. But I give you my word that I'll help you and the hens find a good place to live."

"You're not leaving." Baby turned from the stove with a desperate look on her face. "You can't go yet." Her gaze wandered up to the ceiling.

"Let her go." Minnie reshuffled the cards, the cigarette drooping from her lip. "We should've never contacted her in the first place."

Elizabeth wished they hadn't either. Unfortunately, there was no going back. Ignoring the hens would be like leaving three blind mice in a burning building. Someone had to watch out for the insane women. Elizabeth just wished it wasn't her.

"The Realtor will be back next week," she said as she headed to the side kitchen door. "And stop smoking, Minnie. If you don't kill yourself, your secondhand smoke is going to kill Sunshine and Baby."

"It will take more than a little smoke to kill us hens," Minnie huffed.

She probably had a point. The three would no doubt outlive most of the population of Texas.

The sun had just started to slip beneath the horizon as Elizabeth made her way around the front of the house to her car. Sunsets in west Texas were spectacular, but she didn't take the time to enjoy the vibrant splashes of color.

If she hurried, she would have just enough time to change and get to the First Baptist Church before the wedding started. She'd just as soon skip the festivities and go home and read. But if she didn't attend, questions would arise. And all she needed was the townsfolk finding out about her connection to Miss Hattie's.

Unfortunately, before she even got to her car, a thought struck her. Why would Sunshine want to go upstairs when the only things upstairs were mice and empty rooms? Elizabeth might've attributed the desire to a brain that had been fried by too many drugs in the sixties if Minnie hadn't acted like she knew exactly what Sunshine was talking about.

And if Baby hadn't acted so strange, constantly looking up at the ceiling.

An uneasy feeling settled in the pit of her stomach as Elizabeth glanced up at the second story. A part of her brain told her to ignore the feeling and get out of there. But the logical part of her brain reminded her that her name was on the deed, which meant she was liable for whatever craziness the hens had come up with. Not wanting to get in another argument with Minnie, Elizabeth decided to slip in the front door and tiptoe up the long staircase.

She had never been upstairs before, partly because the hens lived downstairs and partly because of Minnie's mice stories. It was a creepy place, filled with dark shadows and creaking floorboards. She didn't find any mice, but she did find numerous rooms—all of which were empty.

All except for the corner room.

Elizabeth pushed open the double doors, and her breath

caught. While the rest of the house had minimal furniture, this room was filled to the rafters. She didn't know a lot about antiques, but the items in the room looked like they would send the appraisers on *Antiques Roadshow* into conniption fits. No wonder Sunshine had wanted to come upstairs. The room was like stepping back in time. There were beautiful Oriental rugs, museum-quality paintings, heavy brass lamps with stained-glass shades, and beautiful dressers and chests that gleamed in the last rays of the setting sun.

But nothing compared to the huge four-poster bed that covered one entire wall. The exquisitely carved headboard was made of dark walnut, as were the thick posts that came within inches of the high ceiling. Red and gold brocade curtains draped from the canopy, partially concealing a mattress that had to be a good three feet from the floor.

Regardless of all the horror stories her mother had told her over the years, Elizabeth found herself completely and utterly enthralled by the massive piece of furniture. And as much as she tried to convince her brain that it was just a bed, something inside of Elizabeth knew differently. This wasn't just a bed. This was *the* bed. The same bed where the most famous prostitute in Texas history had slept—or not slept. A bed that had entertained outlaws and politicians alike. A bed that some museum curators would give their eyeteeth to have. And there Elizabeth stood not more than ten feet away from it.

Make that seven feet.

Four.

One.

She slid a hand down the brocade curtains and stared

in at the rumpled black satin sheets. What kind of wickedness had transpired there? What kind of depravity? What kind of fun?

Before Elizabeth knew it, she had pushed back the curtain and slipped inside the shadowy cocoon. The mattress was not too soft or too hard, the sheets cool to the touch. She eased down to the pillows and breathed deeply. The smell of lilacs wasn't surprising. Being Miss Hattie's signature scent, it had been worn by all hens, past and present. But the other scent baffled her. It was an earthy scent that she couldn't quite place.

Attached to the canopy was a huge mirror. A mirror painted with a mural of a beautiful woman in a seductive red dressing gown. The painting completely obscured the dowdy old maid in the ugly gray suit, leaving only the other side of the bed visible. It wasn't hard to imagine the shape of a man's body beneath the rumpled satin sheets. Or hear his deep, steady breathing. Was he a filthy-rich oil man? A lonely cowboy fresh off the trail? Or possibly a handsome hero straight from the pages of a historical romance?

As she gave her imagination full rein, a dark head separated from the black satin of the pillow and a deep voice rumbled next to her ear.

"I've been waiting for you."

THE DISH

Where authors give you the inside scoop!

From the desk of R.C. Ryan

Dear Reader,

When my daughter-in-law Patty came home from her first hike of the Grand Canyon, she was high on the beauty and majesty of the mountains for months. Since then, it has become her annual pilgrimage—one that fuels her dreams, and feeds my writer's imagination. I've wanted to create a character with the same passion for the mountains that Patty has for a long time, someone who experiences the same awe, freedom, and peace that she does just by being in eyesight of them. And with JOSH, I think I finally have.

Josh Conway, the hero of the second book in my Wyoming Sky series, is truly a hero in every sense of the word. He's a man who rescues people who've lost their way on the mountain he loves in all kinds of weather. There's just something about a guy who would risk his own safety, his very life, to help others, that is so appealing to me. To add to Josh's appeal, he's a hard-working rancher and a sexy cowboy—an irresistible combination. Not to mention that he loves a challenge.

Enter Sierra Moore. Sierra is a photographer who comes to the Grand Tetons in Wyoming to shoot photographs of a storm. At least that's what she'll admit to. But there's a mystery behind that beautiful smile. She's come to the mountains to disappear for a while, and being rescued—even if it is by a ruggedly handsome cowboy—is the last thing she needs or wants.

But when danger rears its ugly head, and Sierra's life is threatened, she and Josh must call on every bit of strength and courage they possess in order to survive. Yet an even greater test of their strength will be the courage to commit to a lifetime together.

I hope you enjoy JOSH!

P. C. Ryan

RyanLangan.com

From the desk of Anna Campbell

Dear Reader,

Wow! I'm so excited that my first historical romance with Grand Central Publishing has hit the shelves (and the e-waves!). I hope you enjoy reading SEVEN NIGHTS IN A ROGUE'S BED as much as I enjoyed writing it. Not only is this my first book for GCP, it's also the first book in my very first series, the Sons of Sin. Perhaps I should smash a bottle of champagne over my copy of SEVEN NIGHTS to launch it in appropriate style.

Hmm, having second thoughts here. Much better, I've decided, to read the book and drink the champagne!

Do you like fairytale romance? I love stories based on Cinderella or Sleeping Beauty or some other mythical hero or heroine. SEVEN NIGHTS IN A ROGUE'S BED is a dyed-in-the-wool Beauty and the Beast re-telling. To me, this is the ultimate romantic fairytale. The hero starts out as a monster, but when he falls in love, the fragments of goodness in his tortured soul multiply until he becomes a gallant prince (or, in this case, a viscount, but who's counting?). Beauty and the Beast is at heart about the transformative power of true love—what more powerful theme for a romance writer to explore?

Jonas Merrick, the Beast in SEVEN NIGHTS IN A ROGUE'S BED, is a scarred recluse who has learned through hard and painful experience to mistrust a hostile world. When the book opens, he's a rogue indeed. But meeting our heroine conspires to turn him into a genuine, if at first reluctant, hero worthy of his blissfully happy ending.

Another thing I love about Beauty and the Beast is that the heroine is more proactive than some other mythological girls. For a start, she stays awake throughout! Like Beauty, Sidonie Forsythe places herself in the Beast's power to save someone she loves, her reckless older sister, Roberta. Sidonie's dread when she meets brooding, enigmatic Jonas Merrick swiftly turns to fascination—but even as they fall in love, Sidonie's secret threatens to destroy Jonas and any chance of happiness for this Regency Beauty and the Beast.

I adore high-stakes stories where I wonder if the lovers can ever overcome what seem to be insurmountable barriers between them. In SEVEN NIGHTS IN A ROGUE'S BED, Jonas and Sidonie have to triumph over the bitter legacy of the past and conquer present dangers to achieve their happily-ever-after. Definitely major learning curves for our hero and heroine!

This story is a journey from darkness to light, and it allowed me to play with so many classic romance themes.

Redemption. A touch of the gothic. The steadfast, courageous heroine. The dark, tormented hero. The clash of two powerful personalities as they resist overwhelming passion. Secrets and revelations. Self-sacrifice and risk. Revenge and justice. You know, all the big stuff!

If you'd like to find out more about SEVEN NIGHTS IN A ROGUE'S BED and the Sons of Sin series, please visit my website: www.annacampbell.info. And in the meantime, happy reading!

Best wishes,

Anna Campbell

♥ ♥ ♥ ♥ ♥ ♥ ♥ ♥ ♥ ♥ ♥ ♥ ♥ ♥ ♥

From the desk of Katie Lane

Dear Reader,

One of my favorite things to do during the holidays is to read *The Night Before Christmas*. So I thought it would be fun to tell you about my new romance, HUNK FOR THE HOLIDAYS, by making up my own version of the classic.

> *'Twas four days before Christmas, and our heroine, Cassie,*
> *Is ready for her office party, looking red hot and sassy.*
> *When what to her wondering eyes should she see*
> *But the escort she hired standing next to her tree?*
> *His eyes how they twinkle, his dimples so cute,*
> *He has a smile that melts, a great body to boot.*

There's only one problem: James is as controlling as Cass,
But she forgives him this flaw, when she gets a good look
    at his ass.
He goes straight to work at seducing his date,
And by the end of the evening, Cass is ready to mate.
Not to ruin the story, all I will say,
Is that James will be smiling when Cass gets her way.
Mixed in with their romance will be plenty of reason
For you to enjoy the fun of the season.
Caroling, shopping, and holiday baking,
A humorous great-aunt and her attempts at match-making.
A perfect book to cozy up with all the way through December,
HUNK FOR THE HOLIDAYS will be out in September.
For now I will end by wishing you peace, love, and laughter.
And, of course, the best gift of all… a happily-ever-after!

Katie Jane

♥ ♥ ♥ ♥ ♥ ♥ ♥ ♥ ♥ ♥ ♥ ♥ ♥ ♥ ♥

From the desk of Hope Ramsay

Dear Reader,

I love Christmas, but I have to say that trying to write a
holiday-themed book in the middle of a long, hot summer
is not exactly easy. It was hard to stay in the holiday
mood when my nonwriting time was spent weeding my
perennials border, watching baseball, and working on my
short golf game.

So how does an author get herself into the holiday mood in the middle of July?

She hauls out her iPod and plays Christmas music from sun up to sun down.

My husband was ready to strangle me, but all that Christmas music did the trick. And in the end, it was just one song that helped me find my holiday spirit.

The song is "The Longest Night," written by singer-songwriter Peter Mayer, a song that isn't quite a Christmas song. It's about the winter solstice. The lyrics are all about hope, even in the darkest hour. In the punchline, the song-writer gives a tiny nod to the meaning of Christmas when he says, "Maybe light itself is born in the longest night."

When I finished LAST CHANCE CHRISTMAS, I realized that this theme of light and dark runs through it like a river. My heroine is a war photographer, who literally sees the world as a battle between light and dark. When she arrives in Last Chance, she's troubled and alone, and the darkness is about to overwhelm her.

But of course, that doesn't last long after she meets Stone Rhodes, the chief of police and a man who is about as Grinch-like as they come. But as the saying goes, some-times the only way to get yourself out of a funk is to help someone else. And when Stone does that, he manages to spark a very hot and bright light in the dead of winter.

I hope you love reading Stone and Lark's story as much as I did writing it.

Ya'll have a blessed holiday, now, you hear?

Hope Ramsay

Find out more about Forever Romance!

Visit us at
www.hachettebookgroup.com/publishing_forever.aspx

Find us on Facebook
http://www.facebook.com/ForeverRomance

Follow us on Twitter
http://twitter.com/ForeverRomance

NEW AND UPCOMING TITLES

Each month we feature our new titles
and reader favorites.

CONTESTS AND GIVEAWAYS

We give away galleys, autographed copies,
and all kinds of exclusive items.

AUTHOR INFO

You'll find bios, articles, and links to personal websites
for all your favorite authors—and so much more.

GET SOCIAL

Connect with your favorite authors, editors, and
other Forever fans, and share what's important to you.

THE BUZZ

Sign up for our monthly romance newsletter,
and be the first to read all about it.

VISIT US ONLINE AT

WWW.HACHETTEBOOKGROUP.COM

FEATURES:

OPENBOOK BROWSE AND SEARCH EXCERPTS

•

AUDIOBOOK EXCERPTS AND PODCASTS

•

AUTHOR ARTICLES AND INTERVIEWS

•

BESTSELLER AND PUBLISHING GROUP NEWS

•

SIGN UP FOR E-NEWSLETTERS

•

AUTHOR APPEARANCES AND TOUR INFORMATION

•

SOCIAL MEDIA FEEDS AND WIDGETS

•

DOWNLOAD FREE APPS

Bookmark Hachette Book Group
@ www.HachetteBookGroup.com